THE LEAP

THE LEAP

Stepping On Your Other Toes

Blaine C. Readler

Full Arc
Press

THE LEAP
Stepping On Your Other Toes

Published by Full Arc Press

Visit us at: http://www.readler.com

E-mail: blaine@readler.com

An acknowledgement and thanks to Lulu Enterprises, Inc. for making the publishing of this book possible.

You should use them to publish!   http://www.lulu.com

ISBN: 978-0-615-41897-1

Printed in the United States of America

First Edition: 2011

Dedicated to Robert A. Heinlein, who taught me that my head can be used for something other than mooing along with the herd, while all the time leading me to believe that he was merely entertaining me.

The sly bastard.

ACKNOWLEDGEMENTS

Heralding angels to MTB for indefatigable editing.

History always repeats itself twice: first time as tragedy, second time as farce.
—Karl Marx

Well, Art is Art, isn't it? Still, on the other hand, water is water. And east is east and west is west and if you take cranberries and stew them like applesauce they taste much more like prunes than rhubarb does. Now you tell me what you know.
—Groucho Marx

Prologue

At 7:05 AM on October 14, 1947, Dr. William McKinney's telephone rang. He put down his coffee and answered it.

"Bill!" his brother-in-law crowed through the receiver. "It's a boy!"

Bill McKinney smiled broadly. "That's great! How's Helen?"

"She's fine. She's sleeping. Gotta go—a lot of calls to make."

"Of course. I'll stop by the hospital later today."

The young physicist gently hung up the phone and grinned into his cup. He was an uncle. It was hard to believe. Him, an uncle.

One eyebrow went up. If he was going to do it, why not now? Why not indeed? He didn't have to tell anybody. They'd just laugh.

He shrugged, pulled a nickel from his pocket, and flipped it spinning high. He caught it, and clapped it onto the backside of his other hand, splitting the universe in two. He carefully lifted his hand to reveal his new universe. It was tails.

"Counterclockwise it is," he declared to the small dining room.

He slipped the coin back into his pocket, but then reached in and retrieved it. He went to the kitchen and found an envelope in the drawer where his mother had always kept the stationary. He sealed the nickel inside, turned it over, and wrote:

10/14/62.

Fifteen years. It was plenty of time to prepare.

He smiled and shook his head. He was embarrassed that he'd even given it serious thought.

"It's crazy, all right," he announced to the empty kitchen, and then left for his first class.

Chapter 1

"Your uncle's trying to send you to another universe," Alicia repeated as though he'd just told her that he was really a toad masquerading as a twenty-nine year old man.

Will glanced at her sitting in the passenger seat. "Uncle Bill is actually my great-uncle, and yes, once a month he tries to send me to another universe."

He checked the rearview mirror and signaled for a lane change. He knew she would think the whole thing was nuts. He didn't disagree.

"He's my namesake, you know," he reminded her.

"I wouldn't advertise that."

"He was nominated for a Nobel Prize."

"Really? You never told me."

"1970. A Swedish guy named Luis Alfvén won it instead. They both worked out the principles of magnetohydrodynamics, but Alfvén bet him to the punch."

"What in God's name is magnets-to-hydramics?"

"Magneto-hydro-dynamics. It's the study of the kinetic behavior of electrically conducting fluids."

"Oh, thanks. That makes it crystal clear. Now I'm finally ready for *Jeopardy.*"

He chuckled. He enjoyed her sarcasm—when it wasn't directed at him. "Don't worry; I don't understand a bit of it either."

"Save the humility, Math Boy. I've seen your reference books."

He shook his head. "I can follow the math okay. I learned that stuff as an undergraduate. It's the underlying physics that drowns me. Mathematics is just a game until you apply it."

"Ha!" she scoffed. "You're the one who claimed that mathematics is a language that describes the universe. You said— and I quote—that anything that can be mathematically represented should exist, and that if we don't see it, it just means we haven't looked in the right place. It sounds to me like you're all twisted up in your own suspenders, Mr. Smarty-pants."

He smiled. The guy she married would need a thick skin. "Touché," he conceded.

Alicia thought that this guy was him. Familiar spiders crawled up the back of his neck at the thought.

"Your uncle Frankenstein is using this magneto magic to shove you out of our universe?"

"I guess. I don't understand it all. Uncle Bill is either the next Einstein, or completely loony. He believes that there are an infinite number of different universes, each of which is continually dividing into yet more. Every second, hundreds—thousands—*millions*—of new universes split off from ours. Of course, every one of the new ones is also 'ours,' but running off on a different path."

"I don't think your uncle invented this. I've heard it before. There's supposed to be, like, thousands of other Alicia's living other lives . . . some of them maybe even married by now."

He ignored the barb, but the spiders danced a jig. "I know. Science fiction writers have been using the idea forever. The difference is that Uncle Bill thinks he's worked out the details."

"Specifically, that we can travel between them."

"As long as he can make an exchange."

"I would, like, change places with another Alicia?"

He nodded, moving into the exit lane. "The first law of thermodynamics rules."

"Are you trying to make me feel stupid?"

"It essentially says that energy can't be created or destroyed, and as Einstein elucidated, mass—you, for example—is energy. We can't send something from one universe to another without making an exchange the other way."

Alicia was looking at him with a smirking grin, probably wondering if he believed it himself. "So, why doesn't he go himself?" she asked. "Why send his favorite great-nephew?"

"Because the same 'he' needs to remain at both sides to operate the return exchange. He's afraid that one of him would get to the other side and not know how to work the equipment, and it takes precise coordination at both ends. He would—they both would—be stuck in the opposite parallel universe forever."

"That might not be so bad. I wouldn't mind trying out a different universe—way too many Republicans in this one for my taste."

She equated "Republican" with "far right conservative."

The spring Seattle mist coalesced into a drizzle, and Will flipped the wipers to a faster speed as he turned onto the highway. "What about the other Alicia?" he asked. "You want to maroon her here on the conservative side? She's you, you know."

"Better her than me. Plus, you'd get to try out another me. Maybe you'd like that one better."

The constant jabs were getting old. If she kept up the nagging . . . well, she was just shooting herself in the foot.

She must have sensed she'd crossed the line. Her tone softened. "I think it's sweet that you humor your old Uncle."

"It's only once a month. The whole thing takes maybe five minutes."

"Because it never works?"

"Of course."

She'd known about his monthly appointments, but he'd always sidestepped the purpose. He was embarrassed to admit that he was involved in such a cockamamie venture. He'd only brought her along this time because they were going to a birthday party right afterwards.

"Is it dangerous?"

"No. Of course not."

"How many times have you done it?"

"This is the fourth time. My dad did it for . . . gosh, every month for forty years. I took over when he died. Uncle Bill is confident that my mom and dad married in most of the other universes. So, he thinks there should be a lot of me's out there."

"Because they grew up in the same town?"

"Good memory."

His mom and dad both loved horses. His dad worked at his mom's family farm, and they would go out riding together as teenagers.

"Forty years—hey! That means your dad started when he was, like, ten!"

"Fifteen. Uncle Bill would have started earlier, but he wanted to make sure there was enough differentiation between universes."

"Wait a second. Even if they married in the other universes, what's the chance that it was the same sperm and egg?"

"I asked him about that. Uncle Bill explained that the problem isn't that there won't be enough me's, but too many. The farther in time we get from the split point back in 1947, the more millions of universes spawn off. He thinks that the sperm factor actually works in our favor, providing some filtering."

She was grinning at him again.

"I sound like I believe it, don't I?" he confessed.

He took a turn, and braked to a halt in front of a workman holding a stop sign on a pole. Uncle Bill's house used to sit by itself, isolated in the country, but the Seattle sprawl had finally overtaken him, and the farmers' fields had methodically given way to endless rows of track houses. A construction crew blocked the road as a Caterpillar bulldozer tried to maneuver itself onto a flatbed truck.

"Shit!" Will exclaimed.

"What's the matter?"

"We're going to be late!"

It was Alicia's fault. She wanted to come along, but wasn't ready when he arrived to pick her up.

"What's the big deal?" she said.

"The big *deal* is that I have to be there and ready at precisely noon. Both sides have to activate their transfer fields at exactly the same time."

"The other Uncle Bill knows this?"

"Yes!"

He was angry with her and he could hear it in his voice. "On the first day of each month at exactly noon, all the Uncle Bills go through the same procedure. All of them except ours, unless we get past this roadblock."

"All the uncles know exactly what to do?" she challenged.

"Of course! They're all *him!*"

"You really do believe it."

"It doesn't matter whether I believe it or not. All that matters is that Uncle Bill is counting on me." He opened the window and leaned out. "How long will it be?" he called to the sign-holder.

The worker glanced back at the activity. "Dunno!"

"Is there another way around?"

The guy thought a moment. "Go back and take a right on Pickery. That'll take you to old Route 9. Not the new section, the old highway. Take another right on . . . I think it's Fairville . . . or, maybe Meadow. Anyway, there's a gas station. That'll bring you back about a half mile ahead."

Will nodded, disgusted, as he backed the car to turn around. If they were late, it was all Alicia's fault.

ж ж ж

"Where's your new girlfriend?" Uncle Bill asked, sitting on his stool in front of the dusty old control panel crowded with large rheostat knobs and klunky toggle switches. It hadn't changed in forty years. Will's doddering uncle didn't seem at all perturbed that he'd shown up just minutes before noon.

"She wanted to stay in the car," Will replied, tearing off his clothes.

Actually, she didn't really want to, but Will had more or less told her to. They hadn't talked the rest of the way there.

"And how goes your computer programming?" the old man inquired, seemingly oblivious to the unrelenting countdown.

His great-uncle looked every year of his eighty-seven. Will marveled that he managed to get back up the old rickety steps from the basement. Will wondered if the old guy had even the strength to throw the toggle switches.

"It's just a hobby, Uncle Bill. Nobody uses assembly level programming anymore. Now, it's all done in high-level languages using fancy compilers."

"Nothing wrong with a solid grasp of the basics. You never know when they might come in handy."

Will pulled off his socks, and the stone floor felt like ice. Uncle Bill had bought this house specifically for the basement. This end of it had been carved out of the underlying bedrock. "Nothing like granite for stability," his uncle would say.

The illuminated digits of the big clock on the far wall showed 11:58:07, and incrementing. Earlier that morning, Uncle Bill would have calibrated it with the US Naval Observatory signal. Timing was everything.

Completely naked now, Will walked across the bare floor, swept meticulously clean by his great-uncle, and stood under the iron rod hanging from the ceiling between massive coils of finger-thick copper wire. Uncle Bill was pointing at the floor. Will saw that one of his socks was inside the chalk-line arc. He trotted over and kicked it out, then returned to the "transfer" spot. The iron rod was for positioning only, as were the painted outlines of two feet on which he carefully placed himself. Under Uncle Bill's direction, he'd practiced how to stand, his hands flat against his thighs, his eyes staring at a bulls-eye painted beneath the large digital clock on the far wall. He was a good half-inch taller than his dad, and the metal rod poked into the top of his head. He'd asked Uncle Bill if they couldn't shave off a quarter inch, but the old physicist had carefully explained that exchange would occur only if there was greater than 99.98 percent match in both quantity and position of mass at both sides. A smudge of dirt, missed when sweeping the floor, could spell failure.

The bright segment characters of the clock blinked to 11:59:00 and continued counting. Will breathed evenly. Uncle Bill put on his dark glasses against the blinding flash that was to come. Will imagined all the other Uncle Bills sitting on their stools, and all the other Wills standing at this precise same spot. Were they thinking of him? His great-uncle threw a switch, and a deep, ominous hum filled the musty cavern basement. From the barrel-sized capacitors that the old scientist had been charging all morning, thousands of amps of current coursed into the hulking coils hovering like Tyrannosaurus rex jaws about to devour him. Thousands of amps more would have flowed, but his uncle's design specifically limited it. Otherwise, the overly massive amount of energy might arc between the coils, with potentially fatal results to the naked man inside.

Ten seconds left. He let the air ease from his lungs until they were empty, and stared at the wall. Empty lungs were most likely to match across universes. As with the previous month, he felt his heart thumping inside his chest. What about that? What if the other Will's heart was out of sync? What if one heart was expanded, and the other contracted? He knew the answer: there would simply be no exchange. But there was surely more than one other Will out there.

Four seconds. The hum rose to a vibrating whine. The magnetic fields around the coils would be completely established now. As he watched the clock count away the last seconds, Uncle Bill's finger rested on the final switch that would cut the current, causing the powerful magnetic fields to collapse upon themselves in a counterclockwise direction. Somewhere among half of the other universes, maybe, just maybe, another Will matching him by at least 99.98 percent would be standing inside a mating clockwise field.

The old man's finger moved, and Will closed his eyes against the flash. A lightning bolt seemed to explode in the basement as sparks splashed high on each side of him. Will jumped involuntarily even though he was expecting this as the collapsing magnetic fields, releasing the energy they'd stored, created tens of thousands of volts across the circuit breaker.

As his father had done for forty years, and as he had done the previous months, Will was now to utter the one word that would let his aging great-uncle know if the exchange was successful. "Counterclock—" he started to say, but froze as the brilliant light from the arcing sparks faded.

Uncle Bill had disappeared.

Chapter 2

"Uncle Bill?" Will called into the cavernous basement, dark and brooding after the brilliant fireworks.

There was only silence broken by a hissing sizzle of the last dying sparks.

"Uncle Bill!" he called louder. "Where are you?"

Nothing.

A hand-written note taped to the control panel caught his eye. He hadn't noticed it before. Walking over, he saw that it was addressed to someone named Buck. Funny, Uncle Bill had never mentioned any Buck.

His unease swelled as he glanced around the basement. It looked different. He didn't remember the metal shelves in the corner, and he felt goosebumps blossoming when he saw that above the bullseye, where the digital clock had hung, there was now a large, round, industrial-type clock with big black hands on a stark white background. This was the clock he remembered from when he was a child.

He'd gone back in time!

Good Lord! How could this be? Uncle Bill had never talked about the possibility of time travel. In fact, he was adamant that unidirectional time progression was as immutable across all the universes as the law of conservation of energy. The math just didn't allow for it.

Apparently his great-uncle had missed something.

The goosebumps surged back as he realized that Uncle Bill—a younger version—might be right upstairs, unaware of the unexpected visitor. Would he recognize him? How would he convince him that he really was a grownup Will?

Taking a deep breath, he started up the stairs, but realized he was still naked. Blushing, he scampered back down, only to find his clothes gone. Of course. They were still back—forward—in the twenty-first century. He glanced around and found a pile of clothes neatly folded on one of the shelves. The shirt was odd—knit, like his own polo shirts, but the front was divided down the middle by a fake seam and a fake row of buttons. It brought to mind a clip-on tie. It fit though.

When he shook out the pants, however, he found an even stranger fashion indulgence: the thighs were loose and baggy, which suited Will fine, but each leg narrowed towards the bottom, ending in an elastic band that hugged his ankle tight. There was no mirror, but he was sure he looked exactly like a clown. Young Uncle Bill must have been a real wild dude. No, back then he would have been a real cool cat.

His fortune turned when he picked up the shoes and found a very normal pair of sneakers, albeit a bit worn and tired. The luck extended to a perfect fit, as though he'd picked them out himself in the store.

Pausing just a moment to collect himself, he headed up the stairs a second time. At the top he found the door locked, just as Uncle Bill had always kept it to prevent inquisitive eyes from finding his mad-scientist equipment. The hidden key wasn't in its usual spot, though, behind a joist. In fact, the nail from which it normally hung was even gone. Probing around, he found the key on a nail behind a different joist farther away.

He unlocked and swung the door slowly open. The house was quiet. "Uncle Bill!" he called, but there was no answer. "It's Will . . . er, a grown-up Will!"

Either his great-uncle wasn't home, or he was hiding from this intruder claiming to be his great-nephew.

Will walked towards the kitchen. The living room furniture was all . . . flowery. He didn't remember this as a kid, but then again he probably didn't take much notice. The same old rotary dial phone hung on the kitchen wall. He remembered this from before his uncle finally changed to a touch-tone. Next to the phone, where it always hung, was a calendar. On top was a picture of an idealized spring day on a Washington farm, and underneath, in large, bold letters, was the year.

Will's heart seemed to stop when he saw it. The year was 2011.

The kitchen seemed to swirl around him, as though he was spinning his way through the decades back to present time. At first he was immensely relieved, and a little voice said, *I told you Uncle Bill's giant capacitors and coils are nonsense.* But he'd watched his great-uncle disappear along with his own clothes. And what about the clock? And the living room furniture? And the key!

He considered for a moment that Uncle Bill might be pulling some elaborate practical joke, but decided that the old guy wasn't that kind of kidder. He would never go this far.

Somehow, the alternative—that he had actually transferred to a parallel universe—was hugely more disturbing than traveling back in time where at least it was a world he *knew.* He hadn't felt this lost since he was six years old and separated from his parents at the Evergreen State Fair.

He was suddenly afraid now that his great-uncle—*this* great-uncle—*would* show up. He envisioned a monstrous, deranged version of Uncle Bill, complete with a bloody axe raised to strike him.

Calm down, he reassured himself. This would be the same Uncle Bill, but one who had simply lived a slightly different life. After all, they'd started out as exactly the same person. So what if he had a weird taste in clothes?

He suddenly remembered that he'd left Alicia waiting in the car. Dreading what he'd find, he ran to the front window and saw the street forlorn and empty. A car drove by. At least, he assumed it was a car. The shape was bulbous, reminding him of the kind a cartoonist might draw. It didn't seem designed for high speeds. Like the pants, it looked like it should be in a circus.

In a daze, Will made his way back to the basement where it had all begun. If he had indeed made an exchange, a leap between universes, why hadn't this Uncle Bill been here with his hand on the toggle switch the instant afterwards? Other than the shelves in the corner, and the clock, he wouldn't have known that this was a basement sixty years diverged down a different path. The control panel and massive capacitors and coils were identical; the Uncle Bill of each universe had built them to the same detailed plans.

Almost.

He now noticed that sitting next to the control panel was a metal box with tiny dials. Wires fed to the innards of the control panel.

And there was also the hand-written note. He picked it up and read it.

> *Dear Buck,*
>
> *Welcome to my universe. I apologize for the sparse reception (hopefully you are indeed alone), but I have arranged (via a precision timer switch I borrowed from a bouncer's nav assembly) for this exchange to occur absent any knowledge on this side. I pray that you are able to help my world, and that, for your sake, your world has chosen a significantly saner course. I beg of you to help me in any way you can, using whatever unique knowledge you can bring to bear.*

Will realized that the note was for *him*! Whoever wrote it thought that his name was Buck. Wait. Not "whoever." The author was obviously the Will of this universe. His name was not Will, but Buck, and he would have naturally assumed that his counterpart would have the same name.

He read on.

> *Now that the time has arrived, I realize there is far too much to tell properly, so I shall have to summarize. Up until two months ago, nobody knew of Uncle William's experiments, other than father and myself (father passed away four years ago, and I have been working with Uncle William since). At that time, CID claimed to have uncovered a terrorist nest within the university, and in the ensuing interrogations, Uncle came under scrutiny. Having nothing really to hide, he readily explained his quiet work of six decades and the purpose of the odd homemade apparatus they found here in the basement. As expected, the investigating agent, although believing Uncle's ideas a result of senility, immediately declared the equipment to be components of an atom bomb and proof of terrorist activities.*

>*One particularly clever CID agent by the name of Hank Breggart, however, became intrigued, and—alone among his agency colleagues—decided to investigate the possible usefulness to CID of Uncle's work. He managed to convince his superior to delay public indictment of Uncle while he probed the situation. Uncle William, of course, was reluctant to cooperate, but relented when they also arrested Aunt Bettie as a "co-conspirator."*

Will let the letter fall, and looked up in amazement. Uncle Bill got *married* in this world? That explained the flower print on the living room furniture. He realized he'd have to get used to unexpected differences. He continued reading.

>*You should know that Uncle never had any dealings with terrorists. Also understand that CID has claimed to uncovered dozens of terrorist nests in the last year alone. If one believed them—and unfortunately, far too many Americans do—the country is infested throughout with citizens bent on its destruction.*
>
>*Coerced into participating, we continued under Breggart's watchful eye, until, impatient with no results, the agent insisted that Uncle remove the protective current limit to the coils. At first, Uncle refused, unwilling to risk my life, but when Breggart coldly warned that it was either that or Aunt Bettie's life, I convinced Uncle to cooperate.*
>
>*As it turns out, the resulting increased field strength was the key to success. On the very next attempt, the exchange was successful, and I found myself in a parallel universe very different from my own. As pre-arranged, I successfully transferred back the next day to find Breggart nearly beside himself with excitement. The "other" Buck had described a world with far-advanced weapons technology, replete with energy rays able to destroy buildings from space. Unfortunately for Breggart (but fortunately for my world), the Buck of that universe, like myself, was an accountant, and he had no understanding of the principles behind the weapons. Thus, Breggart exchanged me back in order to try again, this time hoping to snag a technical Buck— presumably you.*
>
>*But as you now understand, I've swapped with you without Breggart (or Uncle William) knowing. I gambled that other universes may have switched to daylight savings time before ours, thus attempting*

the exchanges an hour earlier than Breggart expects. I have arranged to delay his arrival by feigning that I need a ride (I, of course, will not be at my house when he comes to pick me up), but I expect that he will arrive here at Uncle's house soon, so you must not dally. You should proceed to a friend of mine to whom you should show this note. He can be trusted, and will help you (for his safety, I have not revealed the whole story to him yet). He can be found at 517 Piccard St., and his name is Phil Cox. You can call a taxi—the number is written above the phone in the kitchen. I've placed money for you in the attached envelope.

Now a word of warning, of which you have probably already thought: I suggest you speak sparingly until you accustom yourself to this world's speech. I noticed in my previous exchange that I barely understood some of the idioms, and they laughed outright at my accent.

Finally, my conscience will not allow me to leave you trapped here, so I will try to arrange with my new Uncle William (your Uncle William) an exchange each day for the next two weeks at this same time for you to come home—your home. I understand that this may well result in dire circumstances for me there, but if you/ we can somehow help end this tyranny, then I will consider my life to have been of sufficient worth.

Yours respectfully,
Buck

Will stood staring at the handwritten words. They looked familiar. They should; the writing was a more precise version of his own, as though he'd taken pains to be neat.

His mind seemed stuck. He was enthralled with the note itself, entranced by the fact that another *he* had written it. He saw the elegant, cursive words, but refused to acknowledge the meaning behind them.

He suddenly shook his head and took a deep breath, breaking the trance. Like it or not, he was not in Kansas anymore, and he had to deal with it.

He read through the note again quickly, making sure he hadn't missed anything. He had no clue what the CID was, but it sounded like a dirtier version of the FBI. Either that or some special "internal security" department—maybe what Homeland Security would have evolved into, given an earlier start. It sounded a lot like McCarthyism, except using terrorists instead of commies as the bogeymen.

And the language! Buck didn't sound like him at all, more like somebody who grew up in Victorian England, exchanging bits of news with Sherlock Holmes over a spot of tea, "don't chew-know." Will decided he would indeed take Buck's warning to heart. Maybe he'd pretend to have gone mute.

He peered into the envelope and saw that Buck had given him a handful of fives, tens, and a few twenties. Accountants apparently were not very well off in this universe. He pulled a five-dollar bill out and looked at it closely. It was a dead ringer for those of his own world . . . except for the back. Instead of IN GOD WE TRUST, it simply read, ONE GOD. That could be interpreted as an inclusive gesture, but it could also be a way of saying the *only* God. Based on Buck's letter, he could guess which way it leaned, and he was glad that he'd memorized the Apostle's Creed as a kid.

Will turned his attention to the subject of clothes. He looked around again, but found no others. He had to face the fact that the circus apparel he was wearing was indeed the ones Buck had left behind when he too stepped naked between the coils. On the other hand, his counterpart might this very minute be protesting to Uncle Bill about the T-shirt and jeans *he* had to wear.

Back upstairs in the kitchen, he found the taxis number among a list of others, including pizza delivery (guaranteed one-hour delivery, or thirty percent off) just as Buck had promised. He hesitated before dialing. He was afraid that he might not understand the dispatcher, or the dispatcher him. He decided that he'd keep the exchange as simple as possible, but found he'd be lucky to make the call at all. He'd never used a rotary phone, and it wasn't as easy as it appeared in the old movies. First, his finger slipped out before he'd finished pulling the dial all the way, and then when he tried again, he wasn't sure what he'd done wrong, but he obviously had a wrong number, because he got a fast beeping tone—no voice mail. On the third attempt, he finally connected, and the man who answered spoke a reassuring form of American English, not at all like Sherlock Holmes. Will gave him his Uncle's address after rifling through the opened mail to make sure it was the same, and when the dispatcher asked for his name, he said, "Will . . . er, Buck!"

"Willard Buck?"

Just then, he heard a car pull up outside. *Breggart!* "Yes," he replied.

"Okay, Willard. The taxi should be there in about an hour."

"An *hour?*"

"Did you want the express rate? That would be twenty minutes."

"Uh, yeah."

"That's an extra two, you know."

He heard a car door slam, and then another. "That's fine. Please hurry."

"Are you asking for emergency service?"

"Er, sure," he agreed, craning his neck to see through the living room to the front window, but bushes hid his view. "How much is that?"

"Are you kidding? That doesn't cost anything."

That didn't sound good. "It doesn't cost *anything?*"

"That's what your tax dollars are for."

Uh-oh. "The express will be fine."

"You got it, Bub."

Will hung up and started for the basement, but just then the front door opened.

"—better be here, Dr. McKinney," a man was saying.

Too far to the basement door. Will ducked down behind the table, praying they wouldn't come into the kitchen.

"I don't understand," he heard his uncle—this uncle—say in the calm and measured voice he was so used to. "This isn't like Buck. He must already be here."

From his crouched position, Will saw one pair of pressed dress pants and shiny black shoes, while the other legs wore what looked like wrinkled pajamas and rubber loafers. He could guess which was his—Buck's—uncle.

The two men clattered down the basement stairs, and Will tiptoed over to the door. Peeking around the frame, he could see them standing below, looking around at the empty room. Breggart was dapper, sporting a thin mustache, like eyeliner for the upper lip. His hair was combed straight back and held in place with some sort of gel that made his hair appear wet, but not shiny. Strapped to his belt was what looked like a WWII-era walkie-talkie in a leather case. Uncle "William" looked pretty much like his own Uncle Bill. He'd apparently tried to use the same sort of hair goop, but then couldn't resist mussing it all up afterwards.

"I'm losing my patience," Breggart warned. "What's that?" he suddenly asked, pointing to the timer box Buck had placed next to the control panel. "I don't remember seeing that before."

Uncle William looked at it blankly. "That," he finally said, "is the paraflux super-surge override." The old man met the agent's eyes with nonchalant calm.

Breggart held his stare for some seconds before asking, "What's it for?"

"We added it when we took out the current limit to the coils. It prevents the whole house from blowing sky-high."

His great-uncle was the same in both universes: sharp and quick. Will could tell that this was the first time he'd laid eyes on the box.

Breggart brushed off the subject with an irritated wave of his hand and paced around the basement. "I told you what would happen if he didn't cooperate. You vouched for him." He looked at his watch. "It's quarter to twelve. If he's not here in fifteen minutes I'm going to declare both you and your wife traitors of America."

"I'm sure he'll show up," Uncle William said, but his brow was furrowed in thought. He was beginning to understand just what Buck had done.

Will's mind raced in circles, trying to decide what to do. Buck hadn't talked about what would happen to their uncle when he didn't show up. What were the consequences of being found "traitors of America"?

Uncle William absently pulled at his earlobe, and suddenly Will's decision was made. This is exactly the unconscious habit his own Uncle Bill exhibited when deep in thought. In this universe, Uncle William *was* Uncle Bill, and he could never betray him.

He looked down at himself. He was already wearing Buck's clothes, and next to Uncle William's pajama bottoms, Buck's pants didn't look quite so silly. But what about his speech? Should he try to imitate Buck's language in the letter? Everybody he'd heard so far seemed to talk normally. But Buck had warned him to speak sparingly. Frankly, he was now afraid to open his mouth.

He waited as long as he dared while Breggart paced and fumed, threatening all manner of doom on Uncle William. When the agent announced menacingly that it was now only four minutes until five, Will tiptoed to the front door, opened and slammed it, and then walked quickly to the basement doorway. "I have arrived!" he called down.

"Judas Priest!" Breggart yelled. "It's about time! Where in devil's name were you?"

Uncle William looked up in surprise, clearly not expecting any "Buck" to show up. His gaze turned to curiosity, though, as his left eyebrow lifted in a familiar arch.

"I fell in with a bit of misfortune," he replied, trying to mimic the flavor of Buck's letter as he trotted down the basement steps. "I happened upon an accident and had to lend a helping hand."

Breggart stared at him. "You look like you just stepped out of a shower," he observed.

Surreptitiously, Uncle William reached up and pointed to his own hair.

Shit! Will thought. Obviously all the men here glopped their hair back. "That is correct. I was running short on time, so I did not . . ." He waved vaguely at his head. He didn't know what they called the glop process.

Breggart glared at him. "You jeopardized the exchange to take a *shower?*"

Why would Buck do that? he thought. "I wanted to present a favorable impression in the . . . other universe."

Breggart's eyes narrowed. "What's wrong with you? Are you trying to ride me? If so, you're going to regret it."

Uncle William was smiling broadly, openly curious. He must have guessed the truth. He put his finger to his lips, indicating silence was best, just as Buck had warned. "We only have two minutes," the old scientist reminded them.

Breggart jerked his thumb angrily towards the coils.

Just as he'd done an hour earlier, Will stripped off his clothes and stood under the rod. Unlike an hour earlier, though, he now *felt* naked with Breggart staring at him. Instead of a digital clock, he stared at an eight-inch second hand sweeping away the last minute. At minus ten seconds, he took a deep breath . . . and held it. Uncle William, enigmatic now behind dark glasses, nodded slightly. Breggart, wearing wrap-around sunglasses, divided his attention between the coils and the clock. At minus five seconds, the agent began counting down, and at the exact instant the second hand swung to twelve, Will closed his eyes, and the basement burst once again with the lightning of arcing electrons.

Chapter 3

When he opened his eyes again, Will saw that Breggart had torn off his sunglasses, and was staring at him.

Will shrugged.

"It didn't work!" Breggart cried, turning on Uncle William in accusation.

The old man lifted his shoulders. "Even with increased coil current, it's still hit-and-miss. We went forty years without a single successful exchange."

Breggart's eyes bored into the scientist for an eternal few seconds, and then he spun on Will. "You're up to something," he hissed, pressing his face close, as though the answer was written in tiny print between Will's eyes.

"I don't know what you're talking about," Will replied, stepping back and giving up the stilted speech. He suddenly felt desperately vulnerable standing there naked, and reached down to gather his clothes.

The doorbell rang upstairs.

The taxi!

"Who in Judas' name is that?" Breggart cried. "Are you expecting anyone?" he asked Uncle William, who shook his head.

Will didn't know what to do. He was naked. He stood, frozen, staring at Breggart.

"Stay here," the agent ordered, and took the stairs two at a time as the doorbell rang a second time.

Uncle William watched Breggart until he was gone and then turned to Will who was pulling on the pants. "Are you Buck?" the old man whispered.

Will shook his head and picked up the shirt.

"Buck did the exchange on his own?"

"An hour ago."

"The rascal! That explains the box—it's a timer control, isn't it?"

Will nodded, sitting on the cement floor to pull on Buck's shoes.

"What's the plan?"

Will looked up. "To get back to my world as soon as you and . . . Aunt Bettie are safe, I guess."

"Of course," the old scientist said. He sounded disappointed.

"Buck asked me to help your world."

"We certainly need it."

Will stood up and looked at the man who had shared a youth with his own Uncle Bill. "I'm afraid I don't have anything to offer," Will explained. "I'm just a math instructor. I don't know anything about advanced weapons."

The old man smiled. Will felt in his bones that he was looking at the same man he'd loved all his life.

"It's not weapons we need," his uncle said quietly.

"I don't know what else—"

Breggart was coming down the stairs. "It's a taxi, for somebody named Willard."

"Uh, that's for me."

Breggart stood before him, hands on hips. "Why did you use a different name?"

"I, uh . . . they must have gotten confused."

He shrugged. What else could he say?

The agent tipped his head towards the stairs. "Well, you'd better get going. The meter's running."

Will was surprised that Breggart was letting him go, but wasn't about to question his good fortune. With a quick glance at Uncle William standing at the control panel, he headed for the stairs. The only sound was the familiar low hum of current coursing through the massive coils. *That's odd*, he suddenly thought. Why would Uncle William be charging the system again?

As he started up the stairs, Breggart called, "You can come out now, Buck!"

Will turned and saw Breggart looking towards the far corner.

Buck is here? Will thought, his mind swirling in confusion. He peered towards the corner, trying to discern his other self.

There was nobody there. He looked at Breggart who was watching him through narrow, furious eyes. "You thought you could fool me," the agent said, his eyes going wide, ". . . Willard!" He reached inside his coat and took out an odd-looking gun. It had sleek, esthetic lines, almost dainty. "When did you make the exchange?"

Behind Breggart, Uncle William had gone berserk. He was rocking his head, and pointing at his squinting eyes as though showing off his stereotypic Chinaman impersonation. Suddenly Will understood and he gave a quick nod. The old scientist immediately reached for the main switch on the panel. Breggart turned to look behind him as Will squeezed his eyes shut, and with a sizzling snap, light as bright as the sun filled the basement.

Will opened them, and even through closed eyelids, the light left a bright after-image. Breggart put his arm over his face, too late to protect himself from temporary blindness. Will turned and ran up the steps. He heard a loud thwip, like the solid crack of a whip, and felt the staircase shudder with the concussion of an impact. Despite its delicate appearance, the gun was apparently deadly. Below him, he heard a thump and a groan as he burst through the basement doorway into the house.

What to do? *Run!* But where?

Behind him, Uncle William came through the doorway.

"What about—"

"I hit him," the old man said as he closed and locked the basement door.

"Did you get the gun?"

The wrinkled face looked at him quickly, surprised, and then wagged a denial. "They're called keepers now," he explained, leading Will to the front door, "and in this world, it's an automatic death sentence for a normal citizen to be caught holding one—at least in America."

"Did you say 'keeper'?"

The scientist snorted. "It's short for peace-keeper. Ironic, eh?"

"Where are we going?"

"You're going to take your taxi and get the devil away from here."

Will glanced out the window. A yellow cartoon car sat out front. "What about you?"

"I'll go and let Breggart out once you're gone."

"But—"

"He has Bettie."

They stood staring at each other. Here was a whole new uncle, with a whole life of which he knew nothing, and now would never know.

"Buck was right in what he did," the old man finally said. "We can't let them get weapons from other worlds. It could mean the end of all free nations on Earth."

Will nodded. He and Buck were essentially the same, after all.

"Do you have money?" the old man asked.

He felt his pocket, and pulled out the wad.

Uncle William's eyebrows shot up. "Well, that should do you for a while."

From behind the basement door, Breggart banged and yelled threats.

"You'd better go," the old scientist urged, smiling at him.

"Right," Will said, and then tentatively held out his hand.

The old man grinned broadly and gave him a hug. "Do good," he said into his ear before pulling away.

Will walked out the door, but then turned back. "How did you know?"

"Besides the fact that you were talking like Shakespeare? You filled your lungs to ensure that the exchange wouldn't succeed."

Suddenly a small hole blew open through the basement door.

"I'd better let him out," Uncle William said, "before he rips apart my house."

Will nodded and sprinted away to the waiting taxi. He climbed in the back and told the driver to go. His new-world uncle waved, then turned and disappeared.

"Where to?" the taxi driver asked, glancing back, and then looked again in surprise. Like Breggart and Uncle William, the man's hair was slicked flat.

He'd have to get some of that goop.

Will read Phil Cox's address aloud from Buck's note.

"You got it, Joe," the driver affirmed, pulling away.

For the first time since arriving in the parallel universe, he had time to sit back and look around. The taxi seemed fairly new, and not very different from cars he was used to, other than the bulging compartment which gave him the sense of being more distant from the terrain sliding by. He wondered idly if there was a reason for the extra headroom. Maybe in this world women wore their hair up in gigantic puffy balls, like the beehive hairdos in the sixties and again in the "big hair" days of the eighties. But then they drove by women walking along the sidewalks, and he saw that the opposite was the case: all had short-cropped, stylishly-cut hair. As if to balance that convenience, though, all the women wore dresses—some long, some short. Apparently Mary Tyler Moore's *Luara Petrie* character hadn't broken the slacks barrier in this universe.

He realized that he was hearing a relentless ticking sound, and looking around, saw that it was the taxi meter. This surprised him; he was used to glowing LED displays. This device looked like it was taken from a museum, except that it was new, like the rest of the taxi.

Motion caught his eye off to the left. It was a rocket! Riding above a billowing plume of pure-white smoke perhaps three miles away, the unmistakable finned V-2 shape rose straight up, then tilted towards him. He scrambled to the other side of the cab as it passed over them, but the smoke trail hid the rocket ship as it gained altitude. An instant later, the taxi shuddered as the sound overtook them.

"Jesus Christ!" he cried. "Did you see *that*!"

Suddenly the taxi driver pulled over to the curb. He twisted around, and his face was red with anger. "Get out!" he cried.

Will was dumbstruck. "What's the matter?"

"What's the *matter*? Are you binny? Do you want me to lose my license?"

What had he done? "I'm sorry. I din't know—did I offend you somehow?"

The driver studied him, probably trying to discern if he was just being a smart-ass. "Where are you from?"

Where, indeed? Another universe?

"I'm not from this country. I'm really sorry if I offended you."

The man seemed to have calmed down. "You can offend me all you want—I get it all day long. Just don't bring down the law."

"Was it what I said?"

The driver sighed. "Yes, taking the Lord in vain is illegal. Not everybody's gonna be as tolerant as me."

He'd have to be careful. Buck had warned him: keep your trap shut.

"I heard someone say . . . Judas Priest."

"So?"

"That's okay to say?"

"Of course."

"How about 'shit'?"

The driver scowled. "It's not against the law, but people will think you're a potty-mouth."

Potty mouth? He remembered the rocket. "What *was* that?"

"What was what?"

"That . . . rocket, I guess."

The man shrugged. "It looked like it was headed east—I guess either the afternoon Chicago or New York jump."

"Did you say 'jump'?"

"Yeah," he replied, clearly getting annoyed with this idiot. "A jump. You know, a . . . jump!"

"It's a *passenger* rocket?"

"I don't know, it might have been cargo—look, you want me to take you to the airport for a schedule?"

"No, no, that's okay. Do they still use jets?"

The driver gave him a distinctly suspicious look. "Where exactly did you say you're from?"

Will's mind raced. He needed someplace that was probably still developing . . . but would speak English. "Botswana."

"Never heard of it."

"It's in Africa."

"So, do they use jets there?"

What was the right answer? "No, of course not."

"Then why would they still use them in the U-S of A?"

Will sat back and crossed his arms. "I was just asking."

He vowed to keep his trap shut even if he had to sew his lips together.

He looked for the rocket—the "jump"—but it was gone. Strangely, even the smoke seemed to have disappeared.

Fifteen minutes later, the taxi stopped in front of a townhouse in the southeastern suburbs of Seattle. The whole row of them looked huge, until Will saw that each had a thin facade that continued up at least a half-story above the actual roof, like the buildings in dusty old-west towns. He was going to comment on them, but remembered the trap-shut rule.

"Can you wait for me?" he asked.

The driver looked at him a moment, and then said, "How 'bout the fare for this leg?"

"How much?" Will asked, pulling the wad of bills from his pocket.

The man pointed at the meter. It read: *1-83*. "That don't include the two for the express service," he added.

Will still wasn't sure what the fare was, but respected the trap-shut rule. He fished through his bills, and pulled out a twenty. He handed it to the driver, ready to pull out another if necessary.

The man looked pained. "Aw come on. You got anything smaller? I ain't got that kind of change."

Will pulled out a five and offered it in exchange it for the twenty, watching for the reaction.

The driver looked satisfied and handed him a dollar and seventeen in change.

Will took it and folded his stack of bills.

The driver watched him. "This Botswana must be one rich little country."

Will nodded again, and opened the door.

"Hey, Joe," the man suddenly said.

"Yeah," Will replied, turning back.

"Listen, you're new in America. Let me give you a tip: keep that wad out of sight. No use tempting some beggar."

Will looked at the fives and tens that were showing. He imagined them with another zero at the end. He smiled. "Right, thanks."

Blaine C. Readler

At the front door he found the doorbell and pushed it. Seconds later the door swung open, revealing a pretty woman with her hair combed back almost like the men's. When she saw him, her eyes went wide in alarm. "Buck!" she cried, glancing around nervously, as though expecting to see masked men hiding in the shrubbery, then turned back to him and glanced, perplexed, at his hair.

He found it impossible to explain the situation. "Is Phil here?" he simply asked.

She stared at the taxi a moment, then said, "Wait here," and disappeared inside.

When she returned a moment later, she stood with her hands on her hips. "Phil's not here," she said meaningfully.

He just looked at her. "When will he be back?"

Her brow furrowed, and she sneaked a glance to each side. "I don't know." Her eyes were saying, *listen to what I'm saying.*

"I see," he said. He didn't know what to do. Why didn't she invite him in?

"Well," she said, suddenly holding her hand out, "it was nice seeing you, Buck."

Perplexed, he shook her hand . . . and felt something between their palms. She gripped his hand and looked him in the eye, then slowly pulled her hand away. Totally bewildered now, he almost dropped the note, but recovered just in time to clench it and put both his hands in his pockets where he dropped it. "Okay," he said, nodding once. "See you."

She quickly closed the door in his face, and he turned and walked back to the taxi.

"Where to?" the driver asked.

"Just go. I have to think."

He took the note from his pocket. Like Buck's, the handwriting was neat and florid.

> *Buck,*
>
> *Please accept my apologies for leaving before speaking with you in person, but as you will see, urgent circumstances demand haste. I know and trust that you did not divulge details about our activities with your uncle, but apparently—somehow—you have attracted the*

28

attention of CID. They are now looking for me, and I must exit the stage post-haste. I will try to keep in touch through Neck.

And now, Buck, to the painful revelation. I implore you to bide your heart and find compassion and forgiveness for what I am about to tell you: Lilda, blessed with our child-to-be, cannot take flight, but must beg ignorance to CID (and mercy, if it comes to that). Therefore, I have instructed—nay, required—that she call CID ten minutes hence as you read these words and report your visit. In this way she may gain some amount of favor with our foe.

Good luck, my friend, and may we someday again share happy times, although, that would now seem to require a miracle.

Favored Regards,
Phil

He scanned through the note a second time. No wonder Phil and Buck were friends; they talked the same Victorian language.

It looked like Buck had become a real liability to his friends and family. But why would Phil have to run? He apparently didn't know about Uncle Bill's project, otherwise he would have known how Buck had stumbled onto CID's radar screen. Maybe Phil and Buck were up to something else. Maybe counterfeiting. A handful of hundreds and they could retire. But who was this Neck guy, if it even was a person? Whoever he was, it was his only lead—

"You want me to stop when I get to Canada?" the driver asked dryly, breaking Will's train of thought.

"No! Turn around!"

"You got it, Joe," the driver said, executing a U-turn.

Back at the townhouse, Will ran up the walk and rang the doorbell. Phil's wife swung the door open and gasped.

"Who's Neck?" he asked.

She stared at him, her eyes a turmoil of suspicion and fear.

She thinks I'm Buck, he reminded himself. *I'm supposed to know Neck.* "Look, it's a long story," he explained, "and for your own sake, you want to remain clueless."

"Clueless?" she asked, more confused.

"Having no clue, ignorant."

She shook her head as though clearing it of unwanted distraction. "I've called CID," she whispered urgently.

"I thought you were supposed to wait ten minutes?"

She just looked at him, distraught.

"Christ!" he muttered.

Her eyes went wide in shock.

"I know, Buck wouldn't say something like that. I'm sorry, it's reflex. Just tell me how I can contact this Neck guy and I promise to leave you alone."

She took a deep breath, and let it out slowly, looking up and down the street. "I don't know him," she said, "but I've heard Phil talk to him on the phone. He works at a privy called Pungent Sound."

"A privy?"

She nodded and stood watching him expectantly.

It suddenly came to him. "You think I'm with the CID, don't you?"

She studied his face a moment, and then gave a little shrug.

He shook his head. "Look, don't worry. I'm not even sure who the CID are."

Her brow was furrowed, but the corner of her mouth curled in a little smile, and she gave a quick nod.

"Right," he said. "I promised." He turned and sprinted back to the waiting cab.

The driver knew the place. "Rough area—Sodo."

That, at least, was the same as his own Seattle. Some things apparently had enough historical momentum to carry on through many universes. "What's a 'privy'?" Will asked.

The driver looked at him in the mirror. "Are you kidding?"

"Botswana, remember? To me, a privy is a toilet."

"It's a bar."

"Where they serve alcohol?"

The driver glanced in the mirror again. "Yeah. Where they serve booze."

"Why do they call it a privy?"

"It's short for 'private club.'"

"It's *private*?" He wondered if Buck had a membership.

"They're all private. Public bars are illegal. Pretty strange you didn't know even that," the man said, studying him in the mirror in a way that was becoming all too familiar.

Trap-shut rule, he reminded himself.

It took them nearly forty minutes, all by highways bristling with traffic lights. When he asked why they just didn't take the Route 5 interstate, the driver had no idea what he was talking about. Sodo was even grittier than the industrial area from his Seattle, and despite the distinction of being a private club, Pungent Sound turned out to look like any other tired and dingy bar. Inside, it was so dark he had to wait a moment for his eyes to adjust. Stale beer and staler cigarette smoke made him resent breathing, and the scattering of sad-looking customers didn't even look up at him. He asked the bartender if Neck was around. The dumpy man wiped his hands on his apron and stared at him. "I know," Will agreed, "my hair's all messed up."

The glazed expression didn't waver as the bartender asked, "You got a card?"

Credit card? ID card? Will remembered—it was a private club. "You mean a membership card?"

"No, a beauty pageant card," the man quipped, staring him in the eye.

"No."

"Stan," the bartender barked without taking his eyes from Will. "This guy's your guest."

The soak sitting a few stools down the bar grunted.

"That'll be twenty-five for a guest pass," the bartender said, holding his hand out.

Twenty-five what? Twenty-five cents, or twenty-five dollars? It couldn't be dollars. That would be something like five hundred "real" dollars. He reached into his pocket, but remembered the cabby's advice and pulled out just the top bill. Holding it under the bar, he saw it was a five. He reached in for another, and this time pulled out a single dollar, which he handed over.

"What'll it be?" the bartender asked, opening the register and depositing the dollar, but then closing it again without taking any change.

He didn't really want anything, but also didn't want to draw attention. Would they have beer in this universe? Would they still *call* it beer? "A beer."

"What kind?"

"Whatever you have on draft."

"Never heard of that kind. Where's it made?"

He took a wild shot. "How about Budweiser?"

The bartender reached down and placed a familiar-looking can in front of him, then set a dirty glass next to it.

Will pulled the tab, and was surprised when it came off. He looked up at the bartender, but he'd already shuffled down to the other end of the bar. Pop-tops. He remembered them from when he was a little kid. Curious, he took a swig. It tasted like . . . Budweiser. Some things were just inevitable.

Enough distractions. "So, what about Neck?" he called to the bartender.

The man stared at the floor a moment, as though the burdens of life were almost too much to bear, then sighed and ambled back. "What about him?"

"I'd like to talk to him."

The bartender watched him impassively a moment. "What's your business?"

"I think that's between me and Neck."

The man shrugged and walked away.

"Okay! Phil said that I should look him up."

He turned around. "Phil Cox?"

"Yeah. Look, it's important."

The doughy face looked at him a few seconds, and then walked to the end of the bar and dialed a phone. Will couldn't hear what was said, but when the man put the handset back on the cradle, he walked back and nodded towards the back of the room. "Neck's upstairs." And with that, the bartender turned and walked away.

Leaving his watery beer on the bar, he found two doors down a short, dark hallway: one was clearly a bathroom, but the other was unmarked. He opened it and found stairs. At the top, another short hall led to three more doors, all closed.

Would Buck have known which room it was? He decided to hedge his bet. Neck would be expecting him; instead of knocking on any one door, he rapped his knuckles on the wall and called out softly. Sure enough, the end door swung open, and Will was looking at an older man, part and parcel with the drab surroundings. Indeed, he seemed to live here. His clothes were wrinkled, as though he had slept in them, and from the room spilled the smell of habitation—cooked fish mixed with sweat and stale beer.

Will now understood where the man had gotten his nickname: his neck was more like a thick thigh than a throat. In reality, he had no neck; the head merged smoothly from the ears into the shoulders.

The rumpled man just stood, looking at Will, waiting for him to say something. "Neck," he greeted, nodding.

The man's eyes narrowed at hearing the name.

Will suddenly realized that just because others use a nickname freely doesn't mean the owner welcomes it. Would Buck have known this?

"Phil suggested I contact you," Will quickly added.

Neck's eyes glared cold suspicion as he continued to stare at him. After an endless few seconds, he stepped back and motioned for Will to enter.

Inside, worn furniture crouched in permanent surrender among threadbare carpets and faded walls. A dirty sheet covered something unrecognizable in one corner.

Neck watched him closely. "I hear the Sabres are playing home," he finally said in a deep, raspy voice.

Will returned his gaze and nodded slowly. Who, or what, were the Sabres? Maybe a football or basketball team. The comment seemed out of context. Neck watched him, dead serious. Why would he bring up sports? Why not ask him why he was here?

The man's eyes moved ever so slightly, focusing just to the left of him, and instantly Will knew that the comment wasn't idle conversation, but a leading phrase. The real Buck would have known the proper response—the password.

Before he could react, though, somebody grabbed him from behind, and the cold, sharp edge of a knife pressed against his throat. Neck's face was suddenly inches from his, and he was yelling at him. "Admit it!" he screamed.

"Admit *what?*" Will cried, his voice trembling.

Neck ran to the door and closed it, then came back. "You're a terrorist," he said more calmly. "Admit it."

Panic clutched Will's chest. He could see that Neck was setting the stage to kill him. But *why?*

"I'm not a terrorist," he pleaded. "Look, I don't even really know Phil. Buck—the real Buck—left a note that told me to see Phil for help. When I got there, he was gone—he had to run from the CID—and *he* left me a note to see *you!* For Christ's sake! I don't know that the hell is going on!"

At his blasphemy, Neck moved back and his face relaxed into curiosity. The edge of the knife pressed harder against his throat, though, as though the owner was anxious to finish the job.

Reckless language probably saved his life.

"What do you mean, the 'real' Buck?" Neck asked.

"I . . . I just look like Buck." They'd never believe the truth. "We're twins, but I'm not from here."

Neck's eyes bore into his. "Where are you from?"

A whole other universe—one that's sane. "Botswana."

"Botswana? Where's that?"

"Africa. Just north of South Africa."

He shook his head. "Never heard of it."

"It's small. Colonized by the Dutch."

"What are you doing here?"

"I came to . . . help Buck."

Neck stared at him, tapping his thumb unconsciously against the dirty shirt across his chest. "Hold him," he finally said to the unseen man behind him, and reached forward and frisked him, feeling carefully—more carefully than needed to find a gun or knife.

They think I may be CID, Will thought. Neck was looking for a wire. "I need help," he said as his captor felt along his legs and ankles. "The CID is probably after *me!*"

Neck froze and looked up at him, then slowly stood up. "Why?"

Will wasn't sure a lie would be any better. "My uncle—Buck's uncle—*our* uncle, has been doing some experiments that they're interested in. I was pretending to be Buck, and one of their agents, Breggart, found out—"

"Did you say Breggart?"

"Yeah. Why?"

Neck stared at him a second, then shrugged and said, "He's a very patriotic citizen—to be commended."

Will returned the stare. The guy wasn't taking any chances in case he really was with the CID.

"Can you help me?" Will finally asked.

Neck looked at him a moment, and then shook his head. "Sorry. It's nit."

Will could guess what the phrase meant. "Then, can I go?"

For the first time, Neck grinned and nodded to the man holding him, and the knife withdrew.

Will took a deep breath, and resisting the urge to look at the Neck's accomplice, started for the door.

"Hold it," Neck said.

He turned and his eyes went wide when he saw that the person holding the knife was a woman, weathered and muscular.

"For the cause," Neck said, holding out his hand, palm up.

Will considered running, but reached into his pocket instead. He felt the wad of bills, and also the loose five that he'd taken out at the bar. He pulled that out and handed it to Neck who raised his eyebrows when he saw the denomination, but took it with one swift motion, and it was gone from sight. "Thank you, brother," the man said.

Will walked to the door, but stopped and turned around. The man and woman stared at him stone-faced. He wanted to tell them that brothers don't extort each other.

Instead, he turned and trotted down the stairs before they changed their minds. Extortion was preferred to a slit throat.

Chapter 4

The taxi still waited for Will outside the Pungent Sound. He was glad to see it—his only haven. That in itself was depressing, though. And frightening.

The driver was content having a live-in, on-meter fare, but the wad of bills would eventually give out, despite the greatly expanded value. He told the driver to find a phone booth, and was relieved when the man didn't ask him what that was.

Three blocks later, Will flipped, ever more desperately, through a phone book attached to a heavy chain. He first looked for Alicia's name, and then several of his friends. He didn't really expect to find them, as they were all born after Uncle Bill's universe split in 1947, but he had to give it a try. The hard confirmation that he was really and truly all alone in this vast universe raised the hairs on the back of his neck. Even his—Buck's—father was dead. For the first time in his life he was totally lost, with absolutely nowhere to go.

He sat down on a low retaining wall next to the phone booth and struggled to keep the panic from overwhelming him. Another car had pulled up behind the taxi, and a woman leaned over into the passenger seat to gawk at him through the open window. She was about his age, with a thin face and a hint of a hawk-nose. She wasn't model material, but he found her attractive, especially the subtle sense of intelligence that animated her features. She looked at him and smiled—the kind of familiar smile that expected a like response. When he just sat staring at her, she wrinkled her brow and waved him over.

He looked around, expecting to find somebody behind him, then stood up, uncertain what to do.

Impatient, she opened the car door, climbed out, and ran to him with arms open wide. "Buck!" she called, "I'm so glad you're okay!"

So, that was it. He let her wrap her arms around him, and he gently returned the hug. It wasn't difficult.

"You gave me a real scare," she whispered into his ear.

He didn't know what to say. "I'm not Buck," would have been a good start, but then she'd let him go.

She pulled away anyway, disconcerted. "You really don't want to see me, do you?"

He shook his head in confusion. He couldn't find any words.

Now she looked angry—a woman scorned. "Then why did you leave me the note?"

His mind raced for something to say.

She tossed her head, spun on her heal, and started back to her car. "It's my own fault," she declared. "I'll never learn."

"Don't go!" he finally blurted.

She stopped and turned, nodding her head as though this was expected. "Don't go, but don't really stay, either. Nothing's changed, has it?"

He sighed. "I don't know your name."

This threw her. She seemed to struggle to understand what he was trying to tell her.

"I mean," he continued, "I really don't know your name."

Understanding dawned, but with it, skepticism. "Are you trying to tell me that you've . . . that you're . . ."

"Not Buck," he finished for her.

She took a few steps back and outright disbelief screwed her face. "What are you trying to pull? Is this some sort of game?"

He studied her a moment. Even when angry, she looked appealing. "What did Buck tell you?"

She seemed to be deciding whether to go along with him. "Then, who are you?" she asked, ignoring his question.

"It would be easier to explain if I had an idea what you already know."

She sighed, and looked at the taxi. "Where's your car?"

He grinned. "No place where I can get at it. If you're talking about Buck's car, I have no idea."

She rolled her eyes. "Come on. Pay the cabber," she said and got back into her car.

He turned his back to the cab, took out his wad, and pealed off a five. He hesitated, pulled off another five, and put the rest back in his pocket. At the cab, he leaned in the passenger window and asked how much he owed. Like before, the driver pointed to the meter, which read *2-58*. He knew now that this meant two dollars, fifty-eight cents. He handed one of the fives through the window and said, "Keep the change."

The driver looked at him in surprise. "Judas, thanks!"

Will straightened up and slid the remaining five back into his pocket, realizing he'd just given a tip worth nearly fifty dollars. He'd have to be more careful with Buck's money.

"Hey, Joe!" the driver called.

He leaned back through the window, and the man winked and handed him a two-dollar bill. "Maybe you're really loaded and I'm a sucker, but it wouldn't be Christian to take this."

Will took the bill and smiled. "I'm not rich, just stupid." He reached in and shook the man's hand. "Thank you," he said, and trotted over to the car where Buck's girlfriend—or maybe ex-girlfriend—waited.

"What's your name?" he asked her as he climbed into the passenger seat.

She searched his face, looking for truth. "My name is Donna," she finally said.

He held out his hand. "I'm Will."

She took a deep breath and accepted his handshake. "My name isn't Donna," she confessed. "It's Francine."

He grinned. "You just wanted to watch my reaction."

She shrugged and nodded.

"Look, I don't know how to convince you that I'm not Buck. There's probably a thousand ways he could prove he *is* Buck, but how do I prove I'm *not*? Under normal circumstances, I could by proving who I really am, but—"

"You have no history."

He stared at her. "You know?"

"Do I *know*? No, I don't *know*. I only heard what . . . Buck told me."

"And what's that?"

She hesitated. It was obviously hard to talk about crazy things. "He was helping his great-uncle with some experiment that's been going on for years—"

"Uncle William."

She looked at him.

"I met him," he explained. ". . . when I arrived."

She gave him that skeptical the-jury's-still-out look. "If I didn't adore Uncle William," she said, "I'd think he was binny—"

"I assume 'binny' means crazy?"

She just looked at him with that doubtful raised eyebrow. "Anyway," she went on, "Buck said that Uncle William was trying to exchange him for his counterpart from another world. This is presumably . . . you."

"Except that in my universe, my name isn't Buck, but Will— short for William. I was named after *my* Uncle William, who goes by Bill."

She stared at him a moment. "Buck's name is actually William."

"Really? That's wild. Why the nickname Buck?"

"Buck Rogers."

"The *comic* book character?"

She snorted. "Buck took his nickname from the first man who stepped foot on mars. He was five years old when that happened, and he insisted everybody call him Buck after that."

"But, he would have been five in 1979."

"So?"

"When did the first man land on the moon?"

"1972"

"And they went to Mars seven years later?"

"Why not?"

"Why . . . in my universe, we *still* haven't been to Mars!"

She just looked at him.

"I *saw* a rocket!" he exclaimed, suddenly remembering. "It went right overhead." He demonstrated by pretending that his hand was the rocket zooming over his head.

Francine stared at him quizzically. "You don't have rockets in . . . your universe?"

"Sure! The Space Shuttle."

"*The* Space Shuttle? One?"

"Heck no! There's *two*! There used to be four, but two were destroyed. Actually, even those two are retired now. But we still have them. Uh, how many reusable rockets do you have that can make it into orbit?"

She sat back in surprise, as though this was a question that she'd never contemplated. "I have no idea. Hundreds, I guess. Probably more like thousands. It depends on whether you include all the jumps, which, technically, could make orbit."

He sat staring at her. Was she pulling his leg?

"Why don't you let that sink in," she suggested dryly, putting the car into gear. "While I take us home."

He tried to let it sink in, but the idea that humans could go to Mars seven years after first landing on the moon bobbed there on the surface, a persistent buoy of incredulity.

Wait, did she say *home*? "Uh, Francine, do you and I . . . I mean, are you and Buck . . ."

"Married?"

"I was going to say living together."

She gave him a quick glance. "First, do you know that an unmarried couple living together is illegal?"

"It *is*?"

"Formally. It's one of those laws they enforce when somebody complains, or you're already on their list. In reality, it happens a lot. You just have to be able to show another address to call your domicile—usually a friend's house."

"So . . ."

"Are we married? No. Promises, promises. Living together? Up until a couple of months ago when you developed chicken feet."

"Uh, you mean Buck."

She glanced over again. "Of course. Buck."

It sounded like he did indeed have a lot in common with Buck. He watched the urban neighborhoods of Seattle roll past. He could easily imagine he was home . . . if he ignored the women dressed in Sunday-best dresses, and the men who all looked like James Dean obsessed with a new hair cream.

"How did you find me?" he asked.

"Your note said that—"

"Uh, you mean Buck's note."

She sighed. "*Buck's* note explained that he was going to attempt an early exchange, and if it was successful, he would send his 'other' self to Canada for help. That was code. We used to call Phil and Lilly Canadians because they were always scheming to emigrate there . . . before the borders were closed."

"Lilly—she's Lilda?"

Francine nodded. "I went to see her," she said, "and she explained that you'd been there acting binny."

"There's that word again. What exactly does binny mean?"

"Binny," she said, as though it was self-explanatory. "It comes from those decorative marks that Hindu Indian women wear on their foreheads."

"You mean a bindi."

"Yeah."

"Uh, isn't that, like, cultural slander?"

Francine gave him a sly sidelong glance. "Are you sure you're not Buck?"

"Why?"

"He refused to use it for that very reason."

"Why *do* people say it?"

She puckered her mouth, contemplating a difficult subject. "America isn't the same country that fought the Germans in the Second World War. Back then, we thought we were better than everybody else, but we were content to let them live their lives. Now we *know* we are better than everybody else, and anybody who doesn't pledge allegiance to the American Value is a *foreigner*—and there was a time when that wasn't even a derogatory word."

He remembered what the cab driver told him about taking the Lord's name in vain. "Let me guess: the American Value is white and Christian."

"If you asked a politician, he would refute that, but in essence, yes."

"Do blacks have equal rights?"

"What do you mean, 'blacks'?"

"African Americans?"

"You mean Negroes?"

"Uh, yeah."

"Again, if you ask a politician, he'll say yes. In reality? Far from it."

"What about the 15th amendment?"

She squinted one eye. "Refresh my memory."

"The bill was passed after the Civil War. It gave blacks—Negroes—the right to vote."

"Some vote, though not enough to make a difference."

"Why only some?"

She looked at him as if confirming he was serious. "They can't pass the test. Most don't even try; they know that they'll be branded as trouble-makers."

"Blacks have to take some sort of literacy test in order to vote?"

"Yeah. Actually, everybody's supposed to take the test, but you can get a waiver if you can show 'civil competency.' This was originally reserved for people with college degrees, but it now includes anybody with a high school diploma, and they're talking about making it hereditary."

"And Negroes don't go to high school?"

She rolled her eyes. "Of course not. Negroes go to Colored School."

" 'Equal but separate.' "

She laughed. "Be careful about what you say. Too much talk about Negro equality is considered insurgency."

"Your world never had a Voting Rights Act of '65?"

She shrugged and shook her head.

"How about a Lyndon Johnson?"

She thought a moment. "The name's familiar. I think he was a vice president."

"To JFK?"

"You mean Jack Kennedy?"

"Yeah! Lyndon Johnson became president when Kennedy was assassinated."

"*Assassinated?*"

"Kennedy wasn't assassinated in your world?"

"Judas, no!"

The worlds had obviously started to diverge considerably after fifteen years. "Didn't Kennedy try to advance civil rights?"

"Civil rights?"

"You don't even know what it *means*?"

"I can guess: more freedom for Negroes."

He sighed. "That would be a start."

"You know," she warned, "you really should watch what you say."

"I know: insurgency. I'm already on the run for kidnapping a government agent. How much worse could talking about a taboo subject be?"

Francine gave him an ominous sidelong glance. "Plenty. Kidnapping is a criminal offense. As merely a violent criminal, you're protected by the court system. What you're talking about would be considered sedition."

"Talking about civil rights is worse than kidnapping?"

She pulled into a parking area next to an apartment complex. Taking an empty spot, she shut off the engine and turned to him. "You could be accused of being a terrorist."

He shrugged. "And that takes me outside the judicial system?"

"You bet," she replied, getting out of the car.

He climbed out and followed her through a door into the building and up two flights of stairs. "What about the First Amendment?" he asked to her back.

She turned and gave him an alarmed look. He understood. Neighbors might be listening.

He nodded and followed her silently down a short hall and through another door into her apartment. What the hell had he gotten himself into? He was beginning to understand that his life was in this woman's hands.

She closed the door and turned to him. "You mean freedom of speech?" she said. "You're free to talk about anything you like, as long as it doesn't denigrate the government or blaspheme religion."

"Christian religion, you mean."

"In America, it's one and the same."

"What about Jews?"

"What about them?"

"Do they practice Judaism? Do they have synagogues?"

"Of course."

"Let me guess: it's okay, though, if I trash Yahweh."

"Now you're getting it. Hold on—I have to use the bathroom."

She disappeared down a hall, and Will took the opportunity to check out the place where his other self had lived. The furnishings seemed normal enough. It could easily have been any apartment from his own universe . . . except for the phone.

"Why all the old-fashioned phones?" he asked when she returned.

She shook her head, perplexed.

"Every phone I've seen so far is a dial type."

"So?"

He looked at her. "That's all you have?"

She shrugged. "Sure. Why not?"

"No cell phones?"

She grinned. "Somehow, I don't think you mean phones in jail cells."

"What about cordless phones?"

"You mean radio phones?"

"I guess."

She shrugged again. "Police cars carry them."

"How could you go to Mars, and not even have portable telephones?"

She just looked at him. His question was obviously gibberish to her.

"Let's back up. Do you have integrated circuits?"

"Integrated? I don't think I understand—all electronics have circuits that are integrated."

"I mean chips. You know, miniaturized circuits. Actually, maybe you wouldn't know."

She gave him a hard look. "You think a mathematician knows more about electronics than a physicist?"

"Uh, you're a physicist?"

She grinned. "There's no law yet banning women scientists. So, what's a 'chip'?"

"Maybe you have another name for it. A bunch of transistors all built up on one wafer of silicon."

She wrinkled her brow. "Transistor?"

He laughed out loud. "You don't know what a transistor is?"

She just stared at him coldly.

"Sorry. A transistor . . . what would you call it here? Silicon doped so that it's a semiconductor with junctions that ... hell, I don't know exactly how they work."

She just shook her head. She had no idea what he was talking about.

"Look, how big are your computers?"

She raised that eyebrow. "I've seen pictures," she said.

He was beginning to understand ... and it was difficult to swallow. "You've never seen a computer?"

She shook her head as though it was a stupid question. "Why would I want to?"

"Where do they keep them?"

" 'Them'? You mean, 'It.' "

"There's just *one*?"

"In America. England has one. And France."

"Let me guess," he predicted, "they fill rooms."

"Of course."

What happened here? he thought. *Where did they go wrong?* "Shockley didn't invent the transistor?"

She shrugged. "He invented the minitube," she offered.

"Minitube? What's that?"

"Maybe it's another name for your ... transmister?"

"Tran-*sis*-ter."

"Right. In the early fifties, he developed the field emitter."

It was Will's turn to shake his head in ignorance.

"Before that," she went on, "tubes were thermionic—"

"Right!" he cried. Finally, common ground. "Heating elements that give off electrons—I think it's called the cathode. High voltage then draws them to the other side of the tube."

She smiled at his description. "Close enough. Anyway, Shockley discovered that electrons could be freed from certain crystalline compounds using voltage fields alone. That, in turn, reduced the power consumption by magnitudes, and allowed the tubes to be made smaller—much smaller."

"The size of a pin head," he offered.

"*No*," she scoffed. "That's ridiculous."

"How small, then? How many could fit on a penny?"

She thought a moment. "Maybe ten."

He was beginning to see the picture. The minitube of this universe was a red herring. It provided a path of progress away from the clumsy thermionic tubes, but was ultimately a dead end miniaturization-wise.

"In your universe," he explained, "you can fit ten minitubes on a penny, but in mine, we can fit hundreds of millions of transistors."

A skeptical smile spread across her face. "Millions?"

"Maybe billions by now. I can't keep track."

"You're joking."

"No. I'm not."

She stared at him a moment. "That's impossible. These . . . transistors would have to be . . . why, they'd have to be maybe microns in size."

"That sounds right. I recall them talking about sub-micron dimensions."

She just looked at him, seeming to size him up, deciding if he was trying to pull one over on her. She finally shook her head. "That's just too incredible to believe. How can you possibly *make* something that small? How do you build the tiny machines that fabricate them?"

"The individual transistors aren't made by a machine. They're etched on a thin wafer of silicon. It's called photolithography."

"Photo . . ."

"Lithography. They shine a light with very precise wavelengths through masks that . . . look, I don't know the details, but I can assure you that we have circuits with millions of switching devices on a surface the size of a penny."

She just smiled at him. She didn't believe him.

"Look," he tried, "I find it incredible that you've gone to Mars *without* them."

She shrugged one shoulder. "What would you ever *do* with that many transistors?"

"Well . . . for one, you could make telephones that you can fit right into your ear."

She laughed. "Or, maybe wear on your wrist like a watch?"

"Sure."

"Oh really? Just like Dick Tracy."

"How do you know—"

He remembered that Dick Tracy's wrist radio went back to forties.

"What else do you do with these tiny things?" she asked.

What else . . .

"Computers! We make computers that you can carry like a book. You can put some in your pocket!"

"A computer in your pocket," she repeated, as though patronizing him. "What on Earth would you do with one?"

"Why, there's a hundred things. You could . . . you could play games—no, forget that. You could send messages to your friends. You could even send them pictures."

She nodded agreeably. "Okay. That could be handy. The computer fills out the envelope and puts the stamp on?"

"No! Electronically." He wasn't sure if she was pulling his leg. "Your friend a thousand miles away could look at the picture seconds after you send it."

"But we have that too. In color, even."

He could guess. "Probably like a fax."

"You mean a facsimile machine?"

"Yeah. But I'll bet that it takes minutes to send a good color picture."

She shook her head. "Maybe ten seconds."

"Well, with a computer, you could send it in less than a second—more than one picture, even. From your car!"

She gave him the eyebrow.

This wasn't going right. "Look, you could write a whole novel, and then send it to your publisher instantly."

She grinned wider. "Let me get this straight: I would spend months, even years writing a book, and then wouldn't want to take a few days to send it to the publisher by mail?"

"But you could send it *electronically*! No paper!"

She shrugged.

"When you're writing the book, you can make corrections without re-typing. You could re-write whole paragraphs over."

"That could be handy," she encouraged.

She was definitely patronizing him now. "You could look up facts just by hitting a couple of keys."

She nodded in agreement. "Sounds like everybody would be writing books."

He looked at her. "Yes. In fact, almost everybody I know has written one, or is trying to."

"People must really read a lot there."

"Not really. In fact, most books are self-published, and nobody reads them at all. Everybody watches movies at . . . yeah! We watch whole movies at home!"

"We do too."

"You do?"

"It's not cheap. Mostly just the well-to-do have home theatres."

"There," he concluded with satisfaction. "Just about everybody in my universe can watch a movie at home any time they want to."

"Instead of reading a book," she added.

He sighed. "Yes. Instead of reading a book."

After a moment she added, "We don't have many authors. They have to use typewriters."

She looked at him earnestly. She wasn't trying to make fun of him. She seemed to be genuinely trying to help. He found that he trusted her. He felt in good hands. She might make fun, but it wasn't mean.

"Before computers," he finally said, "we didn't have many authors either—" Gears suddenly meshed. "That explains the handwriting!"

"What handwriting?"

"Everybody here has perfect penmanship! It's because they don't type everything on a keyboard. People still know how to write—to *really* write!"

She gave a little shrug. She didn't know anything else.

"That's probably why the stilted language as well!"

"You mean letter-talk?"

"Letter-talk?"

"It's what we call the formal speech we use when writing letters. We often make fun of it."

"Why do it, then?"

"When I say we make fun of it, I don't mean everybody. I mean my friends. It's . . . I guess a traditional thing, a cultural habit. People would think you were insulting them if you wrote them a letter in the same way that you'd talk to them. They would think you don't respect them enough to do it properly."

He grinned and nodded. "I always wondered if our forefathers spoke to each other the same way they did in their letters."

She chuckled. "Imagine George Washington calling Ben Franklin a binny beggar who goes cheap on the paper."

"Cheap on the paper?"

She blushed. "It's an expression. It means that someone is too cheap to use enough paper when they . . . when they . . . uh—"

"Wipe their butt?"

She nodded, and her blush deepened to crimson. "And their fingers tear through," she finished.

"I get the picture. Religious jokes are taboo, but toilet humor is open game."

"If you want to be called a Potty Mouth."

"I already have."

Francine went off to make tea, and Will absorbed what she'd told him. He had a hard time imagining how they'd gone to Mars without computers. On the other hand, in his own universe, men had traveled to the moon with computers less sophisticated than modern wrist watches. In fact, the primitive machine had crapped out—overloaded with information—during the landing. All the orbital trajectories were worked out on Earth using mainframes, and he could imagine analog machines that could work out the math, just a bunch of integrals.

He turned on her television, wondering if daytime offerings were the same soap operas and circus-frenzy talk shows. The picture that slowly fuzzed to life was at least in color. It appeared to be a movie, and judging from the cheesy special effects, an old one. An apparent villain, sporting the same pencil mustache as Breggart's, threatened the heroine with smooth words of dire import. As he clasped her in a forceful hug and attempted to plant an unwelcomed kiss, a man burst through the wall. Right through the wall, with large styrofoam chunks falling easily away. The rescuer appeared to be wearing a deluxe-model spacesuit with all top-model chrome, but Will gathered that this was supposed to be a robot. This unusual entrance produced an instantaneous response from the villain, who dragged the heroine behind a dial-festooned contraption and threw a switch, initiating a shower of sparks. At this gala display, our synthesized hero fell back with hands to his head, obviously distressed, as though suffering a robotic migraine.

Francine returned with a tray and two steaming cups. "I would have called you on my wrist phone from the kitchen," she remarked straight-faced, "but I didn't have any spare transistors."

Will nodded, pretending agreement. "Too bad Shockley went astray in your universe."

"I wish he had strayed right off a cliff."

He looked at her quizzically.

She blushed again. "I could be accused of sedition just for saying that."

"Why?"

"He's not a Founding Father in your world?" she asked.

"You mean like Washington?"

"The correct term is New Father. Besides inventing the minitube, he originated the whole field of genetic destiny—although, between you and me, it's not a field of science at all. It's a handy political façade, a justification for class segregation." She sighed. "I'd be hanged for sure if they caught me saying that."

Will remembered Shockley's other interest: eugenics. "In my world, Shockley tried to use genetics to prove that whites are superior to blacks—to Negroes. His racist views ultimately discredited him completely."

"Well, in this world he prevailed. His statue stands on the Mall in DC."

"Saluted by all the Breggarts."

She nodded. "By all the weasels currying favor from above."

She sighed. "You know, until recently, Breggart was hardly more than an annoyance. His own colleagues didn't take him seriously about the whole universe exchange stuff—they thought it was binny. I was more worried about Buck's interest in Phil."

"Phil was snooping where he shouldn't?"

"Worse. He was trying to connect with the Railroad."

Will shrugged his incomprehension.

"It's a lot like the Underground Railroad during the Civil War," she explained. "There are people who help insurgent Negroes escape to Russia. Phil—and Buck—wanted to join."

"That's why Phil had to go into hiding?"

"Yes. We knew they'd catch up with him eventually. I begged Buck to keep his distance, but he never listens." She laughed. "Probably like you wouldn't either."

"This guy—Neck—he's part of this organization?"

"It's more of a secret society than an organization."

Will had a hard time imagining the rough man who nearly killed him risking his life for strangers.

He noticed that Francine was studying him thoughtfully. He felt himself blushing.

"Hold on a second," she said, and ran off down the hall.

On the television, the villain was shooting a gun at the hero's chest, where the bullets met an impenetrable barrier. The robot stood, hands on hips, seeming to revel in the spray of projectiles.

Francine returned carrying a manila envelope. She glanced at the television. "Robots," she uttered dismissively, shaking her head. She handed the envelope to him.

"What's this?" he asked, opening it.

"Buck's papers. I think he wanted you to have them. He left them here yesterday with the note. He asked me to hold them until he came back."

"Papers?" He pulled out a few official-looking documents. Glued to them all were pictures of Buck with intricate stamps overlaid.

"Papers—CID identity documents. They prove you're you."

He looked up at her. "What the hell does 'CID' stand for anyway?"

"Central Intelligence Department. The government merged the old CIA and FBI after Moscow blew."

"Moscow blew? How?"

She grinned at that fact that he was probably the only person on Earth who didn't know this. "Terrorists set off an atom bomb next to the Kremlin in 1967. Half a million people died."

He looked at the green and gray papers and back to her. "What good will these do me? Buck's a wanted man now."

She nodded. "But it will take hours to get that information distributed. Actually, considering that nobody really believes

Breggart, it will probably be a lower priority. It could take days. And by then, you'll be long gone."

He remembered that information here was distributed by fax. "Where am I going?"

"I was thinking—"

A loud banging on the apartment door interrupted her.

She threw him an alarmed glance, then ran to the door and peered through the spy-hole.

"Open up! CID!" Breggart's muffled voice bellowed from outside, followed by the scratching sound of a key finding its hole.

Francine flicked the dead-bolt and turned to him. "Looks like our weasel has found you."

Chapter 5

Francine ran off down the hall, and Will took her place at the peephole. He saw the warped image of Breggart holding one of the slim guns, ready to fire. Will could also see the back of somebody else who was bending over just below his view. Breggart suddenly leaned over the man working at the lock, and one huge eye filled the peephole. Will jumped back in alarm, as though Breggart might somehow reach right through the door and grab his throat.

The jiggling sound of the key stopped, and Will heard a voice outside say, "She must have changed the lock, sir."

"Open up!" Breggart bellowed. "Or I'll break down the door!"

Francine returned carrying what looked like two half-formed space suits. The arms, chest, and helmet were missing, leaving just the legs, waist and backpack.

"What in God's name are those? And why does Breggart have a key to your apartment?"

"Our escape, and he probably got it from the landlord."

She handed one of the spacesuit remnants to him, and told him to put it on. When he protested that he didn't know how, she told him to stop being a baby. "You really *are* Buck's double, aren't you?" she concluded. "Watch me."

She leaned hers against a chair and slithered in like a snake down a hole. Getting it on wasn't nearly as easy as Francine made it look, though. When he tried, he either fell over sideways, or the chair slid away from him and he fell backwards. The legs bent stiffly, reluctantly at the knees, and it seemed impossible. In the end, she wrapped her arms around him from behind and held him as he slipped into the leggings. She yanked a waist belt tight around him, and then a chest belt. Feeling like Boris Karloff in *The Mummy*, he waddled along behind her down the hall, through the bedroom, and out onto the balcony. The sound of Breggart's screaming diminished only slightly as they made their way through the apartment. On the ground a story below them, a man in a black suit stood looking up. Breggart wasn't so stupid to let them just climb down and run away.

"Whatever you do," she warned as she adjusted her own bindings, "don't turn it off until you're back on the ground."

And with that, she flipped open a little door on his leg and threw two small toggle switches. His whole body seemed to vibrate, and a whining sound rose in pitch like a tea kettle coming to boil.

"What do you mean, 'back on the ground'?"

"What do you *think* it means," she snapped, flipping the power switches on her own suit. "These are uniboosts."

"You mean . . . we can fly?"

She threw him a worried glance and shook her head in dismay as she yanked a slide switch on his back. These forced the legs and waist of his suit straight and rigid.

"Hey! Wait a second!" he cried. "I don't know how to use this thing. I could be killed!"

"You won't be killed," she replied soothingly. "Just don't make any sudden moves."

"Oh, that's reassuring. What if I sneeze?"

She ignored him, and explained quickly how the uniboost worked. A knob at his thigh adjusted thrust; this was his lift control, taking him up or down. He steered by merely leaning— slightly—in the direction he wanted to go. It was a model of Spartan simplicity. She handed him a fifteen-pound dumbbell, calling it his ballast, and explaining that it would stabilize him in flight.

Breggart was now pounding on the door, and they looked at each other when the booming suddenly stopped, filling the apartment with ominous silence. A moment later, a loud crack announced a bullet coming through, followed quickly by another.

"Come on!" Francine called. "Let's go!"

Holding her dumbbell in one hand, she used the other to ease her thrust knob on until she rose slowly off the balcony, then leaned forward and glided away across the swimming pool. Lounging people jumped up, yelling excitedly, as she flew over. A uniboost apparently wasn't an everyday event.

He realized that the wild animation below was spurred by more than just a desire to get a better look; the sunbathers were knocking over chairs in their haste to get out from under Francine. And then he felt a wet, tropical wind wash his face, and he realized that the exhausts from her uniboost's twin nozzles must be hot—*very* hot— steam. That also explained the thick leg coverings of the suit. They insulated him from occasional stray blasts of his own scorching propellant.

A loud thump boomed within the apartment, followed by the sound of splintering wood as Breggart broke through the door.

Alarmed, Will gave his thrust knob a quick turn, and a second later felt himself jerked violently upwards. *Slowly*, he reminded himself. But he panicked as he rose into thin air, and he twisted the knob in the opposite direction, falling heavily back onto the balcony and losing his balance so that he crashed into the railing.

Through the open balcony door, he saw Breggart stride into the bedroom and stop short upon seeing him. "Where in Judas's face did you get *that?*" the agent exclaimed in shock.

Another man came through, nearly knocking Breggart over. "Glory bile!" he breathed hoarsely. "A uniboost!"

Will pushed himself upright, turned his back to the men, and engaged his thrust . . . slowly. A deafening high pitched whistling swelled as hot, humid air filled the confined space of the balcony, gently lifting him off.

"Stop!" Breggart screamed from behind.

Will's stomach clenched tight and he urged his butt sphincter to follow suit. Not only was he suspended in midair, but there was a man pointing a gun at him with a proven proclivity to use it.

On the other hand, the whole flying thing wasn't so difficult after all. Like skiing, he just had to lean into the turns.

Suddenly one of Breggart's bullets slammed into the top of his head, and his vision spun in a kaleidoscope of motion.

But only for a second. It wasn't a bullet. He realized that his head had hit the edge of the balcony roof.

Woozy, he looked down and saw that he was gliding out over the swimming pool . . . but he was also falling, heading for a crash dive into the apartment patios on the far side. Disoriented from the blow, he'd leaned too far forward. The cement ground and pool furniture were coming at him at an alarming and lethal rate. He had only a second to counter his course. He pulled his dumbbell ballast tight against his chest, and twisted his torso up, throwing his head back as though trying to do a backward summersault. It wasn't like floating in free fall, or what he'd imagined free fall to be; the boost thrust provided something to push against, something against which to maneuver. He also understood now why the suit was stiffened and made rigid for flight. Otherwise it would have been like trying to balance on a surfboard made of flexible rubber.

His maneuver tilted him backwards so that he was looking at the sky. Something clattered next to him, and he saw that he had collided feet first with some patio chairs before coming to rest. He hovered there a second among the aluminum furniture before slowly rising again, backwards towards Francine's apartment. Below him, the chairs were melting from his exhaust—no, just the plastic webbing. It was a wonder that his legs didn't burn as well.

He was looking at the sky again, still flying backwards like an Indian baby in a papoose. He tried to turn so that he could see where he was going, but found that this axis of rotation was nearly impossible to control; he couldn't find purchase against the thrust to rotate. He could hold his ballast out and lean forward, though, so that he was more vertical.

As he tilted the uniboost into an upright position, he found that he had crossed back over the pool, and was continuing to glide slowly backwards, carried by momentum. It was like trying to ice-skate for the first time—everything was slippery and movements produced unexpected results. He heard Breggart's curses coming closer from behind. He felt a bump, and simultaneously the hissing steam changed pitch as it splashed against something solid. He'd returned to Francine's building, and come to rest against the wall of a balcony.

"Got you!" Breggart yelled with glee, and Will felt the painful tug as the agent yanked his hair from above. He tried to grab the balcony wall, but the smooth surface offered no handhold as he was hauled upwards. When he rose above the wall's edge, an arm wrapped around his neck, and Breggart leaned out and reached down. Will realized that his attacker was trying to turn off the thrusters. He used the dumbbell to knock the agent's arm away from the throttle knob, but Breggart tightened his headlock, cutting off his air. Will squirmed with growing panic, but the slim agent's strength was surprising, and Will clawed fruitlessly at the iron-gripped arm as his last seconds ticked away.

He knew that he had died when an angel floated slowly down in front of him. The angel looked a lot like Francine . . . and held a stick like a bat, which she swung with conviction at his head! He closed his eyes, but the blow never came. Instead, he heard a solid thunk and groan, and the strangling grip slipped away.

He opened his eyes and sucked a lung-full of air as Francine dragged him painfully by his hair up and away, aided by the thrust of his uniboost. Ever since arriving, his hair was getting an extraordinary amount of attention.

"Thanks!" he called hoarsely.

She nodded a quick acknowledgement, and then looked down and winced. A second later he felt a sharp pain in his thigh, as though a bee the size of a golf ball had stung him. "I've been shot!" he cried in surprise.

Francine ignored him as she reached down and twisted her thrust control, and an instant later Will thought the scalp was going to be pulled right from his skull as she hauled him ever higher. Something whizzed past his ear, but that was the last bullet from Breggart.

Many seconds later, Francine finally let go later and glided away. He started to reach around to see how much blood was flowing, but Francine's cry stopped him. He'd forgotten about the steam exhaust. It would strip the flesh from his hand, just like the plastic webbing on the patio chairs.

She leaned to the side and circled around behind him. He could hear her whistling exhaust approaching.

"The bullet didn't puncture the suit," she said right behind him.

"Well, it hurts like hell!"

"You'll have a good bruise," she replied, "but you'll live."

"What is it made of?" he asked, trying ineffectively to twist around to see.

"Asbestos mostly, held in a carbon filament mesh," she replied distractedly, keeping an eye out below them.

"Asbestos? That stuff causes lung cancer."

She circled back around in front of him, and he looked down. "Yikes!"

He was floating in thin air, hundreds of feet up. The people standing around the pool gazing up at them looked like little toy action figures—action figures pointing straight up in the air with their mouths open. Breggart watched from the balcony, talking into the quart-sized walkie-talkie device that had hung from his belt.

Will had dropped his dumbbell ballast when Breggart choked him. He now found that without it he tended to tilt backwards, and the angled thrust obediently carried him away from Francine. He was once again flying in the ignoble papoose position, unable to turn around.

Francine seemed to abandon him, but after a couple of minutes suddenly appeared above him, holding out a rock. He took it, and she turned over on her back. "Watch!" she cried, and extended her dumbbell and matching leg out to the side. Gravity took its cue, and like a graceful ballerina, she spun, pulling in her ballast and extending the opposite leg momentarily to stop the roll when she was again facing forward.

He tried it, and found that it worked perfectly . . . except that now he was forced to contemplate the nothingness between himself and the very hard ground far below.

"You're falling!" she called from above.

After a moment of panic, he realized she just meant that he was losing altitude. He tilted back, directing his thrust more downwards. He found that he had to use the tops of the tallest trees as a reference to keep from drifting up or down. "Do these things have altimeters?" he called as she swooped in next to him.

"Don't be silly," she replied. "We're not going to fly that high."

She showed him how to adjust both his thrust and tilt to navigate in three dimensions. As a final demonstration, she did a perfect 360-degree loop-de-loop, which made his stomach do its own somersaults just watching.

A sudden thought caused him to glance down fearfully at the ground gliding by below. "How much time do we have?"

"Before what?" she called, swooping in close again.

"Before we run out of fuel."

"You mean propellant. Your exhaust isn't burning."

"Fine. Propellant."

"A full tank lasts about twenty minutes."

At the thought of suddenly falling like a stone, he fought the sudden urge to reach out and grab Francine as a drowning man might claw at a lifeguard.

She must have seen the fear in his face, for she added, "Don't worry. The thrust doesn't stop instantly. It begins tapering about three minutes before you're totally depleted."

He tried to gauge their height. "What if you're too high?"

She shrugged. "You fall the final distance. We should keep an eye out for an opportunity to refill."

"What does a uniboost gas station look like?"

She rolled her eyes, and glancing around to get her bearings, flew off, waving for him to follow.

Will increased his thrust and tilted accordingly to compensate. He found that it required constant attention and adjustment to keep a steady altitude and speed. It seemed that he was always too low, too high, too close, or too far from Francine, and at times his arms became tired from holding his ballast. Also, the wind burned his eyes. He needed those big goggles the WWI fighter pilots wore. Maybe a long, flowing scarf as well.

After what seemed more than twenty minutes, he called to Francine, but she was too far ahead to hear. What if he didn't detect the decreasing thrust as the propellant gave out? The thought of falling brought a wave of panic, and he had just decided to descend on his own when Francine finally motioned to him and sank away towards the ground.

Will miscalculated his descent and had to pull up and fly back around for another try. Francine had landed next to a small stream winding through a suburban development. Backyard fences crowded the banks on both sides, limiting Will's approach angle to one that was nearly vertical. As he tried to maneuver into position, he gained full appreciation for just how much finesse precise piloting required. Each time he managed to position himself over Francine and reached down to reduce the thrust, he would inadvertently lean one way or the other slightly and glide away.

He remembered learning to ski, how complete mental focus was required just to stay on his feet until his body learned the proper reflexes. Afterwards, it was hard to remember *not* knowing how to ski. Francine seemed to have developed that body knowledge.

But he definitely didn't have it yet. On his third try, it suddenly dawned on him that he had been continually increasing his thrust just to stay airborne. Just as he'd feared, he had run out of propellant and hadn't even noticed!

Feeling like he was falling through thin ice, he sank. He tried desperately to maneuver over to Francine, but the uniboost was too pooped, and he came down right on a fence. One foot slipped off the top as he tried to perch himself, and he came down straddling it like it was a horse. Surprised, but supremely thankful that the asbestos-carbon-filament material saved his groin, he fell backwards, arms windmilling, into a yard.

Catching his breath and wondering whether he'd ruined his flying machine, he rolled over to find a preschool girl sitting in a sandbox staring at him with wide eyes.

"Hello," she said.

"Hi," he replied, using a fence post to haul himself slowly up. "Francine!" he called over the wall.

"Get out of there!" she called from the other side.

"Good idea!" he yelled back. "I wouldn't have thought of that."

He saw a gate leading out, but it was padlocked. The fence was five feet high. He couldn't possibly scale it with the uniboost. "Is there a key for this, little girl?" he asked, pointing at the lock.

"I'm *not* a little girl," the girl chided, brow furrowed in indignation.

"Who are you!" a woman's hysterical voice demanded.

He turned to face the interrogator, obviously the girl's mother, standing in the patio doorway. She was holding a dishtowel, and she had twisted it as though ready to use it as a weapon.

"Will," he replied. He realized she was probably looking for more than just his name. "I'm, uh . . . on a mission."

The anger in her face suddenly turned to caution. "Are you CID?"

It was too easy to resist. He looked her in the eyes and nodded.

She gestured at him. "That's a uniboost?"

He nodded again. "Yes, ma'am."

Her mouth pursed as though struggling to contain what she really wanted to say. She ran to the girl, picked her up despite protests and deposited her inside, then closed the patio door and turned to him once more. "I don't care who you are, you have no right bringing that . . . that thing near here."

He looked down at his astronaut-suit legs. "You mean the uniboost?"

Her eyes flashed with anger. "Don't ride me. I'm not an idiot." She glanced inside through the patio door at her daughter. "Look, I'm not afraid of you. I won't stand for this. I'll . . . I'll call the police. I'm sure they'll arrest you."

She held her head high, and Will suspected that she didn't really believe that. CID personnel weren't arrested by mere policemen.

"Look, lady, I want to leave as badly as you. If you'll just unlock the gate, I'll be gone."

She glared at him a moment, disappeared inside, and returned seconds later with a jumble of keys. She took off the padlock, and swung the gate inward. As he waddled past her, he heard her whisper, "Pilot."

He glanced back, but she just stared him down.

Free once more, he found that Francine had released the stiffening mechanism of her suit and was squatting next to the stream. She held a hose in the water, and when he approached she took it out and stood up. "Done harassing the local citizens?" she asked, twisting the hose somewhere behind her. "Your turn," she said, pulling down on his stiffening lever so that his suit suddenly felt like it had melted. He'd gotten used to the support, and almost fell over when he suddenly had to hold himself up with his own knees.

He squatted down next to the stream, and Francine handed him his own hose, which she'd extracted from somewhere on the back of his suit. She fiddled some more, and the hose started making a sucking sound. He stuck the end into the water and watched it swirl up the clear conduit. He noticed a tiny logo on the suit: a heart with a stream of increasingly smaller dots falling away behind. Above the symbol was an even smaller word that read, *Readion*. He wondered if that was the name of the company, or the model.

Francine sat down next to him to wait.

"If water is only the propellant," he said, "then what's the fuel? What heats the water?"

"The energy is stored."

"Like, with batteries?"

She shrugged and looked off into the distance.

It didn't make sense. The energy that lifted them, and held them in the air, was obviously delivered as heat that turned the water into super-heated steam. But that was a *lot* of energy. Using the most efficient fuel, the rocket packs in his universe were barely able to keep a man aloft for a minute—and the fuel tanks alone were twice as big as the whole uniboost. It was incredible that they were able to store that much energy in a battery. Even assuming significant advances in battery technology, it seemed too fantastic. Hell, why would their cars still burn gasoline?

"What kind of batteries *are* they?" he asked.

She shrugged without looking at him. It was an annoyed shrug.

"Seriously! This is the greatest thing I've seen here so far. Don't you have any idea how they work?"

She finally turned to him. "They're not batteries in the normal sense."

"I guessed that. So, what *are* they made of?"

It was a few seconds before she spoke. "Anti-matter," she finally replied, and looked away again.

"*Anti*-matter?"

She didn't answer, but just stared off at the horizon.

"Are you *serious?*"

She sighed and looked directly at him. "Yes, I'm serious. Complete annihilation of matter is the only possible way to store that much energy."

He stared at her and blinked. "Where do you get the antimatter?"

"They make it."

He nodded slowly. It made sense. What better receptacle of energy than matter itself? Nature's own super-battery.

"Wait a minute, how do you store it?"

The antimatter would self-destruct and take along any normal matter it came in contact with.

"Magnetic fields."

He blinked again. "The antimatter is ions?"

"Positrons," she said as though she'd rather be talking about something else.

He shook his head. "But it would take a lot of power just to keep the magnetic fields energized . . . oh, I see. You probably burn some of the antimatter itself to create the energy needed to contain it. Sort of the chicken or the egg."

He suddenly had a disturbing thought. "Uh, what happens if . . ."

She looked at him and nodded with resignation. "What happens if the magnetic fields fail?" She sighed. "Boom."

"Boom? You mean . . . it explodes?"

"Spectacularly."

"Like an atom bomb!" he exclaimed, wanting to get up and run away from the monster that seemed like such a wonderful miracle just seconds before.

"Not like an atom bomb at all," Francine said. Her reticence was gone; the cat was out of the bag. "In nuclear reactions, less than one percent of the matter is converted into energy. One hundred percent of the antimatter, on the other hand, becomes energy. More importantly, an atom bomb—at least a fission bomb—requires a minimal amount of mass, the critical mass, to produce the runaway chain reaction that creates the explosion, and that's twenty-five pounds of Uranium 235. Also, whereas all sorts of energy is released in a nuclear reaction, antimatter annihilation produces pure photon energy."

Will nodded, still wanting to run away, but trying to let her convince him it was okay. "So it's clean energy. No fallout—secondary radiation, I think it's called."

She shrugged and carefully folded her feed-tube back into its storage slot.

"That's not exactly an enthusiastic confirmation," he observed.

She turned to him again with another sigh. "The annihilation energy consists of gamma rays."

She just looked at him, as though the rest was self-explanatory.

"I'm a mathematician, not a physicist. Gamma rays are bad?"

"It's the most damaging emission from nuclear bombs—at least to living tissue."

He stared at her. "So, it *is* like a nuclear bomb."

She waved her hand in a dismissive gesture. "It's all just matter conversion."

Just matter conversion. The desire to run was overwhelming. "So . . . I'm being bombarded by gamma rays as I sit here."

"Mostly when you're in flight. That's when the antimatter feed is greatest. But something like ninety-nine-point-nine percent is captured by the uniboost. After all, that's the whole point. That's its source of energy. And that's also the real secret to its design; the material surrounding the annihilation chamber that absorbs the gamma energy and turns it into heat. Creating and storing positrons is child's play in comparison."

"But even at rest—right now—it's emitting some gamma rays."

She shrugged.

"I could get cancer."

She busied herself putting his tube away, ignoring his comment.

"Has any uniboosts ever exploded?" he asked point-blank.

"Of course."

"People were killed?"

She just looked at him. The answer was obvious.

"They probably have all sorts of built-in safety features, though . . . right?"

"The only uniboosts that ever self-destructed did so because the unit itself was damaged in an accident."

"So, for example, if I let all my water run out and fell to the ground, I could destroy a whole town."

"A very small town, and mostly through ionizing cellular damage—but you'd be dead anyway."

"Or, maybe a fall from, oh say, a backyard fence?"

"You should be a little more careful, yes."

The mother's reaction to a uniboost falling into her backyard was now perfectly clear. "I can understand why the sky's not filled with people commuting to work in them."

"A uniboost is many times too expensive for general use," she explained as she pulled the lever to stiffen her suit. "Plus," she added casually, "they're illegal."

"You need a special license or something?"

"No, they're just illegal. It is against the law for anyone to be in possession of one."

It wasn't like they were talking about marijuana that anybody could grow in their backyard. "It must require a whole industry to manufacture them; who would go to all the trouble to make something nobody can buy?"

"The Dingoes."

"The *what?*"

"Australians. The last free democracy on Earth, and I could be jailed for saying that."

"They're legal there?"

"Along with almost everything else, except maybe murder. Unless it's justified."

She motioned for him to stiffen his suit.

"I think the woman who lives here called me a pilot," he said, pulling up on the lever and feeling the uniboost go erect, "but she said it as though it was a curse."

"It is."

"People really hate uniboosts, don't they?"

"She wasn't referring to piloting a uniboost," Francine explained, as she turned her thrust knob, being careful that the exhaust splashed away from him. "It can be used in a derogatory way when talking about the Pilots Union, but in this case I think the source is two thousand years old. She was comparing you to Pontius Pilate, the man who ordered Jesus Christ's crucifixion."

She gave her knob another turn and lifted away into the afternoon air.

"Hey!" he called after her as he turned up his own thrust, remembering to grab his ballast rock. "How did you happen to own two uniboosts?"

But Francine had already tilted up and away, swooping like an oversized hummingbird over backyard fences and suburban rooftops.

Chapter 6

Will thought he was finally getting the hang of it. His body was learning to ski like a bird. His arms ached, though, from constantly holding the ballast. It seemed like a design flaw. He wondered why the engineers couldn't have designed the suits to be inherently balanced. One advantage, he realized, was that this way the flyer could carry things.

He eased in next to Francine, careful of his lethal exhaust. "WHERE ARE WE GOING?" he called.

"You don't have to yell," she said in a normal voice. "We're not sitting on the tail of a jump."

She was right, of course. Will just naturally associated flying with lots of noise: turbo-jets or the Space Shuttle. Away from the confines of the balcony, the whoosh of his steam exhaust was no louder than the whirring of car tires on pavement.

"We're going to Evergreen College," she added.

"Why?"

"To borrow the physics department's jump."

"As in rocket?"

"Yes, as in your ticket out of here."

"We're just going to . . . fly it away?"

She shrugged. "I have a set of keys."

He looked at her, trying to decide if she was kidding. "How do you happen to have *keys* to a rocket ship?"

She glanced over, as though surprised he'd ask such a question. "I teach there. I'm head of ionospheric studies. And nobody calls jumps 'rocket ships.' You sound like a fifties movie."

The Evergreen College of his universe was totally Liberal Arts. The only physics classes he knew of focused on environmental problems and the role of philosophy in science.

"So, how do you happen to have two very expensive and highly illegal uniboosts just sitting around in your closet?"

She suddenly looked alarmed and pointed down at the choppy waters of Puget Sound below them. An official-looking powerboat emerged from a side-channel and took off north towards the main waterway, pounding along from wave to wave, seemingly on urgent business. Francine motioned for him to follow her south as she lost altitude.

"Do you think they're looking for us?" he asked when she leveled off again after the boat disappeared behind a stand of pines.

"I wouldn't doubt it. That woman almost certainly called the police."

"So, what about it?"

"What about what?"

"How do you come to have the uniboosts?"

She scanned the complex terrain beneath them. Fingers of thick pines were separated by a thousand myriad tentacles of the Sound's watery grasp. "Buck," she said.

"They're his?"

She didn't answer, apparently engrossed in watching for other boats.

"How did Buck get them?" he pressed.

She finally turned to him, and her brow was furrowed with impatience. "The less you know, the better it will be if . . ."

"If they catch and torture me?"

She turned back to her surveillance, but her answer was clear.

He didn't like it when she was angry with him.

"Fuel calculator!" he said, changing the subject.

She looked at him.

"A microcomputer could track how much propellant was left so that you wouldn't have to worry about falling out of the sky, killing thousands of people in the process."

She grinned at his enthusiasm. "The water sloshes around. There's no way to accurately measure the level."

"No. You have to change the approach. A microcomputer can think—"

"They *think?*"

"Okay. They calculate, but at millions of operations each second. It could gauge the exhaust flow and calculate the amount left."

"The result is only as accurate as the precision of the exhaust measurement. An error of only two percent still means falling from the sky. Besides, you don't always start with the same amount of propellant."

"Details. That can all be worked out."

She shook her head and laughed. "Why bother? I can tell perfectly well when it gets low. After a while, you develop a feel. A Dingo would consider you a sissy, you know, for using something like that."

Will chewed on that. What was she saying? That she admired the manly cowboy bravado of a rough-and-tumble Australian man? Maybe sporting bulging shoulder muscles to boot?

"My point," he finally continued, "is that there's many things that microelectronics enable that aren't necessarily obvious at first." He sounded defensive even to himself. "Take, for example—"

Francine cut him off with an upraised hand. He heard it, a sound behind them like a blender struggling against thick ice-cream. He turned his head, but it wasn't far enough to see.

His fellow fugitive rocked and tilted, executing a smooth 360 degree spin, ending at her same position next to him. "There's a copter coming up from behind!" she cried urgently. "Come on! We have to get to the trees." She pointed to the shore where old pines stood thick and welcoming.

"Uh, oh!" Will said. He nodded towards where they wanted to go. There, a second helicopter was coming towards them low over the treetops. These were no ordinary copters, though; in addition to the blur of rotating blades, the blinding white fire of rocket exhaust issued from its tail. They *loved* rockets in this universe.

"Judas curse!" Francine cried. She looked around, pointed towards a small, bare island—not much more than a granite outcrop—and flew off, tilting almost horizontally as she jerked her thrust to maximum.

"There's no trees!" Will cried, following as best he could.

He caught up with her as she hovered a hundred feet over the rocks.

"Whatever you do," she yelled above the swelling roar of the two approaching copters, "stay away from the water!"

He looked down at the intimidating jumble of boulders. "I think I'd rather fall into water than here!"

She eased up next to him as the first copter slowed, coming in at their level. "Exactly," she said. Her face was set with dead earnestness. "They're less likely to risk one of us falling over hard ground."

"But . . ."

And then he understood. A fall unto rocks might damage the uniboost, with catastrophic results for anybody within miles.

"I guess we also want to stay at least a hundred feet up!" he yelled.

The pilot had shut down the copter's rocket, but the beating blades were still deafening.

Francine nodded quickly with mouth set firmly. "I'm sorry!"

"For *what?*"

"Getting you into this!"

He glanced over at the massive machine, which eased in closer. "Uncle Bill got me into this! And it's not over yet!"

But as the copter's downdraft tossed his hair into a frenzy, he saw Breggart through the window gripping his gun with both hands aimed straight at them.

"I'm going to take off over the water!" Francine cried next to him. "They'll probably go after me! When they do, you try to get away! Got it?"

"No way!"

Breggart ended the discussion when he kicked open the copter door. Instinctively, the two solo fliers had leaned away from the down-rushing air, slowly moving away from the hovering metal monster.

"*You're not going to get anything by killing us!*" Will yelled through the storm to Breggart.

In answer, the agent lifted the gun, aimed carefully, and pulled the trigger. At the same instant, Will felt a massive blow to his thigh. The bullet's impact spun and tilted him so that the uniboost's redirected thrust carried him slowly away. Seeping through the white-hot pain, he heard the copter pilot screaming to Breggart that these were *uniboosts*, for Judas sake—did he want to get them all killed? Will watched as though in a dream as Breggart carefully moved the gun towards Francine and squeezed off another shot. Out of the corner of his eye, he saw his companion lurch, then fall away, dropping in a slow, downward spiral. Breggart had been careful not to kill him, but showed no such mercy for Buck's ex-girlfriend.

Francine's limp form, now just unresponsive cargo for the unbalanced uniboost, sank away below him in widening circles. She would either smash her skull on the waiting rocks, or drown in the rough waters.

Will let his newly learned skills take over, and he tilted over hard so that his thrust pointed up. He plummeted at a dizzying rate, but it was already too late. He watched in horror as his guide and only friend in this entire universe smashed headfirst into the sound a hundred feet from the rocky island, leaving behind a plume of water a dozen feet high.

Will's heart-stopping grief was replaced an instant later with the realization that he was heading for the same fate as his uniboost joined forces with gravity to hurl him headlong into the angry waves. He somersaulted backwards, throwing his legs forward beneath him, but only managed to turn himself into a sitting position before colliding with the water. As his legs met the wind-churned surface, momentum carried him violently forward so that the last thing he saw was one instantaneous glimpse of the rippled surface of a wave flying up to meet his face.

He woke coughing salty water, the brine burning his nose. He was looking up at puffy cumulous clouds. The next instant, a new cascade of Pugent Sound washed over his upturned face, and he choked and coughed as his throat filled with ocean again. He had to get his head out of the water, but something was dragging him by his shoulders through the waves, leaving him to flail helplessly like a downed water skier tangled in the tow rope.

It was the uniboost! The rocket pack had not only survived the impact, but was still thrusting, pulling him inexorably along through a medium a thousand times thicker than the air it was designed for. The Puget Sound was bone-chilling cold, but he felt warm washes bathe him sporadically as the super-heated steam mixed with the salt water.

Coughing and blinking the water from his eyes, he reached down, found the thrust knob, and spun it to minimum. Within seconds he came to a stop . . . and sank. The uniboost was heavier than water, and its thrust had been keeping it, and him, afloat.

The world turned darker as he sank. He groped madly again for the knob and, finding it, twisted it on full. Slowly, almost grudgingly, his descent halted, then reversed, and he felt the water flowing down across his face, and the world once again grew lighter. Just when he thought his lungs would burst, his head suddenly broke free, and afternoon sunshine flashed in his eyes. An instant later he was rising into the air, the waves falling away below him. He turned down the thrust, and although the receding waves slowed their mad rush away from him, air continued to flow across his face as though he was still rocketing skyward. It came to him that a roaring sound filled the air. He looked up. It was the helicopter immediately above him. It tilted and glided away, obviously attempting to avoid mincing him in its blades and releasing billions of ergs of antimatter energy. Through the window he could see Breggart screaming, red-faced, at the pilot.

Francine! What had happened to her? Her uniboost had evidently not failed, otherwise he wouldn't be alive. But where was she? Ignoring the copter that was maneuvering into position above him again, he scanned the rough waters of the sound. Had she sunk? He saw her. Now and then something made a splash in a wave, and like a pointing finger, the telltale remains of a small wake defined a travel direction aimed away from the small island.

Breggart's voice, tiny and distant amidst the roar of the copter, called out to him, using the name Willard. Will glanced up at his nemesis, hair tossing about in the open door. An instant later Will tilted over and dove after the inert human torpedo. This time, though, he was careful to execute an arc that brought him up just ahead of the tip of the wake. He could now see that it was indeed Francine, and that, like his own unconscious encounter with the Sound, she was riding on her back, the uniboost pushing her along like a miniaturized jet-ski. Her body undulated with each wave, limp and lifeless.

Will positioned himself over Francine and was about to lower himself to her when he remembered his destructive exhaust. He moved fifty feet ahead, and let himself down into the cold water. He found that he could adjust the thrust so that it suspended him out of the water from the waist up. The scalding steam bubbled madly behind him, like a powerful motorboat in idle. Seconds later, Francine glided past him, like Sleeping Beauty towed by submerged dolphins.

He reached out and grasped her arm, resulting in them both making a lazy turn back towards the island. Will was heartsick when he saw a large red blotch of blood covering the right side of her chest, but miraculously she opened her eyes and looked at him, then smiled wanly.

"*You've been shot!*" he yelled above the bubbling steam and roar of helicopter blades. It sounded like a stupid thing to say, as if she wouldn't know this.

She nodded. "The suit—" she started to say, but gasped and groaned with pain.

He saw that the main strap of the uniboost suit ran through the middle of the red splotch. "*Are the suit's straps also made of that carbon filament?*" he shouted.

She nodded, squeezing out another smile, even though her face was scrunched in agony.

The strap had stopped the bullet. At least it had stopped it from penetrating her body, but her chest had still absorbed all of its kinetic energy. Some of her ribs were probably cracked, or even broken.

A plunk and little plume of water erupted next to her head, accompanied by a swishing whistle. He looked up. The copter hovered directly above them, and Breggart leaned out aiming his gun for another shot. He was trying to finish Francine off without hitting Will.

Very well then. He flicked off his thrust knob and pulled Francine under him as he sank into the wind-churned water. His intention was to lie on top of her like a human shield, but the thrust of her uniboost rotated them both into a vertical position. He wrapped his arms around her neck, trying to protect her as best he could from Breggart's aim. He heard her cry out in pain as the monstrous thrashing of the copter settled in even closer. Another whistle, and a second plume of water erupted just inches from his arm. Breggart didn't want to kill him, but apparently was willing to wound him in his efforts to get Francine.

"Take a deep breath and hold it!" he shouted into her ear.

He felt her chest start to expand, but then she cried out again in pain.

A third plume, this time on the other side.

"Come on!" he pleaded. *"You have to do it!"*

She nodded, her face white like death. This time he felt her chest expand fully as she twitched at the torture it caused.

He sucked in a lung-full as he reached down and turned off her thrust. Immediately, they sank below the surface and the roar retreated to a distant throbbing. Like a roof made from shattered glass, the surface of the water was an impenetrable crowd of ripples agitated by the copter's blades. The two of them would be equally invisible from above.

Still hugging Francine's neck, he kicked until he was again horizontal, with the wounded woman beneath him. He reached around and turned her thrust knob slowly. Bubbles streamed frantically from her pack, then disappeared as the steam condensed back into liquid form. He felt the water glide slowly by as they moved forward through the sound. He found that he could bend his legs up or down like the rudder of a submarine to control their depth. All too soon, his lungs begged for a fresh load. He prayed that Francine hadn't already passed out and taken a lung-full of water. Bending his knees sharply, he forced their headlong rush upwards, and seconds later they broke the surface. Both of them gasped and sputtered, and he kicked frantically to keep them positioned upright.

They had gone barely twenty feet, and the helicopter still roared a blast of air directly down on them. But whereas before their dive they had been under the front where Breggart could shoot at them through his open door, they were now behind it. The rear stabilizing rod between the landing skis was right above their heads.

Will had an idea.

Clasping Francine's arm, he reached up, but the metal rod was just out of reach. He turned on his own thrust slightly, and was able to grab the bar as his uniboost lifted him a foot higher.

He had a problem, though. He needed a third hand. Cursing, he let go of the metal rod and sank back into the bitter cold water. Francine's eyes were closed, either from concentration against the pain, or unconsciousness. He reached down and turned up her thrust, then quickly trimmed it back as she started to lift completely out of the water. When he was done, she hovered with just her legs in the water up to her thighs. He decided that was about right: the uniboost was lifting all but maybe twenty pounds of her weight.

He did the same with his own thrust, found they had drifted away from the truss bar and barely caught it in time. Grasping the bar with one hand as they swayed up and down with the waves, he clutched his partner's arm with the other.

They didn't have to wait long, as Breggart apparently decided that the two fugitives weren't going to resurface within sight. The helicopter lifted slowly, taking with it the two aeronaughts.

Will immediately found that twice-twenty pounds of leftover weight was not easy to hold with one hand, particularly when it was augmented by the drag of their inertia as the copter pulled them along, lifting and turning in a slow circle, watching for some telltale sign of them in the water or air. After the first complete turn, though, the helicopter slowed its rate of rotation, which was a blessing, as Will couldn't have hung on any longer.

Suddenly, the copter started forward towards the rocky island. Will clenched his jaws and clung to the bar even though he expected his arm to pull right out of the shoulder socket. The pilot circled the island slowly, checking to make sure they hadn't somehow made it there. After inspecting the complete perimeter, he began a second round for good measure.

Will had another idea. It seemed like a flash of genius, until he realized there really wasn't any other choice. He waited, praying his shoulder ligaments wouldn't rip, until their unsuspecting chariot once again reached the far side of the little island. The shore was irregular so that sometimes water lay below them, but other times unforgiving jagged granite. "Francine!" he called above the maelstrom. She opened her eyes, looked at him, and the barest smile woke on her lips. "When I tell you," he called, "lean back! Got it?"

She closed her eyes and the smile disappeared. Crestfallen, he realized that her wound was more serious than he'd thought. But then she opened her eyes again and nodded.

He waited until the next miniature bay lay just ahead, then let go of the bar and yelled, "Now!"

They dropped like stones despite the partial uniboost thrust. He leaned backwards, never letting go of Francine's arm. It seemed impossible that they wouldn't fall onto the rocks below, but their forward momentum carried them to the water's edge and beyond just before Francine was torn from his grasp, and he was slammed nearly senseless as the bitter-cold water enveloped him once more. The world faded to darkness, and a second jolt told him he'd found bottom, but the reduced thrust finally asserted itself. Light returned, and seconds later his head broke free.

He looked around frantically for Francine. He'd forgotten to tell her to take a deep breath. Had she understood what he was planning to do? Her drowned-rat head popped up twenty feet from him like a breaching whale, and then slowly moved off towards the far shore, carried along by the tireless uniboost. He leaned forward to catch her, but found that he was fighting the pack's desire to be DOWN. He gave up and rolled over on his back while increasing his thrust. Peering over his shoulder, he reached her, lowered his throttle, and rolled back over. He pulled her upright, causing her thrust to raise her up from the surface like a mermaid spirit ascending to some oceanic heaven. He reduced her thrust until just her shoulders bobbed in the water, calm now in the leeward side of the island.

She looked really dead.

The machine roar of the copter receded away around the island. "Francine," he said. She floated lifeless, a corpse buoy. Despair pulled from him whatever warmth the chilling waters hadn't already stolen. He couldn't bear this much longer, having her die like this over and over. "Francine! *Say something!*"

She finally opened her eyes and immediately started to shiver. "We ca-an't seem to sta-ay out of the wa-wa-water," she managed.

The shivering grew until her head shook uncontrollably. Instinctively, he drew her to him and hugged her tight, giving up whatever warmth he could. She gasped in pain, but settled in, holding his shoulders. After a minute, she gently pushed back. Her dark hair lay plastered against her forehead and cheekbones, but despite the quaking shivers, her eyes were bright with life.

These were eyes he could stare into forever. Buck was an idiot for letting her go.

"This is ni-ice," she said, teeth chattering.

He nodded, smiling with contentment.

"Bu-ut, there's a better wa-ay to get wa-warm."

He just looked at her.

She tapped his pack.

His pack. *Of course!* He nodded sheepishly, and let her turn him around. She held on to his shoulders and let the heated water from his exhaust well up and envelope her.

"What if they come back?" she asked, her shivering already subsiding.

"They've already circled the island twice."

"Really? I must have been out."

"When I was a kid, we used to play hide-and-seek. My secret strategy was to sneak to a place where the seeker had already looked."

"Child's play."

"Uh, okay."

"I keep forgetting you're not from here. It's an expression: 'A child's play portends the adult's way.' "

"Commendable. Our expressions go something like, 'Thank God it's Friday! Party hardy!' "

He tried to find the helicopter, but the island blocked their view. "We should try for a getaway, but I'm worried about that second chopper." He hadn't seen it since their interception.

"A chopper is a helicopter?"

"Yeah."

"I suspect that the other one is watching the shore."

"In case we miraculously escape?"

She didn't answer at first. "They'll be watching for my friends," she finally explained.

He waited, but she didn't offer any more. "I don't get it," he said. "What friends?"

Behind him, he heard her sigh. "Co-conspirators would be a better, I guess. Academic traitors. Filthy atheist Satan worshipers."

"Uh, I think that last one's a contradiction—these are Buck's friends? The ones who are helping blacks—Negroes—escape to Russia?"

For many seconds, all he heard was the bubbling of his steam exhaust from behind. She sighed again. "I lied when I told you that the uniboosts were Buck's."

"I'm listening."

"I was trying to protect you in case . . . in case they captured you."

"I see. I think."

"Oh fiddle! Look, that's a lie too. I misled you about the uniboosts to protect me, and my friends. Buck didn't even know what was going on. He didn't know about the uniboosts."

"What about Phil? Buck sent me to him."

"Phil was keeping an eye on Buck—playing along, pretending to be a fellow neophyte trying to help Negroes. He was really just making sure Buck didn't draw attention to the others."

"Where these 'others' include you?"

He felt her shrug.

"And what about that Neck guy?" he asked.

He only heard the steam bubbling from behind him.

"Francine?"

When she answered, her voice sounded tired. "Neck's not part of the group. He's just a thug."

"So, why did Phil send Buck—me—there?"

Silence.

"Francine?"

"Phil was taking care of a problem before going into hiding."

"Uh, the problem was Buck, and the solution was . . ."

"The solution was Neck. They were afraid that Buck was starting to draw too much attention."

"He was expecting that Neck would . . . *kill* Buck?"

"Look, I didn't know Phil was going to do that! They didn't tell me because they knew I'd interfere. When you . . . when *Buck* left me that note, I suddenly suspected what they had planned. Buck explained in the note that he was going to his Uncle William's house, but I thought he was just saying that to throw me off the track, that he was really going to try to connect with the Railroad."

"That's why you went to the Pungent Sound."

"That's right. I got there just as you came out, and then followed you."

"Wouldn't it have been easier for them just to let Buck into the group?"

"It would have, but they didn't think he was trustworthy."

"I see. What do *you* think?"

"Well, as I found out, he obviously has problems making commitments."

The bubbling steam filled the silence as he let that one sink in. Had he been born into this universe, it would have been him who they sent off to Neck for a "solution." It would have been him who had broken up with Francine. Because, of course, until a few hours ago, he and Buck were the same person living their lives along separate paths, otherwise they would never have made an exchange. He wanted to deny it, but he knew it was true.

"Look," Francine said, pointing.

Off to the west loomed the unmistakable dark wall of heavy rain. A squall was approaching. "It looks like we've got our escape after all," he said.

Escape. Retreat. It was the one thing he had down cold.

Chapter 7

"Stay low!" Francine called to Will.

He kept drifting higher. He couldn't help it; it made him nervous weaving around the trees at full speed.

How did birds do it? Their reactions were awfully quick for such small brains. Maybe that was their advantage: less mental nooks and crannies to get caught up in. A bird thought, *tree—move right.* His own brain went something like, *Oh shit! There's a tree right ahead! Should I go left, or right? I went right last time. Maybe I should go left this time, or I'll go around in a big circle. But there's that other tree pretty close on the left—maybe I should go to the right. Ahh! Too late! Damn, I'll just go up.*

At least the breeze was drying him off. The cover of the heavy rain had made for an easy getaway, but it felt even colder than the water of the Puget Sound. The squall line was behind them now, though. The air was clear and dry, and there were no helicopters in sight. If he could just keep up with his guide who seemed determined to lose him in the pines, this woman who first revealed herself as Buck's ex-girlfriend, then a physics professor, and now an insurgent bent on . . . what? Overthrowing the government? Or just changing the laws so couples could live together and once in a while take the Lord's name in vain?

Suddenly the pine forest fell away behind them, and they were cruising over ploughed fields. Francine pulled up and peered about.

"Where are we?" Will asked as he tried to stop next to her with one deft maneuver, but missed her reply as he sped past, totally miscalculating his momentum. They carried bags of water for ballast, and flying with them was like balancing a plate of jello while snowboarding, except that this snowboard rode on a slippery cushion of air.

By the time he adjusted his drift and worked his way back with jerky, drunken swoops and swerves, his companion must have gotten her bearings, for she pointed and sped off again. Muttering an illegal curse, he leaned over and increased his thrust to catch up. He followed her over a farmhouse. In the backyard, a woman was mowing grass. She stopped, looked up at them in surprise for a few seconds, and then ran for the house, covering her head with her arms.

He wasn't a bird, or a plane, or superman. He was a flying Hiroshima-sized bomb.

"How's your chest?" he asked, easing up next to the attractive physicist insurgent.

"It hurts like Satan. Excruciating pain makes me grumpy, so don't ask any stupid questions. Hey! I just remembered—Breggart shot you first. Did he wound you?"

"My uniboost suit came to the rescue again. I think I have an even nastier bruise on my leg though. In fact, sympathy would be in order."

"I'll let you know when I have some to spare. He could have killed you if he wanted to. It appears that he wants you alive."

"I guessed as much. He thinks I have some valuable knowledge about futuristic weapons."

"You don't?"

"I'm a mathematician, for Christ's sake!"

She winced at his blasphemy.

"Sorry. We may have to put duct tape over my mouth. Did your friends—your comrades—know that Buck was supposed to be exchanged with some military savior? That would be quite a boon for the cause."

She shook her head. "They thought the whole thing was binny. They don't know yet that Buck made the exchange, that he's no longer even a part of this universe."

It made sense. Phil's wife thought he was Buck. She didn't know she was sending some stranger off to Neck for elimination.

Francine looked at him curiously. "On the other hand, maybe you *do* have some knowledge that could be useful."

He wagged his head with determination. "Uncle William asked the same thing. I'm telling you, all I know is mathematics—differential calculus as applied to multi-dimensional arrays."

"Sounds like tensor fields."

"You know tensor calculus?"

"I know *of* it. I've never used it."

"Anyway, I know as much about weapons as an accountant."

She watched him a moment, and then shrugged. "There," she said, pointing to a developed area off on the horizon.

"Is that the college?"

In answer, she twisted her thrust knob to maximum and pulled away.

That was the end of conversation, as he couldn't catch up with her. Even though straight flight was infinitely easier than hovering in one place, her experience gave her an edge even for this. He found that he was constantly drifting either too high, or too low, and had to lean down or up to compensate, losing a bit of forward speed with each adjustment.

When they finally crossed a last Puget Sound inlet and came to the campus, he recognized the state capital building of Olympia some miles farther ahead sitting on its lone hill, just like in his own universe. Instead of flying on to the Red Square of the campus proper, his comely guide veered off to the right where a headland forced the inlet to divert and curve off to the west. As they cleared the boundary of tall pines, Will thrilled at the sight of an honest-to-goodness spaceport—a small one, judging by the jogging trail that hugged the trees around the perimeter, but a spaceport nonetheless. Like a cover from a forties pulp magazine, half a dozen rockets sat proudly upright on their tail fins. The bodies bulged sensuously amidships, tapering to noses that looked sharp enough to impale a bull.

Francine flew straight for the smallest rocket, sitting by itself off to the side with the name *Verdad* printed in script along the side. Like a life-sized Tinker Bell, she swooped to within a yard of the ground, pulled up, rotated, and then with arms extended like a ballerina for balance, settled gently onto the pavement.

Will took a deep breath and steeled himself for his arrival. Determined to demonstrate his improved proficiency, he also dove to skim the ground before looping up into a vertical descent. The ground rushed up at him at surprising speed, though, and panicking at the last minute, he leaned back reflexively so that the ground and Francine disappeared below as he looped up . . . and up. All he saw was the deep blue of the sky. He lost all sense of orientation as his uniboost carried him along on a trajectory only to be guessed. Suddenly, alarmingly, trees appeared above him. The entire spaceport rotated into view like a canopy pulled over his head from behind, and then, as though forced to repeat a horrible nightmare, there was the pavement rushing up at him once again. He leaned back as far as he could, and Francine flashed by on his left as the pavement became a blur beneath him.

This time, though, he broke out of the 360-degree loop by leaning forward so that, instead of rolling in a circle backwards again, he shot straight up. Momentum carried him a hundred feet into the air where he slowed to a stop looking sideways at the rocket's needle-thin nose, then sank a few dozen feet until his thrust buoyed him, bobbing him slowly up and down like a puppet suspended by rubber bands. He looked down at Francine who stood with her hands on her hips. The whistle of steam fell in pitch, octave by octave, as the last of his propellant was vaporized, and he plummeted the final ten feet to the ground where he bounced once within the stiffened suit, and landed on his face.

"Are you done?" Francine said from above.

He lay there and let his heart rate return to something under 200.

"How'd I do?" he asked, rolling over so that he could unstiffen the suit. His bag of water had burst beneath him, soaking his whole front.

"Like somebody who's decided they have nothing more to live for."

"I'll have you know that required careful calculation."

"Is that why you were screaming the whole time?"

Was I? he thought. "Those were shouts of exhilaration," he explained, standing up painfully on his bruised thigh.

"Well, your exhilaration nearly killed you."

"We should be wearing helmets, anyway."

"You're not supposed to need them. You're supposed to fly like an adult."

"Yeah, well accidents happen."

"Don't be a sissy."

"This is your ship?" he asked peering up at the brushed metal, gleaming in the sun.

"You are binny, aren't you? Would I live in an apartment if I had that kind of money? *Verdad* belongs to the college. The rest of the jumps belong to various rich or politically corrupt people from Seattle."

A shout from across the pavement interrupted them. A young man, young enough to be a student, waved and trotted over. "Hey, miss Sewer!" he called. "Haven't seen you in a while."

"Miss *Sewer?*" Will chided.

"Can it, Mr. Acrobat," she shot back. To the approaching student, she called, "Hello, Harold!"

The young man stopped short when he saw the blood covering her chest. "Good Ford! You're hurt! Should I call an ambulance?"

"It's okay," she said, waving it off. "I fell . . . on a chair."

As she talked, she casually, but quickly, pulled off her suit, nodding curtly to Will to do the same. Considering the reaction of everybody else who'd seen the uniboosts, he was surprised at Harold's complete disregard, as if they didn't exist at all.

"Carter's not here," the student informed. "Should I see if I can call in a sub?"

"No," Francine replied, opening a hatch near the bottom of the compact rocket and shoving her suit into the small compartment. "We're not taking *Verdad* up. I'm just showing off her new seats to Buck." She gave Will a knowing glance.

Apparently Harold had previously met Will's double. "Yeah," Will said, handing his suit to her so she could jam it in the storage compartment as well. "She's been bragging about them. Brag, brag, brag. Now maybe she'll shut up."

Francine rolled her eyes. "You expect Carter back anytime soon?" she asked.

"He went into town to catch a movie. That was a half hour ago."

"Okay. Thanks Harold," she replied, climbing a ladder that was set into the side of the rocket. "I expect to see you in next semester's ozone studies class." She paused and nodded for Will to follow.

A *ladder?* Where was the launch tower? The white room? The spacesuits, for God's sake! He followed her up, wincing each time he lifted the bruised leg.

The student walked away, back towards the small building near the spaceport entrance. On the way, though, he detoured and spoke briefly to a couple of men working among the unfathomable jumble of wires and pipes revealed by an open access plate on one of the larger ships. The two mechanics glanced briefly their way, then wiped their hands and trotted off towards the building as well.

Will paused. The amidships bulge, which looked so esthetic at a distance, now presented a problem: ladders weren't supposed to lean backwards. Francine had continued up and around the slight overhang without even pausing, so he continued on. It was easier than he'd imagined. The rungs were flat, and tilted inward near the middle for gripping with the feet, while round at the edges for comfortable handholds. Easy, that is, as long as he didn't look down.

"Who's Carter?" he asked.

"The port pilot."

"Bad news that he's not here?"

"Good news."

"I don't get it."

"It means nobody will be following us."

"Nobody else here can fly a rocket?"

"That's not the point. It's illegal to fly one without a union pilot on board."

"But we are?"

The absence of an answer was his answer.

He heard sirens—several—off in the direction of Olympia. "It sounds like they've found us."

She stopped above him and pulled a ring of keys from her pocket. "They won't be here for a few minutes," she replied, fitting one into the hull, and then sliding aside a hatch.

From their high perch, he could see across the treetops to Olympia. Three police cars topped a hill a couple of miles away. "Won't the police just take off in one after us?"

"Not without Carter," she replied, grabbing an overhead handle and pulling herself inside.

"None of the police know how to fly a rocket?"

"I told you," she said from the darkness within, "they're called jumps, not rockets, and it's not a matter of knowing how to fly. Nobody—*no*-body—violates union rules." Her face appeared above him. "And if you continue asking stupid questions, they won't need a union pilot to catch us."

When he climbed up the last steps and pulled himself inside, his fugitive cohort had turned on the interior lights. Raised on fifties science fiction movies, he'd was expecting the control cabin to be all bare, riveted metal, with metal seats bolted to a metal floor. Instead, the cabin looked like the inside of an upscale SUV. Two black leather captain's chairs invited him to settle in and relax. Francine flicked a switch, and the control panels glowed life. Dials sprang to indicative positions, and a myriad of little lights glowed yellow and green—one flashed an insistent red. Directly in front of Francine, who had flopped into the left chair, a CRT screen was filled with a wide-angle image of the spaceport.

"Take a seat," she said, flipping more switches, and turning down the volume of a radio that squawked to life with static and broken pieces of monotone conversations. "We're taking off as soon as the fields are stable."

He slid into the chair on her right, and found that it wasn't exactly like an automobile seat. Between his legs was a flight stick, replete with finger and thumb buttons. An identical one lay between Francine's knees.

"What fields?" he asked, peering at his own CRT screen that showed a blue sky with scattered clouds—obviously a view from the nose.

"Containment fields."

"What do they contain?"

"Plasma," she replied, adjusting a knob while watching a dial that responded accordingly.

"What's the plasma for?"

She glanced at him. "What's with all the questions? You sound like a four year-old."

He realized that he was nervous. He'd never flown in a rocket before—or a jump, or a hop, or a skip. "I know what it's for," he said, coming to his own defense. "It's part of the nuclear fusion drive."

It was just a guess. He was surprised when she said, "You get a cigar—put on your belt; I don't want you floating around later."

"Where are we going?" he asked, reaching around for the webbed belt.

"Still with the questions? India."

"Wow! Half way around the world!"

She glanced at him. "Not the country, the station."

He looked at her with wide eyes. "Like a *space* station?"

"Yes, Willy" she said as though indeed talking to a young child as she slipped on headphones with an attached microphone. "We're going into space—*outer* space!"

On her screen, he saw the three police cars careen onto the field, stopping in front of the small building.

"You don't have to get snotty," he objected. "Shouldn't we be wearing, like, spacesuits?" He was babbling, but between police cars and a fusion rocket engine, there wasn't much room for calm deliberation.

"Why?" she asked distractedly as she studied a dial whose needle seemed to be reluctant about progressing further.

"What if we lose pressure?"

"Spacesuits aren't going to help us if we lose the hull. That's like taking a pillow along in a car in case you're in an accident—by the way, you're going to navigate. I'll show you more later, but for now, just keep an eye on the nose radar and holler if you see anything within sixty degrees."

"*I'm* going to navigate? Are you nuts! Where's the nose radar?"

"See that switch there?" she said, pointing.

"The one that says, 'nose rad'?"

"Another cigar."

He flipped it up, and the clouds became superimposed with a bullseye target of concentric dotted circles. "I don't get it."

Francine sighed, reached over, and flipped off a switch that read, *nose view.*

His screen went dark, except for the dotted circles. He saw now that they had numbers next to them—obviously angles off the nose. Near the edge of the screen was a small white bar. As he watched, it got shorter. "The length indicates distance!" he said, proud of his discovery.

She glanced over. "Of course. Haven't you ever seen radar before?"

"Our radar screens are only two-dimensional. The distance from the center indicates how far away an object is."

She swung open a little plastic protection window and flipped a switch painted bright red. He felt the ship vibrate beneath him, and heard a powerful whooshing sound. "But you have computers that you can put in your pocket," she observed dryly.

"What's that sound?"

"Air intake."

On Francine's screen, Will saw that Harold stood in front of the building shaking his head at a policeman that was pointing in their direction. The student shook his head one last time, waved his hand dismissively at the cop, and ran into the building. The officer looked in their direction, then ran for the building as well.

"What's the air for?"

"You'll see in a minute."

A man's excited voice broke through over the radio. "Miss Sewer! Shut down that vehicle—now!"

She flipped a switch and said calmly, "*Verdad* jump here. There's someone on the air unaware of radio protocol—over."

The whooshing sound tapered off, and the whine of some powerful motor below them trailed off as well. A green light on the panel glowed to life.

"Cut the poop, Sewer! I'm serious. CID has ordered us to shoot you down if you try to take off!"

"If the FCC is listening," she replied, lifting another plastic window over a large red pushbutton, "there's a potty-mouth on the air who continues to ignore protocol. *Verdad* over."

She flipped the radio switch off and said, "Radar clear, navigator?"

"Huh?" he said, looking quickly at his own screen. "Uh, yeah."

"Okay, you're about to find out what the air is for."

Holding her thumb over the large pushbutton, she took the flight stick in her other hand. "Geronimo!" she yelled and pushed the button.

Nothing happened, other than a deep groan somewhere below, sounding like a subterranean giant waking from a long sleep. Then, with a startling crash, he was smashed into his seat. He couldn't turn his head, but out of the corner of his eye, he saw the space port receding alarmingly fast in Francine's screen. Before he even had a chance to adjust to the acceleration, it was over, and he was floating against his straps, weightless.

"Wow!" he exclaimed. "That's it? I thought it would have lasted longer!"

"That's all it takes," she replied distractedly, peering at one of the dials. "Come on, baby!" she implored. "Don't let Mama down!"

"We're, like, in orbit now?" he asked

He was feeling a tremendous exhilaration.

She glanced quickly at him. "Are you binny? That was just the air boost. We're barely a half-mile up."

"Air boost?"

She sighed with exasperation. "We have to gain altitude before the main drive kicks in. Otherwise, we'd blow away the whole port."

Will felt a gentle pull draw him back into his seat.

"Ahh," she said, wiggling the flight stick experimentally, "there we go."

"That's the main drive?"

"You bet. Just like clockwork. Now we'll see how she flies."

"Uh, you haven't flown this ship before?"

She looked at him as though to confirm that he was serious. "You really are binny aren't you? Nobody but union pilots fly ships."

"Wait! You're telling me that you've never flown *any* spaceship before?"

"Of course not. Don't worry. I've watched them—it's no problem."

He suddenly felt every foot of the three thousand between them and the Earth. "Do we have parachutes?"

"Who needs parachutes? We have the uniboosts."

"We can get to them from up here?"

She waved her hand. "Don't be such a worry-wart. Nothing's going to happen."

"We can't, can we? We can't get to them from up here."

She pretended to study a dial that clearly wasn't moving at all.

The acceleration had increased to the point where it took effort to lift his head. "How many G's will we reach?"

She gave up her absorption of the frozen indicator. "You mean equivalent gravities?"

"Right. G's—gravities."

She shrugged. "Maybe one and a quarter. I never thought about it."

He'd had images of himself flattened into the seat, holding out against the almost unbearable pressures pulling his cheeks down to his ears. The ability to withstand extreme acceleration had seemed nearly the primary requirement of astronauts in his universe. "We can make it into orbit with only one and a quarter G's?"

She shook her head sadly. "What kind of mathematicians do they train in your universe? Think about it: what's the minimum amount of acceleration that would be required to reach orbit?"

"Theoretically? Well, anything above one G, I guess . . . as long as you had enough time. Anything greater than one would result in a steadily increasing speed against gravity."

"So, there you are."

"But that's just theoretical. That assumes, like, infinite fuel."

"Infinite fuel? Then your vehicle would weigh an infinite amount—not much acceleration there."

"Uh, of course . . . it's energy. It's a matter of how much energy."

"And how efficiently it can be applied to the propellant."

"Specific Impulse!" He wasn't exactly sure what it was, but it seemed right in the context.

"Exactly. How much acceleration—change in momentum, actually—you get from a certain unit of propellant. And that, in turn, is proportional to the exhaust velocity of the reaction propellant. Early chemical rockets—Von Braun's rockets of the fifties—had exhaust speeds on the order of 30,000 feet-per-second. That was barely enough to make it into orbit. In fact, the chemical fuel didn't contain enough energy-per-mass to even carry all of itself into orbit. It was only the fact that it was continually used up during the ascent, making the whole rocket lighter and lighter. It's amazing when you think about it: they used massive vehicles weighing upwards of a million pounds, burning hundreds of thousands of gallons of fuel just to get a little satellite weighing maybe a hundred pounds into orbit. *Verdad*, here, has an exhaust velocity of 150,000 feet-per-second. That's why we had to gain some altitude before lighting her fuse. Steam traveling at that speed would strip the flesh off your bones in milliseconds. Efficient interplanetary ion drives have exhaust speeds above half a million feet-per-second."

She looked at him and grinned. "Your universe still uses chemical rockets, doesn't it?"

He lifted his head and pretended indignation. "We prefer the esthetics of a classical approach."

"Right. And every household has a dedicated servant who walks behind the family buggy cleaning up the droppings from the horse."

"Jumps use nuclear fusion?"

"All Earth-accessible vehicles use both air boosts for initial take-off, and then fusion cores for driving the reaction propellant—almost always water. In addition to regular old-fashioned reaction mass, IP—interplanetary—ships use the nuclear energy to power ion drives."

"Because ion drives are very efficient, but don't provide very much instantaneous thrust," he finished smugly for her.

She raised eyebrows. "I thought you only had chemical rockets?"

"That doesn't mean we didn't study the theory of other methods. Mostly, we haven't figured out how to make nuclear fusion work under controlled conditions."

She grinned. "You were too busy making little telephones that you could stick in your ear."

He chuckled. "There's probably more truth in that than I'd care to admit. But wait a second—why not use antimatter for your spaceships as well?"

"How much do you think it costs to make a uniboost?"

"I have no idea."

"Take a guess."

Remembering his cab fare, he mentally divided his guess by twenty. "Ten thousand dollars."

"Not a bad guess. The actual number is about twice that. Now guess how much it takes to add half a gram of antimatter."

"I don't have a clue."

"Ten times the cost of the uniboost itself. Almost all of the cost in operating a uniboost is in the creation of the antimatter. There's no free energy. Antimatter is simply a way of very efficiently compressing a whole lot of energy into a very small package. Nuclear energy, on the other hand, is already packaged, ready to use. There are proposals to build interstellar ships that would use antimatter, but they're just pipe-dreams, since it would take more than a human lifetime to reach the closest star anyway."

Will tumbled some mental arithmetic around: his uniboost, loaded with antimatter, cost over two million of his own universe's dollars. Either Francine was one savvy thief, or somebody considered her important enough to trust with astoundingly expensive hardware.

"So, why no wings?" he asked.

"On the uniboost? I thought that was obvious—"

"No. On the jumps. They still look like the V2 rockets the Germans—Von Braun—designed during WWII."

"What's wrong with that? Why would we want wings?"

"Well, how about the fact that Von Braun's V2's could only land nose-first . . . traveling at full speed."

"So what? That wasn't a result of the vehicle's shape, but just that the chemical fuels weren't efficient enough to do more than get the rockets into the air. Wings are fine at slow speeds—subsonic—but they just get in the way at jump speeds."

Will had noticed one dial that read in increments of 1,000 up to 20,000. The needle was just passing the 3,000 mark. "Is that our speed?" he asked, pointing.

"Yeah. We need 17,000 to reach orbit, but we'll take it higher since we're going out to India Station in synchronous orbit."

They were already traveling at nearly Mach 4. They'd broken the sound barrier, and he hadn't even noticed.

"How do you re-enter? How do you come back from orbit?"

She looked at him as though she wasn't sure she understood. "You slow down . . . and come back."

"What about air friction? Why don't you burn up in a fiery flaming ball?"

"You would if you didn't slow down. It happens every once in awhile; a pilot has a hangover and miscalculates."

"But coming back from orbit, you're traveling at over 15,000 miles-per-hour. How can you slow down enough before you . . . burn up?"

She shrugged. "Same way you went up." She obviously didn't understand his confusion.

He realized that his trouble stemmed from a lifelong assumption that rockets carried just barely enough fuel to get them up and away. "You use the main engine to slow down enough *before* entering the atmosphere? But as soon as you start to slow down, you'll fall out of orbit . . ."

The look on Francine's face told him that he was missing something fundamental.

He took another shot. "Once you hit the atmosphere, do you use the engine to slow down quickly before you heat up too much?"

She grinned at this. "At 15,000 mph, the fins would be torn off the first second, and the main body would break up within five seconds after that. The remaining pieces would burn up in that fiery flaming ball. We know this thanks to those hung-over pilots."

He was beginning to see the light. "The main engine not only slows your tangential orbital speed, but is angled so that a vertical vector also maintains your altitude. Ultimately, you could end up just hovering in one spot as the Earth rotated beneath you."

"Now you're thinking like a mathematician. You could take it to that extreme, but that would be a real waste of propellant. In fact, you probably wouldn't even have enough for that—at least to also lower you to the ground afterwards, unless you tanked up first at a station. Instead, you slow down just enough to do a flip. At about 3,000 mph the thin upper atmosphere catches the tail fins and spins you around, nose-first. At that point you shut down the thrust and let air friction slow you to below Mach 1. Then you light the candle again, fly to your landing site, do a nose up, and settle gently down on your butt."

"That easy, huh?"

"No. Not at all. That's why the Pilot Union is so exclusive."

The cabin was silent for a moment except for the confident, distant roar of hellish steam pushed away at hypersonic speed. "And you can bring us down?"

"I don't intend to try. I'm neither that stupid nor that brave. We just need to make it to India Station. Going up is the easy part. Like sailing: getting *away* from the dock requires hardly any skill."

"Speaking of pilots—or the lack of—who's flying the ship now?"

He'd noticed she hadn't been using the flight stick.

"We're on autopilot for the time being. It's programmed to take us up on a standard orbit trajectory."

"These things are standardized?"

"It's just an aid. Most flights start with a low-altitude equatorial orbit. You dial in your latitude, and the autopilot takes it from there. If we sat back and took a nap, we'd end up in a stable, somewhat elongated orbit 150-miles up, crossing the equator every forty-five minutes or so."

"I thought your computers were as big as buildings?"

"Who needs a computer for that?" She scoffed. "The autopilot simply uses nav beacons to follow a defined trajectory. The beacons transmit from each of the six synchronous stations." She checked one of the dials labeled *longitude*. "But India is our destination, and we have some calculations to make to get there. If you reach behind you, there's a book titled *Primary Orbits* . . . Will?"

Something had caught his eye. On his screen a glowing bar floated, unmoving. It grew perceptibly as he watched.

"Is it moving?" Francine asked peering over his elbow.

"No, it's just getting longer—that means it's coming directly at us, doesn't it?"

"It does," his partner said with furrowed brow.

"Is it another jump?"

She shook her head. "Too small."
"What do you think it is, then?"
"Probably a missile."
"Like, with a bomb at the end?"
"A big bomb. And it has us in its sights."

Chapter 8

"Is it an atom bomb?" Will asked, his voice mirroring the tremor he felt in his throat.

"Depends," Francine answered as she grabbed the flight stick in one hand and placed her other on a panel switch, ready to trip it.

"On what?"

"How desperate Breggart is. We're forty-two miles high, coming up on Minneapolis. He'll take people out on the ground if it is."

"Doesn't, like, the President have to push a button or something to launch nuclear weapons?"

There was a sense of unreality at the idea that a nuclear bomb could be launched to stop two people.

"What are you babbling about?" she shot back irritably.

He remembered. Moscow blew up in the sixties. With no cold war, there were no warhead arsenals aimed at each other ready to destroy the world with a single mistake or miscalculation. Atom bombs could be used casually.

"Can we go faster?" he asked. The question sounded dumb.

She bit her lip, and then, closing her eyes, flicked the switch. A light on the panel blinked red urgently for a few seconds, then turned blue.

"What did you do?" he asked.

She looked at him with eyes that were seeing their own execution. "I disabled the autopilot."

She turned her attention back to the panel indicators as she gripped the flight stick with white knuckles. "There are two possibilities," she elaborated. "The first is that the warhead is loaded with normal munitions and Breggart is counting on the fact that we'll follow a standard orbit trajectory. The missile can sense the infrared from our exhaust to close in and make final contact."

"The second possibility is that it's a nuke?"

"In that case, it doesn't have to make contact. In fact, once it's within a certain range, it will automatically detonate if it loses contact with us."

"How soon will it be in range?"

In answer, she reached over and flicked a switch on his panel. "Use your stick to move the crosshairs over the missile."

Once he had the cursor positioned, he could read a distance figure from a meter beneath the screen. "Twenty-three miles."

"It's already within range."

The roar of the steam exhaust had become distinctly muted. He wondered if it was because they were leaving the atmosphere. "Why would Breggart assume that we would stay on a standard trajectory?"

She seemed not to hear him. He didn't press it. The white bar had grown significantly larger. "We're going as fast as we can?"

She shook her head. "It wouldn't matter. That missile is made for speed. We couldn't possibly outrun it."

The distance meter now read thirteen miles. His heart thumped in his throat. "What are we going to *do*?"

"I'm doing it," was her curt answer.

"*What* are you doing?"

"What's the range?"

He looked again. "Seven miles—it's coming *fast!*"

She took a deep breath, as though preparing to dive into cold water, then punched a large red button with her left thumb. With her other hand, she flipped the plastic cover of the original launch button, and hesitating just a moment, punched that as well.

Nothing happened for a second, and Will tensed for an eminent explosion as the missile finally caught them, then was thrown forward against his seatbelt.

"What happened!" he yelled.

"I cut the drive."

The missile was heat-seaking. She'd obviously waited until the last minute so that it wouldn't have a chance to readjust its sensitivity and home in on their residual heat.

He felt odd, light headed, like he'd just topped the hill on a roller-coaster. "Hey! We're actually in free-fall—"

A concussion slammed him sideways in his seat.

"Shit!" he screamed. "It was a nuke!"

Even if the shock wave didn't kill them outright, the radiation would hours or days later.

"Look at your screen," she said.

Where the bar had been, there were now a handful of smaller ones surrounded by a cloud of points.

"So?"

"A nuclear explosion would have vaporized the entire missile."

He closed his eyes, and took a deep, thankful breath as he floated against his straps. "What now?"

Francine's lips were pursed tight as she threw a series of switches and flipped open the firing button cover. "We try to make orbit," she replied and punched the big red button. The distant roar of steam returned, and he was pulled gently back into his seat.

"Try?"

"We've lost the standard trajectory," she muttered, eyes glued to an artificial horizon ball as she worked the control stick.

"Was the autopilot damaged?"

"No—I don't know. What difference does it make?"

"Why can't we just turn it back on?"

She threw him a glance as though checking to make sure an actual person with a brain sat next to her. "If we had a few hours to reprogram it to pick up where it left off, and if I *knew* how to program it, and if we could stop *Verdad* so that it floated in this exact spot while I learned, then, yes, we could turn the autopilot back on. Now, if you'll stop asking stupid questions, we *might* make orbit."

Will pouted and watched the radar reflections of the disintegrated missile fall away behind them. "In my universe," he said matter-of-factly, "the computers could have easily figured all that out."

"In your universe," she reminded him, "you don't have jump ships to get back on track. Look, if you're just going to keep bothering me, I might as well put you to work. Grab the *Primary*

Orbits book behind you, and find the perigee sector for a Number Six orbit."

Will found that the thick book was essentially a compilation of tables. Following an introduction section crammed with flurries of equations, were twenty-seven chapters for twenty-seven different types of orbits, each containing dizzying crowds of values associated with every imaginable attribute. There were orbital periods for apogee altitudes in increments of five miles, the same for perigee altitudes, eccentricity expansion referenced by delta miles-per-second at both perigee and apogee, and even tangential angles relative to Earth's leading and lagging horizons for every degree of the orbit in increments of ten miles of altitude out to fifteen thousand miles where the whole Earth was only thirty degrees wide and the accuracy needed to measure the angle of the horizon became impractical.

It was the last category that his harried pilot sought. Will was not versed in orbital mechanics, had barely ever given it much thought, but the geometrical mathematics were straightforward, and he had little problem grasping the relevance of the tables. He knew that at any point in time, the orbit of an object could be exactly defined given three attributes: the object's distance from the Earth, its direction of travel, and its speed. At both apogee, when the object was farthest from the Earth, and perigee, when it was closest, the direction of travel was exactly at right angles, i.e. level with the Earth's surface.

Verdad had continued to rise, and was now forty-six miles high. Francine told him to find the orbital speed for a Number Six orbit at sixty-five miles of perigee while she took *Verdad* higher. Once she reached sixty-four miles, she watched the speed and direction indicators, while he read off the altitude. At 64.8 miles she was satisfied that she was within one percent of the 4.97 miles-per-second shown in the table, and as close to an easterly direction as her indicator could define, and she punched the shutdown combination with satisfaction, and the steam exhaust faded to silence.

In forty-one minutes they would cross the equator and slow to 4.81 mps at an apogee of 160 miles, and then another forty-one minutes after that, they would cross the equator once more and return back to perigee, heading in the same easterly direction, although over a different spot on the Earth.

Will continued to study the table as he floated inside his seat straps. "The pages in this section are pink," he observed.

"That means that those orbits are unstable," she replied merrily. She was obviously relieved.

"And that's supposed to be good?"

"Don't worry. The thin atmosphere here at perigee would eventually drag us out of orbit, but I don't intend to be this low that long."

"We're still going to India Station?"

She nodded. "Now comes the real orbital navigation. Getting off the Earth was the easy part."

Will continued to work the book's tables while Francine piloted *Verdad*. The simple analog calculators of the ship used the beacons beamed from the six stations to provide altitude, spherical position in latitude and longitude, and speed. The first maneuver was to move their orbit to one that was equatorial so that they were in the same plane as the geosynchronous stations 22,000 miles above them. They thrust laterally in a northward direction when they reached their southern-most part of their orbit, and then again southward for another bump when they eased north of the equator again. Then, after twenty-five minutes of cuticle chewing, Will came up with a crude, highly eccentric orbit that would take them out to India Station.

This was orbit type Number Nine in the book, and Francine explained these were Hohmann transfer orbits, elongated orbits whose perigee coincided with the starting point on the inner orbit, and whose apogee just touched a point on the outer destination orbit. The trick was to increase speed at the precise amount at the precise point on the inner orbit to put you on the track of the Hohmann transfer.

It was impossible, of course, to do all this precisely enough to arrive at India Station some six hours and 70,000 miles later without some adjustments, so at the predetermined time, Francine hit the ignition button and brought the thrust up to Will's calculated value on a Hohmann orbit that would bring them to apogee just ahead of the station and a hundred miles below, where the station would then pass over them as they started their long fall back to Earth. They would then fire *Verdad* once more to increase their speed, breaking out of the Hohmann orbit into one that was circular, and slowly catch up with the station.

When Francine shut down the thrust, silence returned to *Verdad's* tiny cabin, interrupted now and then by the soft tick of some buried relay as the navigation calculators continued to track their position. His screen was completely dark; there were no other vessels within its three hundred-mile range. He changed to visual mode, and the brilliant blue Earth filled half the screen, fading to the blackest of black above. That's where they were headed, into a blackness, the nature of which his distant ancestors had only guessed at, gazing up from the warmth of their fires.

"We're in space!" he said, amazed at the revelation.

His companion glanced at him with a look that was becoming familiar. But then she smiled. "That's quite a feat in your universe, isn't it?"

"Reserved for a lucky handful of astronauts who train for years for a chance at it."

"Well, it's not cheap here, either. Most people are lucky if they can afford one vacation trip off-Earth in a lifetime."

He smiled. "Actually, in our universe, the Russians will take you up for a price. The last one I heard about carried a seventy-five million dollar ticket."

She snorted. "You aren't serious. You could buy a fleet of jumps for that."

"But in the currency of your universe, that would only be about four million dollars."

"Only four million? Gee, that one joyride would buy you a mere ten *Verdad's*."

Francine sat back and closed her eyes. Her face seemed pinched, as though she was contemplating something unpleasant. After a minute, she opened her eyes and smiled at him. "The problem with having time to relax is that you then notice all the pain you've been ignoring."

The blood on her blouse had dried, but she seemed pale, drained.

"Do you have a first-aid kit on board?" he asked.

"You mean like bandages?"

"Yeah. I'm thinking more along the lines of ibuprofen."

"What's that?"

"Pain killer."

"Like aspirin?"

"Yeah, only better."

She shrugged and pointed over her shoulder. On the wall was a panel with the universal coiled snake and staff symbol of medicine.

Will released his strap and floated out of his chair . . . and immediately knew he was in trouble. Strapped in the chair, he'd felt unquestionably weightless, but it was somewhat familiar, the sensation that he was poised over an endlessly long dip in the road. But this—this was altogether different. His mind couldn't ignore the fact that he was suspended in air with no support whatsoever. Suddenly, the panic of falling overwhelmed him, and he thrashed about madly as though his very life depended on finding some anchor. His foot connected with something soft and he heard a yelp, and then Francine's face was inches in front of him upside down. It was an angry face.

"You kicked me!" she cried. "Will you calm down, already?"

He grabbed her shoulders, and having her upside-down head firmly locked in his view reassured his ten million year-old instinct that he wasn't actually falling out of the family tree.

Inches from his nose, she arched one upside-down eyebrow. "Getting a little familiar, are we?"

He realized that what he thought was one of her shoulders, was actually her breast. He quickly let go with both hands and slowly floated away. "Sorry."

"No harm. You okay now?"

He nodded, and proceeded to wave his arms in a futile attempt to swim through the air.

"Stop it before you hurt one of us!" his erstwhile victim cried. "Here," she said, grabbing him by his shirt and throwing him backwards, over her head. "Grab one of the handholds."

As he flew through the air with the greatest of ease, he saw that the walls were indeed fitted with inset handholds. Fending off the far bulkhead, he quickly grabbed the nearest handhold before bouncing away. Using others, he pulled himself to the medical panel and tried to open it, but it was locked. Francine told him to yank it hard, and when it sprang open, he tumbled away and hit his head on the far wall. Vertigo, pain, and dizziness begged him to question whether space travel was as wonderful as he'd imagined as he carefully made his way back to the medical cabinet.

Inside was an array of little tubes and plastic-wrapped packages, all held in place with straps. He found a container of aspirin, but next to it was one of codeine. When he expressed his surprise, Francine explained that pilots had legal authority to administer drugs from the supply. He looked at the cornucopia and said, "We weren't supposed to open this, were we?"

"They can add it to the other dozen charges they already have against us," she replied.

He left the aspirin, and brought her the tube of codeine pills instead.

Hell, why waste a windfall?

When she saw what he'd given her, she glanced at him questioningly, then shrugged and opened the tube. He floundered his way to another closet and returned with a pint bag of water from which she sucked a mouthful through a sip-spout to wash down the pills.

"How many did you take?" he asked, looking at the tiny writing on the container.

"Three."

"Hmm, the instructions say to take one or two."

She snatched the tube back. "You can't believe that," she countered, squeezing another pill through the elastic mouth and tossing it into her mouth. "The guy who wrote those didn't have a bullet wound," she added after taking another swig.

Will returned to his seat, rotating himself so that he could position his butt down and buckled himself back in. The straps were comforting; when secured in his seat he was no longer falling into infinity.

Francine seemed to have fallen asleep, and he was admiring her comely profile when she suddenly opened her eyes and looked at him. "Sorry," she said. "I'm not a very good host. I suddenly feel so . . . drained."

"That wouldn't be from a drug overdose, would it?"

"I'd have to take the whole tube to overdose. Besides, they obviously haven't taken effect yet."

"How do you know?"

"I still hurt like Judas."

"Right."

Despite her obvious distress, she smiled at him. "Thank you, Will."

"For what?"

"Letting me drag you into so much danger."

"As I recall, I was already on the run when you caught up with me."

"Still. You're being a very good sport about it. It can't be easy popping up in a whole new universe."

He wanted to tell her that he'd do it again if she would be there to greet him, but he didn't, probably just like Buck wouldn't have either. Instead, he asked, "Where did the name *Verdad* come from?"

She closed her eyes again and her face seemed to relax. "It's Spanish."

"What does it mean?"

"Truth," she said softly.

Her breathing slowed.

"How do you know about the military's missiles?" he asked. "And how did you get so experienced using uniboosts?"

She just floated there, fast asleep. The codeine had finally pulled down its comforting blanket.

She looked like a sleeping princess.

Ж Ж Ж

Will decided to familiarize himself with the army of indicators and controls staring him down. He found that his radar had multiple modes. He'd been operating in close range—up to two hundred miles. Medium range scanned out to eight hundred miles, while the long range mode sent tenuous radio tentacles out fifteen-hundred miles. At orbital speeds, two hundred miles represented less than forty-five seconds of travel time. He left the dial set on long range, providing a whole five minutes of warning.

Every so often, a bar of light—fuzzy with the reduced resolution of long range—appeared near the periphery of the screen, grew a bit in size, and then faded away. He assumed that these must be other ships or perhaps satellites. What if one appeared dead ahead? Should he wake Francine, or try to take evasive action himself? Space was enormous, he reminded himself. The chances against actually hitting something must be huge. His screen represented a diameter of space three thousand miles across. Assuming another ship was, say, a hundred feet long . . . he slid his mental slide rule around: the chances of hitting another ship that appeared on the screen were one in two hundred billion, give or take a few billion. He relaxed, satisfied. But then another thought arose: those were the same odds they had to overcome to rendezvous with India Station.

He had over five hours to kill. His renegade captain had mentioned something about a mid-course correction. At the time, he had been agonizing about his orbital calculations, and hadn't really been listening, but now he wondered when that needed to happen . . . and what preparations they needed to perform. There was plenty of time, he decided. Francine would have told him if it were imminent. He should get some rest, maybe take a nap. He closed his eyes and tried to let his mind float free along with his weightless body.

It was no use. He was traveling through space, for God's sake. He picked up the orbital navigation book and studied the tables associated with their Hohmann obit. In increments of ten minutes, he noted their position as derived from the station beacons, and then normalized them for their expected degree of eccentricity. Finally, he extrapolated the normalized point of apogee back to their actual path. He frowned at the result, and then went through the calculations a second, and then a third time. There was no doubt; on their present course, they would overshoot India Station, arriving fifteen minutes too early and sail on past its orbit.

They really needed that mid-course correction. He looked at the clock. They were nearly halfway. At Hohmann breakout, he'd wondered what they would do for the six hours of travel, but now he was sweating, wishing the trip was twice as long.

He worked feverishly, checking and double-checking his scribblings. He calculated how much velocity they needed to kill, and the fractional degrees of direction offset. At one point he stopped and gazed wonderingly at the pencil in his hand. He was managing with paper, pencil, and logarithm tables what he would normally have taken for granted on his computer.

No time for philosophy, though. His carefully worked orbital correction was only valid for a precise point in their path . . . and it was coming up—he looked at the clock—in eight minutes!

His pretty captain had slept for nearly three hours. That would have to do. "Francine," he said softly. "Wake up."

She didn't stir.

He jiggled her shoulder. "Francine," he said louder.

She took a deep breath and snored once, but otherwise could have been in a coma.

The codeine. Plus exhaustion.

He glanced at the clock. Seven minutes. "Francine!" he yelled.

She finally stirred and opened her eyes, but he wasn't sure they really saw anything.

He shook her shoulder. "Wake up! We have to make the course correction."

"Hmmph," she muttered nodding in agreement, and then closed her eyes.

Shit!

He shook her shoulder roughly. "Francine! Listen to me. How do I know how much thrust *Verdad* develops?" This was a crucial part of the correction.

She opened her eyes again, although it seemed to be a tremendous struggle. "Trust?" she mumbled.

"Thrust! *Thrust*, Francine! Where's the thrust indicator?"

She turned bleary eyes on him. "Thrust?"

"Yes! Where's the goddamn indicator!"

She looked hurt. "That's blasphemous."

"I don't give a shit! I'll tell you what's blasphemous! Missing the space station and becoming lost in space! We'll spend the rest of our miserable short lives until the air gives out listening to a fake robot yell 'Danger! Danger! Will Robinson!' "

She seemed to be finally waking up. "What are you talking about?"

"Never mind. Just tell me where the thrust indicator is."

She blinked a few times, looked at him a moment, then studied the control panel as though seeing it for the first time. "Thrust," she finally said, and pointed to a vertical indicator off to the side with a label under it that read THRUST. The needle rested at zero.

He'd completely missed it in his frantic haste. The meter was marked off in increments of 'Tlbs'. He asked her what that meant.

"Thrust," she said dreamily.

"I know that. What are the increments?"

"Thousands of pounds."

That made sense. He needed one last parameter, though. "How much does *Verdad* weigh?"

She smiled as though he'd just told her a joke. "Trick question—nothing."

"What do you mean? Christ, Francine!" He was feeling panic clawing at his back. They had just two and a half minutes left.

"We're in free fall. The ship is weightless. You'll get in trouble for cursing, you know."

He put his hand to his forehead and tried to stay calm. "Francine, listen to me. How much does *Verdad* weigh when on Earth?"

She smiled and pointed again at the thrust meter.

He wanted to scream, but then he noticed that under the label was a little plate that slid into a grooved holder. It had a date and '32.743T'

"That's our weight in thousands of pounds?"

She shook her head, grinning.

"What *is* it, then?"

"You forgot about us. That weight doesn't include us."

"Oh for Christ's . . ."

He took a deep breath. It was true that their own mass was part of the total, but that tenth of a percent difference was a factor too small to worry about.

He didn't have time to deal with his loopy companion. He ignored her stream of flippant remarks, and concentrated on calculating a thrust value appropriate for the ship's mass. The seconds ticked away, and when he came up with a value, he realized that the burn period would have to last for nearly twenty minutes. That would never do. The course correction was calculated assuming a certain point on their present orbit. They couldn't produce the needed velocity change in just an instant, of course, but the longer the thrust was applied, the farther they moved from the assumed point in the orbit . . . and the greater the error in the correction.

He started over. He tried not to look at the clock, but each second clicked audibly from the mechanical device, and his stomach tightened a little with each one. Sweat from his forehead found its way to his eyebrows, and then launched itself when he moved to become annoying obstacles which floated before him to be swatted away, only to be broken into a dozen smaller watery flies.

He finally had a new thrust value, and saw that he'd already missed the target time by six seconds. He cursed mightily, as he worked his control stick to turn *Verdad* into its tail-first position for the firing. The curses swelled when he found that it was nearly impossible to nudge the ship into a precise orientation. It was like trying to balance a pencil on its point. As the vessel swung along one axis into position, he either overshot the mark, or corrected by too much so that it swung back the way it had come. It was like trying to land the uniboost . . . while carrying bags of cement.

The target time had passed by a whole minute and a half when he glanced over and saw that Francine had stopped her rambling nonsense to watch him amusingly. He knew that she was only marginally cognizant in her codeine state, but he snapped at her. "What's so funny?" he snarled

"You. What's the rush? You act like this course correction is a matter of life and death."

He fired the tiniest burst from the steering jets and watched as Verdad missed its mark yet again. "Damn it!" he hissed at his stick. "Without the correction, we're going to miss India Station by a couple of hundred miles."

"So what? We can correct anytime. It's actually easier later on. You don't have to be so precise then."

"But it takes a whole lot more propellant if you wait until later . . ."

He remembered. This wasn't his universe where the inefficient chemical fuels required exacting navigation, where failure to account for every possible economy could mean an empty fuel tank and missed target.

He sighed and took his hand from the stick. "I feel like a fool," he said, looking at her. "I spent all that time calculating a correction and . . ."

Francine was staring at the control panel, a look of utter horror gripping her face.

"What's wrong?" he asked.

Without breaking her gaze, she pointed. Under a small, circular indicator off to the side was the word PROP. The needle hovered a sliver above zero.

"Does that stand for propellant?" he asked, fearing the answer.

She nodded slowly and looked at him, her eyes vacant, like a zombie's.

"Where did it all go?"

The question sounded silly.

Her nod froze, and she just looked at him. "I took for granted that the tank was full," she finally said faintly.

The oversized codeine dose would be ameliorating her anxiety. Her numb distress was therefore the equivalent of screaming hysteria.

"We're up shit creek, aren't we?" he said.

She looked at him with furrowed brow.

"Without a paddle," he added in explanation.

Her eyes suddenly went wide. "We need that course correction *now!*"

Chapter 9

Will turned his attention back to the control stick.

"What are you doing?" Francine snapped.

"I'm trying to get *Verdad* lined up tail-first, but it's almost impossible to—"

"Forget it," she barked, all business now. "Once you fire up the main engine, you'll be able to control her attitude easily. Do you have your reference?"

She meant the stellar landmark he would use to orient *Verdad*. "Antares," he replied.

This was the bright star at the head of Scorpius. It was the object he'd been trying in vain to center in the crosshairs of his screen.

"Then, what are you waiting for? Fire!"

He hesitated with his finger hovering over the big red button. He turned to her. "You should do it."

She thought a moment and then said, "No. I feel binny from the drug. Just fire—you'll do fine."

He punched the button, and felt the gentle grip of false gravity pull him down into the seat. As he increased the thrust to his calculated value, he found that Francine was right: the steady push of the exhaust made child's play of keeping the crosshairs on Antares.

As the woozy physicist counted down the minutes and seconds, Will realized that it might be better if they didn't fire through the entire period. His calculated course correction should line them up with the original orbit, which peaked at an apogee just ahead and a hundred miles below the station. But if they reduced the burn time, they might arrive closer to the station. He didn't have nearly the time to redo his calculations. He'd have to make a guess. He decided he would cut the thrust fifteen seconds early, but *Verdad* had already decided on something a bit different. When Francine reached twenty-five seconds in the last minute of her countdown, he heard the distant rush of steam subside, and felt the rocket's thrust ease off. The propellant tank was dry.

He let go of the stick and took a breath. For better or worse, it was at least over. "We were three minutes late starting, and a few seconds short, but I think we're still pretty close to the original orbit now."

Francine didn't look as happy about the burn. "Which puts us a hundred miles inside India Station."

In three hours, the space station would pass just beyond sight above them as they slowed and started their long fall back to near-Earth orbit. And now they had no way to speed up to catch it.

"The tank is normally always kept full," she said, rubbing her eyes as though trying to make them work. "I forgot that some grad students were doing ionosphere measurements that require precise maneuvering. A partially full tank makes the ship lighter and easier to handle."

The young insurgent looked genuinely sorrowful, and a sorrowful captain generally portended bad news for the crew.

"We can't think of everything all the time," Will consoled. "A hundred miles isn't very much in space, right? Maybe there'll be another ship at the station that can come and get us."

Francine just held her face in her hands. He wasn't sure she'd even heard him.

With a sigh, though, she lifted her head. "Oh, there'll be lots of other ships there," she agreed. The words were sardonic rather than affirming.

"I don't get it. Then, what's the problem?"

She adjusted her strap, and winced at the pain. Muttering an unfamiliar curse, involving monkey rear-ends and Satan's proclivity for cleaning them, she unstrapped herself completely so that she floated slowly out of her seat. "No pilot at India Station will come for us."

"Why? It seems like a relatively easy maneuver."

"It's not that. We're not sanctified."

"Not sanctified? What the hell! They'll let us die because we don't belong to their religion?"

"It's not about religion . . . at least not the kind you're thinking of. We have no pilot on board."

"You mean one that's a member of their union."

"As far as they're concerned, that's the only kind. From their perspective, we're just tainted garbage floating by."

"But just leaving us . . . that's murder! Aren't there any laws in space?"

"There's international treaty doctrines that serve the same purpose, but believe me, no nation is going to interfere."

"*Why*, for heaven's sake? Are pilots some kind of gods?"

After thinking about it for a moment, she nodded. "That about nails it."

"But that's crazy! Why would whole countries kowtow to a bunch of overstuffed rocket jockeys? Why don't countries just tell them all to go to hell and train their own?"

"You don't understand. It's more complicated than that. First of all, the Union would boycott any country that broke ranks. That would mean no other country would fly into the breakaway territory, and no other country would allow the non-union pilots into theirs. The intransigent nation would find itself totally isolated. They couldn't even dock at any of the stations."

"So, what if countries banded together? What if, for example, all of Asia just thumbed their noses at the snob club?"

"Okay, let's say they decided to do that. Piloting a space ship is not easy, as you've found out. How is an entire continent going to train thousands of pilots in secret for the day that they raise their thumbs to their noses? In any case, they wouldn't have any ship to fly *with*."

"Why not?"

She sighed, weary under the burden of explaining what every school child already knew. "Every spaceship that exists was built by one of just three companies: Ford, Boeing, and SCI. These three corporations own every single one. They never sell them; they only lease them. The engine designs are tightly kept trade secrets. They place sophisticated seals on the engine access panels, and only their own employees are allowed inside. This is all spelled out in international treaties."

He shrugged. "What does this have to do with the pilots . . . wait, I'll bet they all work for the three companies as well."

"Almost. The Big Three control the Pilots' licenses. The Union is separate from the manufacturers, but they all form a symbiotic relationship. Limiting the number of licenses ensures the Pilots' security, while tightening the companies' mutual monopoly."

"In my universe, people wouldn't put up with it. They'd force the government to break up the gang."

"Yeah, well in your universe, Shockley invented the transistor."

He shook his head. "I don't get it."

"You said that in your world, Shockley's ideas about genetic destiny never caught hold. Remember that here they build statues of him. Americans—at least the ones who have any say—have been brainwashed into protecting his ideas. The thing with rigid class structures is that, although there are those above you, you know that there are also those below you. There's a security, sick as it is, in knowing just where you stand. The Pilots are near the top of the heap, and knocking off the top threatens the whole pile."

He suddenly felt tired. Tired and depressed. As bizarre as it was to be flying around in space, it was the differences between their societies that brought home the fact that he really wasn't in Kansas anymore.

"In my world, Ford builds cars, and Boeing makes airplanes."

She nodded. "Here too."

"We don't have an SCI, though."

"It's a conglomeration of the old military manufacturers: Northrop, McDonnell Douglas, Lockheed, others I don't remember."

"You don't make military equipment anymore?"

"Not nearly as much as before Moscow blew. After that, there just wasn't any need for that many giant companies."

His light bulb lit up. "I see. You turned your ICBMs into spaceships."

"Not at all. ICBM's were old fashioned chemical rockets—"

"I meant figuratively. In my universe, most of the nuclear research went into weapons development. Here, you were free to stretch out."

She shrugged. "You may be right. Nuclear ships started to fly just about ten years after the blow."

"So, what does SCI stand for?"

"Space Craft, Incorporated."

"Huh," he grunted and looked at her. "Sort of says it all."

Ж Ж Ж

Francine had fallen asleep again. The codeine was taking a long time to wear off. He envied her. In less than two hours they were going to slow to apogee, and soon after, India Station would pass by twenty miles below them. It was maddening to float here just waiting for their only chance at salvation to sail by. His leg still hurt where Breggart had shot him, so he'd taken one of the codeine pills as well. It seemed to help the pain, but apparently he wasn't lucky enough to be affected with drowsiness. He'd considered taking a second pill, but the idea made him uneasy. It smacked of euthanasia.

He thought about going through his calculations for their corrected orbit a third time, but decided to hell with it. He was sick and tired of plodding through the formulas, moving back and forth between the dozen tables. Besides, they wouldn't be able to do anything about it now anyway.

Would they?

He couldn't stop thinking about it. They would be so close. They'd be able to see the station as it sailed silently by. Tourists in the observation galleys would see them as a small shining dot moving gracefully, inexorably against the backdrop of pinpoint stars, a dot containing two lost souls falling forever in an orbital destiny that would eventually bring the station and spaceship together again long after *Verdad*'s oxygen had run out.

Twenty miles. On Earth he could run that far. Okay, he could walk that far. In space, twenty miles was but a skip and a jump. It was a nudge, and then you sat back and waited until you floated over.

Their propellant tank was out of nudges, though.

Verdad's nudges were ordinary water. He scratched out the arithmetic to approximate how much they would need to catch up with the station when it passed by: around four hundred pounds, give or take a hundred, and they had barely twenty pounds of drinking water on board. Twenty pounds of propellant was the equivalent of a canoe paddle on an eighty-foot yacht.

But what if the yacht had a canoe?

Francine floated, sound asleep, behind him. He unbuckled his strap, and hooking his foot under his armrest for an anchor, he reached out and caught her pant-leg. "Wake up!" he called, shaking her leg.

Her whole body waved back and forth like a trout swimming against the current, and her head banged into the wall.

"Ow!" she cried, looking around bleary-eyed, holding her head. "For Judas' sake! What's the matter with you?"

"Does the ship have an escape pod?"

"Escape pod?" she repeated, looking at him as though she was trying to figure out what language he was speaking. "Do you mean a lifeboat?"

"Uh, yeah."

She gave him a disgusted look that made him wish he could erase the last two minutes of his life. "Don't you think I would have thought of that? A lifeboat is an optional accessory. The college never planned to take *Verdad* outside the atmosphere. We use the lifeboat compartment to store research equipment."

She kicked his hand away. "Now leave me alone."

Taking a deep breath, she closed her eyes, and soon her breathing became slow and regular again.

Fatigue pulled at him, seeming to drain the last of his strength. Francine looked so peaceful. Women were lucky. They didn't have to always be the strong ones. Granted, she was wounded. Still.

It wouldn't hurt if he just closed his eyes for a minute. It felt nice. He unbuckled his strap and let himself float free. Lacking visual cues, free fall was a lot like floating in water. He could easily imagine that he was lazing around a Caribbean lagoon on an air mattress. Maybe the codeine pill was performing some magic after all.

He was ice-skating. Or, at least, he was trying to ice-skate, but it was a whole lot more difficult than he remembered. It was as if he were six years old again and attempting for the first time to use grownup skates, the kind with just one blade. Each time he stood up, the frozen lake slipped away, almost on purpose, as though it didn't like having him standing on it. Strangely, however, he never actually fell. Rather, he seemed to just float in mid-air until he tried yet again to get his feet unto the slippery surface.

Suddenly the ice was gone, and he was standing over infinitely deep water. Water so deep, that he was in mortal danger of drowning. Swimming was not an option, though. He didn't know why. But running was. Running over water. Running so fast that he could maybe, just maybe, stay above the surface. He tried. But like so many times before, his legs resisted as though pushing through taffy.

Complete and utter terror now engulfed him as he struggled vainly against this inevitable doom. As though handed down by God, however, a point of clarity appeared among the chaos of his fear, and he realized with relief and desperate hope that there was a sliver of chance against the dark depths. It was his heels. Somehow—he didn't really care how—they could keep him suspended above the malevolent doom patiently waiting to swallow him. It was as though the blades of his ice-skates were magnetically repulsing the dreaded water. And as with the ice, they slipped away at the slightest distraction. He focused his mind, giving his feet his complete attention . . . or almost complete. From behind him someone called his name. He forced himself to ignore it, concentrating on keeping his magical feet beneath him. But the calling was insistent. Try as he might, he couldn't shut the voice out. Finally, an urgent shout made him flinch, and like watching the first card of a carefully constructed house tumble, he felt his feet slide away, and he fell. But not into water—now it was the maw of a black pit that had no bottom. He fell and fell, and heard himself yell out in terror, and then he was inside Verdad, but still falling endlessly away.

"Will!" Francine shouted again.

Her face floated there before him, apparently falling along with him. He flailed, trying desperately to grab onto something, but the solid interior of the ship remained maddeningly just out of reach. His hand struck something soft, and he heard Francine cry in pain, and then his arms and legs were wrapped around her, clinging reflexively to the cosmic lifeguard come to save him.

Francine placed her hand behind his head and pulled him into the crook of her neck where it was close and warm, and then wrapped her own arms tightly around him.

It came to him where he was. It was the damned free fall again. She had warned him to stay strapped in his seat. He'd made the mistake of falling asleep "flying free," as she had put it. She had looked so comfortable floating there, though.

After a minute, his heart slowed, and he took a long, deep breath.

"You okay now?" his comforter whispered an inch from his ear.

"Yes," he replied in a muffled voice, feeling the rise and fall of her breast against his chin.

She loosened her hug but kept her arms ready to snatch him up should he loose it again. "If you hit me one more time," she warned grinning, "I'm going to break your nose."

He nodded, reaching for the back of his seat so that he could pull himself into its safe grasp. "Sorry about that," he said. "I had a nightmare."

"Freebie-jeebies," she explained. "Even experienced spacers get them occasionally if they're not strapped in when sleeping. You were either falling off a cliff, trying to fly with dire results, or drowning."

"Uh, the second and third, I guess. Why don't you get them— the freebie-jeebies?"

"I'm a woman."

"Women aren't susceptible?"

"Women have more grit," she replied, pulling herself into her own seat. "We're a half-hour to apogee. I'm going to call India Station."

"I thought no pilot would come to save us since we're not 'sanctified'?"

She winked. "Says who?"

She explained that they were going to try to bluff their way in. She showed him where Carter had penciled his ID number on the console, apparently too lazy to memorize it. She also explained that Will would have to make the call.

"Why me? You know the procedures."

"I understand that this detail may be easy to forget, but I am a woman."

In fact, this detail had become increasingly more difficult to ignore. "Women aren't Pilots?" he asked.

She gave him one of her looks. "Does a bear squat in the woods?"

He smiled at the euphemism. "At least we're straight on which of us is demigod worthy. So, what do I say?"

She briefed him on the protocols. They seemed bewilderingly complicated. He knew he was tired, but it was like starting a complicated game for the first time, except that the outcome of this game was their lives.

"Can't you just talk in a deep voice?" he finally asked.

"Getting cold feet? Don't worry; I'll be right here to help you."

Hesitating just a moment, he thumbed the button on the microphone and said, "Private vessel *Verdad* calling India Station."

After an eternal few seconds of static, a voice broke through. "India Station here. Entry? Over."

Will looked questioningly at his coach. It sounded like the duty officer was asking whether they wanted to dock. She nodded.

"Yes . . . er, affirmative, India Station. Uh, over."

Francine rolled her eyes.

"ID?" the voice prompted. "Over."

Will leaned in so that he could see the penciled writing and read it off into the hand-piece.

After some seconds of static, the voice asked, "Tim, is that you? Over."

Francine made a painful face battered by cruel destiny.

"Who's Tim?" he asked her, making sure button was off.

"Carter—Tim Carter. The duty officer must have recognized the ID."

"What'll I say?"

She shrugged. "Improvise."

Improvise. Okay. He pressed the microphone button. "Uh, yes. Um, over."

The static noise that had plied the vast empty spaces between the stars for millions of years hissed lonely and forlorn from the panel speaker until the duty officer finally spoke. "You're not Tim, are you? Over."

Improvise. "Yes I am . . . over."

"Do you know that it is a violation of Part Three of the International Space Statutes to impersonate a pilot? Over."

"Uh, sure. Of course. I know that. Over."

Static filled the cabin for a second. "Who is this? Over."

Francine grabbed the microphone from him. "This is Francine Sewer and Buck Peters from Washington State, USA. We request emergency entry under the Disabled Pilot Protocol Amendment of '83. Over."

"Uh, right. Confirm: did you say emergency entry? Over."

"Emergency entry, affirmative. Over."

"What's the nature of the emergency? Over."

Francine filled the duty officer in on their situation: orbit parameters, fuel status, and air supply, leaving out any explanation about how they happened to be here in the first place.

"Got it," the officer said. "Why is there no pilot on board? Over."

She glanced quickly at Will, and then said, "Sir, we are less than thirty minutes to apogee. I don't think we have any more time for discussion. Over."

Through the static, they heard a sigh from the officer. "Understood. Hang tight. We'll get you in. I need to alert the ranking exec first. I'll be back in a minute. Over."

Francine sat back and closed her eyes.

"You okay?" Will asked.

Without moving, she said, "Yeah, just relieved . . . and hurting . . . and tired as Satan."

"You want more codeine?"

She opened one eye and peeked at him. "You trying to kill me?"

"I'll take that as a no. Now that we're almost there, maybe it's time to answer the question you've been avoiding ever since you demonstrated your acrobatic prowess with the uniboosts."

She closed both eyes. "What are you talking about?"

"How does a physics professor become so proficient with illegal James Bond technology? You can go to sleep and avoid it again, but I'll just keep asking."

Still sitting back with her eyes closed, she asked, "What's James Bond?"

What a sad universe, he thought. *How do they define cool?* "A fabrication that Hollywood devised in order to make an endless series of teenage-mentality movies. He's a super-spy."

She opened her eyes and gave a resigned sigh. "I took a two-year sabbatical in Australia. This was before Congress required US citizens to obtain a special visa to travel there."

Will waited, but she just sat back and closed her eyes again. "And that's supposed to explain it?" he asked.

She studied him critically. "You know, when you're being tortured, the more you know, the more likely you'll be tortured to death as they try to squeeze the last bit out of you."

With that, she turned and closed her eyes again.

Tortured?

"Francine," he said softly, placing his hand gently on her arm, "did they torture you?"

She opened her eyes and looked at him, surprised, and then her face softened. "You're worried about me?"

He took his hand away, and sat back. "Nah. I was just . . . curious."

She was grinning. She didn't believe him. "That was sweet."

She looked tired—tired, and dirty, and weary. And beautiful. There was an inner radiance that animated her weary eyes and dirt smudges so that they seemed cute.

Cute? *Watch it, Will old boy*, he thought. *This isn't your universe, and you're not Buck.* Well . . . not exactly. After all—

"I'm talking about *you*," she said, breaking his swirling thoughts.

"Huh?" What the hell had they been talking about?

"The less you know, the better for you."

"Torture!" he proclaimed, getting back on track.

Her grin broadened. "Have you been sneaking some of the codeine?"

A crackle of static interrupted them. "India Station calling private vessel *Verdad*. Over," came the duty officer's voice. He sounded irritated.

Francine thumbed the mic button. "*Verdad* here. Over."

"Uh, we have a little problem, *Verdad*. Over."

Verdad's pirate captain gave Will a worried look through her cute smudges. "What sort of problem, India Station? Over."

"Actually, the problem isn't all that little." He cleared his throat, as though stalling. "It's the steward. He says he can't let any of his pilots come out to get you."

Francine closed her eyes, as though calming herself. "The emergency protocol amendment requires you to provide assistance. Over."

"I know the protocols by heart," the officer responded, more resigned than defensive. "The steward maintains that the protocol applies only when a pilot was originally on board, but is now disabled. Over"

"What makes you think we don't have a pilot on board? Over."

"Er, the steward has talked to somebody on Earth—"

A banging and rustling indicated that the mic at the far end was being handled. The next voice was different. "This is Ignatius Rye Lee, Pilot Steward Class One for India Station. I'm sorry for your situation, but it seems you brought this upon yourselves. Over."

He didn't sound at all sorry.

"Ignatius?" Will blurted. "He's got to be kidding."

Francine shushed him and thumbed the mic. "Did it happen to be Hank Breggart you spoke with on Earth? Over."

"I am not under interrogation. You are hardly in a position to warrant queries." After a second of static, he followed with, "Over," spoken as though delivering a poke in the eye.

Will uttered a scathing curse and grabbed the mic. "You son-of-a-bitch! You're just going to let us die out here? What a bastard!"

"I take it that this is Willard? I was warned about you. 'Seriously binny' was the description, as I recall. Also, you should learn proper radio procedures before commandeering the airwaves. O-ver."

"Oh Christ!" Will spat into the mic. "You can take your 'over's' and stuff them up your fat, pompous ass—"

Francine snatched the mic back. "I'm sorry about that. Breggart was right—my companion is very seriously binny. I hope you'll forgive the outburst. Over."

"Like I said, I was warned. Fortunately for you, I don't have judicial jurisdiction over citizen blasphemies. Over."

"So, it *was* Breggart you spoke with. Over."

There was a pause, then, "I didn't say that. Over."

"Right. So I guess that's it, then. There's no way to change your mind? Over."

"Oh, don't be so dramatic. You aren't going to die. I am assured that your little ship will be intercepted at perigee and you will be returned to Earth. Over."

Francine's eyebrows went up in alarm. "I see. Thank you. Could I bother you to put on the Station Master, please? Over."

"A Pilot Steward does not take orders from the Station Master, you know. Over."

"I understand, Steward Rye Lee. I'd like to speak with him anyway. Over."

"Very well."

Seconds later another man's voice broke the static, "This is Station Master Kirkenich. Over."

Francine just sat, looking perplexed for a moment. "Excuse me. What happened to Fred . . . er, Captain Jenkins?"

"Station Master Jenkins is Earth-side for a bimonthly staff meeting. I'm his second in command. Is there something I can do for you? Over."

"Yes. Come out and get us. Over."

They could hear the Pilot Steward protesting in the background. "I really wish I could," Kirkenich said, "but you heard Steward Rye Lee. The Union won't allow any pilots out. Over."

The pretty smudged pirate sat staring at the speaker, fuming. "It doesn't have to be a pilot."

The Station Master sighed audibly. "I wish I could allow that, Miss Sewer, but my primary responsibility is for the operation of the entire facility, and I can't jeopardize the safety of everybody on board, let alone risk international complications. Over."

"Cut me a break!" Will cried. "How would we jeopardize the safety of the station?"

Francine shook her head. "He's right. The Pilot Union could call a strike and cripple the station."

"But that's extortion!"

"Very perceptive." She thumbed the mic again. "What if there was UN Court precedence involving life threatening conditions? Over."

"Miss Sewer, believe me, I would have already pursued that avenue, but you heard Steward Rye Lee. The US has already offered to send a ship to rescue you at perigee. Over."

"Right," she said, defeated. "Very well, then. Over."

"Miss Sewer, I am really very sorry I couldn't help you. I'll, er, give your best to Captain Jenkins when he returns. Over."

"Thank you, Station Master Kirkenich. This is *Verdad* signing off."

"God be with you. India Station, signing off."

Will's tired companion reached over, switched off the radio, and sat starting at it.

"So, it's going to be okay, then," Will confirmed after a few seconds. "They'll have a ship rendezvous with us in six hours."

She looked at him as though she'd forgotten that he was there. "No. It's not okay at all. It looks like we're both going to find out just how much torture we can take."

Chapter 10

"Why do you kowtow to that jerk?" Will complained. He was trying to avoid, without much success, thinking about the types of torture that might be applied to him.

"You mean Ignatius? The union steward? You don't want to get on the wrong side of the Pilot Union."

"Since when did you become cowardly?"

"There's nothing brave about being stupid."

"Well, when Breggart is jabbing you with a red-hot poker, I hope it brings you peace of mind that you didn't offend some Pilot snobs. If they're not willing to help us, then I say to hell with them. In any case, we're on our own now."

As he said that he suddenly an image of his feet floating in cold darkness.

Francine sat back and closed her eyes again, as though too tired to argue.

Will floated in his seat and rewound the conversation with Ignatius. Breggart had known enough to contact India Station. They should have expected that since *Verdad* had probably been tracked on US radar after the missile.

Also, Francine had explained that the pilots were in bed with the three US rocket manufacturers, and the government was likely tied right in from top to bottom as well. He wouldn't expect this universe to be any different from his own: despite the noble intentions of constitutions, governments were manifestations of politics, and politics was just another word for influence.

Torture. He couldn't get it out of his mind. It made him queasy. At least he didn't know anything. That was apparently good according to Miss Bond . . . but did that make sense?

Wouldn't they just dig deeper, thinking he was holding out? And digging deeper wasn't just a metaphor in this case.

Christ.

How could Francine be so calm? A near-death state of exhaustion helped, but there was something she'd said that kept tapping him on the shoulder. She'd asked if he was getting cold feet when he was preparing to call India Station on the radio. That was probably where that image of his feet floating in space came from.

Maybe he should try to get some sleep as well. It might be his last for a long while. The government in his own universe used sleep deprivation very effectively. Of course, they insisted that it wasn't torture. Just like Breggart would insist that jamming bamboo shoots under his fingernails wasn't either.

Yep. They were on their own, now. Don't get cold feet.

Why did that keep coming back? Cold feet, on their own. Floating in space. Floating around in space outside *Verdad*. Space Shuttle astronauts floated around in space. They used jetpacks.

The uniboosts!

"Francine! Wake up!"

She opened one eye, and then closed it again.

"The uniboosts! We don't have to watch while our arms are pulled from their sockets!"

This time, she opened both eyes.

"We need spacesuits," he said. "Please tell me there are some spacesuits on *Verdad*."

She blinked and turned to him. "There are some spacesuits on *Verdad*."

"Uh, did you say that because I asked you to?"

In answer, she unbelted and pulled herself to a hatch near the door. It looked far too small for one spacesuit, let alone two. From inside, she pulled out what looked like a nylon ski outfit. He expected her to reach in deeper and extract the bulbous, Pillsbury Doughboy suits he was used to. Instead, she tossed him the crumpled mass. It looked like a deflated gray blow-up doll as it spun slowly towards him.

"This is a spacesuit?"

"Of course," she replied, pulling out a second one. "They're not the fancy models like the upscale yachts have, but they'll do. Each ship is required to carry enough for each passenger in case of an emergency."

"Space life jackets," he observed wonderingly, examining the flimsy article. "Where's the air bottles?"

He saw that the helmet was just more of the same material with a flexible plastic window where his eyes would be. It looked like it was just glued on. He wasn't feeling so great about this.

"As I said, these are just meant for emergency escapes. They don't have fixtures for external tanks."

"So, like, we hold our breaths? How far can we get in two minutes?"

"Don't be dumb. The suits have integral reservoirs. What are you waiting for? Put it on. We'll be at apogee in no time."

She was already pulling on her suit, starting with her feet. The front zippered from crotch to chin. It was like putting on the snowsuits his cousins in Minnesota wore as kids. The disposable spacesuits were one-size-fits-all, and he found that they "fit all" by stretching. He couldn't see how they would work. A space suit had to do more than just hold air to breathe—they had to maintain pressure.

"How am I going to keep from blowing up?"

"What do you mean?" she asked, pulling on the head piece.

"Uh, there's no air out there, remember? No pressure?"

"Dmph wmff brmph'nt."

Her suit muffled her voice. She pulled the top up, uncovering just her mouth. "Don't worry about it. Now come *on*!"

He tugged himself into the space tights. It was as difficult as getting into a wetsuit. When he was finally all zipped up, he imagined he knew what a sausage would feel like if it could feel.

His suited companion—whose figure, he noticed, looked just fine in the skin-hugging material—pulled at a ring under her armpit, and motioned for him to do the same. He found the plastic ripcord and gave it a yank. He felt motion at his back, and saw that Francine's suit was bulging out between her shoulders like a big balloon filling with air. And that, he realized, was exactly what it was: the air reservoir she mentioned. His must be doing the same thing. Her balloon grew and grew, until it was as big as a beach ball and he thought it would explode. Something pushed him forward. He realized it was his own suit expanding against the control panel behind him.

Francine extracted a spray can from the hatch, pushed herself over to him, and pulled his head up against her mouth. "Once I spray this on," she said into his ear, "the suits will seal, and you'll have about forty minutes of air. That's how long we have to get the uniboosts and make it to India Station."

He nodded. He was suddenly scared. They were really going to leave *Verdad* behind and rocket out into black, empty space.

"Are you ready to navigate us to India's orbit?" she asked.

He looked at her in surprise. He hadn't thought past dying of suffocation in vacuum. Through the plastic window, her eyes were serious. This was life and death.

He held up his forefinger, indicating he needed a minute, and then pulled himself back to his seat. His bulging hunchback prevented him from sitting in his chair, so he had to hover above his station as he reviewed the star charts. His mind didn't want to work. Adrenaline urged him to *move*, to *do* something, not float there and ruminate abstractions. He closed his eyes and took a couple of slow breaths. It was clumsy working through the suit's window. He had to pick everything up and hold it directly in front of his face.

In the end, he decided that there wasn't any navigation that they could reasonably do. And he wasn't happy about that. They wouldn't have *Verdad*'s beacon monitors to provide precise three-dimensional positions. They'd have only their eyes and the stars, and they didn't even need the stars. India Station would pass directly below them; they'd have the giant ball of the Earth to guide their direction.

He tossed away the charts, spun himself around to face his companion, and shrugged. It was time to go.

She handed him the can, and he sprayed her from head to toe, then gave it to her so she could reciprocate. As the atomized chemical coated him, he felt his suit stiffen, losing its stretch. Some chemical process was turning his flimsy skin tights into a rigid spacesuit.

But how was he going to move? As a test, he tried to twist his body a little. *Ouch!* Hairs on his chest and calves had caught in the fabric and now tore away from his skin with every motion. These were details you didn't bother about when leaving a spaceship in an emergency . . . which they were, so he ignored the pain.

Although most of the fabric became as stiff as hard plastic, he found that ribbed seams at his elbows, knees, and fingers allowed him to bend his appendages, although only with some effort. There were no seams at his ankles, but he would hardly need them floating in space. A stiff neck was another matter, though. If he wanted to look in any direction other than directly forward, he had to turn his entire body. And, once stiffened, the front of his headpiece pressed painfully against the bridge of his nose. To top it off, he had difficulty taking more than shallow breaths, as the stiff suit constricted his chest, so that he constantly fought the sensation of smothering. He didn't think he could stay in the suit more than forty minutes, regardless of the limitations of the air supply.

His curvaceous, balloon-backed partner placed her feet firmly against his midriff and launched herself towards the main hatch. This spun him around, and he bumped up against the cabin's wall, trying not to be miffed that his most useful role was as a free fall stepping stone.

He pulled himself around and found Francine at the main hatch, working at controls exposed behind a little door. She pushed a series of buttons, but was rewarded with only a blinking red light, apparently the ship's way of shaking its head "no." She kept at it, though, and eventually the light blinked green.

She turned her body around to look at him, and made a motion for him to hang on to something. When she saw him grasp the arm of his seat, she turned back, and holding on to a handhold next to the hatch, she punched a big red button. An instant later the hatch flew open with a bang that he heard through his suit, and he felt a breeze pull against him. A second later, his ears popped. *Verdad* was spilling its precious air. Only larger ships could afford the luxury of airlocks.

Primed by Hollywood movies, he expected a hurricane-force blow, but after a few seconds, the breeze tapered off, and he floated again free in the cabin. The only indication that the cabin was evacuated was the open hatchway to black emptiness and Francine, who was halfway out the hatch, apparently having been caught in a stronger rush near the exit point. She let go of her handhold, and turned so that her feet dangled in the hatchway a moment before she disappeared completely, making her way along the hull ladder to the aft compartment where she had stored the uniboosts.

Will pulled himself to the opening. He paused a few feet away. It felt like approaching a well with no discernable bottom. Strangely reluctant, he peered over the edge of the hatch. *Verdad* was slowly rotating, and there, moving majestically out of view, was the three quarter-full Earth, appearing both huge and small at the same time. Huge because he was used to seeing the moon, and from geosynchronous orbit, his home planet appeared a hundred times as large. Small and distant because just seeing the entire world at once brought home the fact that he was far, far removed.

A moment later, a searing light blinded him. He squeezed his eyes closed, but the white-hot light seemed to be permanently burned into his retina. For an unreasoned instant, he had the horrifying thought that India Station had set off an atom bomb, but he realized that it was just the sun. *Just* the sun? Earth's life-giver, worshipped by man for thousands of years, was nothing but one gigantic atom bomb that never stopped exploding.

He pulled away from the hatch and opened his eyes. Panic mounted as he realized that he couldn't see. His vision was obliterated by the hellish after-image. On Earth, the miles of atmosphere filtered most of the deadly ultraviolet radiation. Spacesuits of his universe included dark shades that could be pulled down over the faceplate. How could the engineers of this one be so negligent? He knew what Francine's response would be: the suits were meant only for emergencies. He was probably supposed to avoid looking at the sun.

To his great relief, the lava-hot image faded, and his vision slowly returned. He was surprised when he realized that Francine had already returned, and was holding out one of the uniboosts for him. He pointed to his eyes and made flashing gestures with his hands. She shook her head in reprimand and wagged her outstretched finger at him. He should have known better. He wanted to tell her that there was no way he could have avoided it, but with no air in the cabin, it wasn't possible to talk to her. Spacesuits in his universe, he noted with pique, had radios.

As he took the solo rocket, he wondered idly if the water in the tank had boiling away in the vacuum.

And then he caught his breath. His uniboost was empty! In the rush of the last ten minutes, he'd forgotten that he had used the last of the propellant with his ignoble landing at the Olympia port.

Francine, meanwhile, had opened yet another of the seemingly endless doors built into the cabin walls. She extracted a clear, plastic hose, held its mouth against that of her uniboost's fill-tube, and motioned to him with her head. When he'd pulled himself over to her, she let go of her hoses, grabbed his head, and jammed it against her own. Faintly, as though listening to somebody while holding a phone receiver a foot from his ear, he heard her shouting. She told him to dump the damn deal.

What deal? he thought. Perhaps his story about transferring here from another universe? She didn't believe him? This was a hell of a time to bring it up.

"Handle!" he heard her shout. "Pump the handle!"

He looked to where she was pointing. Next to the hose in the wall compartment was a switch set to "expel," and next to that, a small pump handle, all obviously part of the ship's potable water system.

Bracing himself, he pumped while Francine held the hoses together. The water flowing between the two roiled with bubbles as it boiled briskly in the room temperature vacuum. After a few minutes, seething froth issued from an exhaust port of her pack, and she reached over and turned a lever, sealing the tank.

They did the same with his suit, and then Francine grabbed his head and mashed it against hers again. "We can't fill the tanks completely in a vacuum," she shouted from a distance, "so take it easy out there."

Take it easy. Sure. He would abstain from showing off his fancy acrobatics.

It might have been just his imagination, but it seemed to Will that the voluminous tumor on his counterpart's back had shrunk. He imagined that the engineers would incorporate some amount of oxygen supplement, but ultimately spent air would have to be released until finally there was none left. The thought made Will shiver with a coldness more chilling than mere temperature.

They took turns helping each other into the uniboosts—no easy task, Will discovered, in their lobster-shell spacesuits in free fall. He found it nearly impossible to bend his elbow enough to tighten the rocket pack's shoulder straps, made even more difficult by the air reservoirs. They had to extend the straps to their maximum to fit around the sides of the bulbous projection, like suspenders pushed to the side of a portly man's protruding belly.

Francine waited at the open hatchway through which he saw the Earth, blue and kindly, glide majestically by, as though it were an obedient satellite of *Verdad*, or maybe a cosmic mother goose watching over its new-hatched chicks. He pulled himself to the black portal, and she again butted their heads together. "Lead on, Navigator!" her tiny voice called.

This was it. He could feel his heart thumping against the hard carapace of his suit. A terror huddled inside of him, shivering in a place as old as the stark cliffs of Kenya's rift valley where his long-distant ancestors had peered furtively over the edge towards vistas new and dangerous. He gave a last look around *Verdad's* small cabin. Although he'd only known its finely engineered efficiency a handful of hours, it had been their home and haven in the cold of infinite space.

He grabbed the edges of the hatch, ready to launch into the void . . . and stopped.

He hadn't thought about ballast. On Earth, he'd needed the extra weight in front for balance. For a brief moment, he thought that they wouldn't need it here in free fall. Tumbling immediately on top of that thought was the realization that he was mistaken about that. Once they fired up the uniboosts, they would generate their own personal artificial gravity, and they would have effective weight, just like on Earth. The same reasons for needing ballast while fleeing from Breggart across the Puget Sound still held as they fled the disabled *Verdad*.

He felt his partner's hand on his shoulder, and then her head mashed against his in the now routine mode of communication. "What are we going to use for ballast?" her distant voice shouted.

Their coinciding thoughts, more or less intertwined, created a vivid image in his mind, one that might solve both this and another problem that had come to mind, which was how to keep from getting separated out there in the vast expanse of nothing.

"You'll be my skating partner," he called back.

They could use each other for balance, become a single human spaceship with two rocket engines.

In answer to her perplexed look, he reached down, unstiffened both of their uniboosts, and then clasped his hands in hers. He wrapped his feet around her ankles so that they were facing each other as though engaged in a pushing contest. From across two feet of vacuum, he saw his counterpart peering at him intently, trying to understand what he was trying to do. Suddenly, her eyes went wide, and she smiled broadly. Without waiting for clarification, she unclasped one hand and pushed against the hatchway, sending them off into the darkness. *Verdad* moved slowly away, continuing to spin gracefully so that the hatch disappeared from view. They had only each other now, and each other was exactly what each needed.

Mesmerized by the sight of *Verdad* drifting away, he was vaguely aware that Francine had bent away out of view. Suddenly, though, she gripped his hand again and shook it urgently. A moment later, *Verdad* spun wildly away, and the Earth followed, and then he squeezed his eyes shut as the scorching light of the sun swept past.

He realized that Francine had turned on her uniboost, expecting him to do the same. The lone rocket now spun them in cartwheels, since their combined center of gravity was not in line with the direction of thrust. Faster and faster they whirled and Francine was pulled from him at the opposite side of their freewheeling centrifuge. One of his feet lost its hold, and an instant later, the other followed, so that only his desperate grip on her hands held them together. He cried out in dismay when she inexplicably jerked one of them away so just one was left clutching his only contact with humanity. Soon, though, he felt her free hand groping again for his, and he grabbed it and held on with a terrified determination.

She had reached down to turn off her thrust. He could tell because the flashing bursts of light as the sun swung past remained steady, the rate of rotation no longer increasing.

She had killed the spinning force, but a significant amount of energy had been converted to angular momentum, and in the vacuum of space there was no air drag to bleed it off. If he could hang on that long, they would continue spinning forever.

Fighting the resistance of his emergency spacesuit, he bent his elbows and pulled Francine closer. Then, with every ounce of strength he could muster, he bent his legs forward, and with one desperate lunge wrapped them around her thighs. Conservation of angular momentum dictated that the spin had to increase accordingly, as a twirling skater speeds up when bringing in her arms. He saw the sun flashing through his tightly closed eyelids like a discotheque strobe light. He pulled Francine in and wrapped his arms around her. The sun now strobed so quickly to be almost a continuous blur. He felt her head push up against his. "I'm sorry!" her far away voice said. "That was really dumb."

"I shouldn't have been daydreaming," he called back. "Keep your hands high on my shoulders. I'm going to try to stop the spin."

He reached down and engaged his thrust the minimum possible. Instead of slowing, the flashing sun began to smear around in all directions. It was too much to expect that the direction of his thrust would lie exactly in the plane of their spin. He might indeed be slowing their rotation, but he was also adding his own component of spin to the mix.

He despaired. They might never stop it. Think! The problem couldn't be that complex. It was a straightforward exercise in spherical vectors. If he could somehow track the sun and determine the spherical angle offset that his thrust was applying in relation to their original spin . . . and then it dawned on him. He didn't have to do anything at all. As long as the force was applied by his uniboost, it would eventually counter any original component. If they just waited, they should stabilize into a steady spin induced by his own thrust.

Of course, they would then continue to speed up in that spin direction as well as time went on. But he saw a way out. He could visualize it as neatly as the 3-D models he used on his computer at home . . . wherever that was.

It didn't take long. After a minute, the scribble of random, flashing sun streaks slowed and coalesced. When it had contracted to a band, he reached down and turned off his thrust. Immediately, the band contracted to a single orbiting flash. However, it had now slowed considerably, completing a revolution perhaps only twice each second. He described his plan through the thin membrane of their suits, and smiled when Francine called back that he was a genius.

"Okay," he yelled, "now *just a little*."

He felt her move as she reached down to engage her thrust. A moment later, she wrapped her arm around him again, and he was gratified when the thin line of circling sun began to wander once more. But this time, they were going to counter the imbalance. "Left," he called, reminding himself that his right was her left. He slowly extended his right arm and leg, and his partner followed along like a hand on a Ouija board. They were moving their center of gravity. The circling flashes began to spread quickly. Wrong way. "Right!" he yelled, and pulled in their extended appendages while slowly extending the other side. Dutifully, the scatter of light smears contracted, but after a few seconds, began to slowly expand again. Too far. He pulled their counterweight in a bit, and the flitting atomic fireflies steadied. He would have whooped with joy if he didn't fear that it might jinx their fragile balance.

He made minute adjustments as the circling sun steadily slowed until it moved so lethargically in its virtual orbit that it became impossible to gauge how far to extend their arms and legs for balance. He called to her to cut her thrust.

Their rotation period was down to nearly a minute. That would have to do. He ventured opening his eyes during his mini night periods when the sun was behind him. Through their plastic windows he saw Francine's eyes tightly clenched. The sight overwhelmed him in a totally unexpected rush of tenderness. Cocooned within his embrace, she seemed vulnerable and totally given up to his protection. An instant later he clenched his own eyes again as blinding radiation swung into view.

During the next faux night he tried to get his bearings. He saw the Earth angling by to his left, but there was no sign of *Verdad*. Either it was on his dayside, or they'd strayed away beyond sight. It didn't matter, as their little ship was of no more use . . . except that now he had lost all sense of direction.

How, for God's sake, were they ever going to find India Station?

Chapter 11

Will tried to calm himself with a deep breath, but his unyielding hard-shelled suit intervened. He wanted to scream. *Think!* Although it seemed like hours, he knew they'd only left *Verdad* just minutes before. If his calculations were at all accurate, the space station would pass below them in the next five to ten minutes.

But from which direction? Before they'd left Verdad, it had seemed a simple task to find the quarter mile-wide space station— they just had to go "in". Space was three-dimensional. What he really needed to know was the orbital plane that India Station would be on—in this case, the equatorial plane intersecting the Earth. The lava smear of sun drifted off the curtain of his closed lids, and he opened his eyes to study the Earth before it too drifted out of view. He saw a large white patch that could be either the North Pole or Antarctica. Even if he knew, it was too indistinct, too big to offer a definitive orientation of the equator. He needed to identify some continents. It sounded easy, but from space the Earth didn't look like the globe standing in his living room. Lacking the benefit of colored political demarcations, and with cloud masses covering a third of the surface, he might as well have been looking at some alien world.

A fiery glow at the edge of his suit window heralded the return of the sun, and he clenched his eyes once more.

The damn sun. What a pain.

Wait! The sun! Of course!

He felt himself flush at his idiocy. The Earth orbited the sun in the same plane as the equator, or close enough for now. It had been late afternoon when they'd taken off from Olympia. That was something like six hours ago, say an even one fourth of a day. The sun would have been directly over the Pacific Ocean. That would put it . . . east of India now, where it would be mid-morning. Francine had said that India Station was actually positioned west of the Indian sub-continent, so if he put the sun on his right hand, and the Earth on his left, his home planet would be oriented with north "up." India Station's orbit followed the rotation of the Earth, so the space station would pass below them from west to east, from left to right.

He had it!

He wondered how much air they have left. Better not to think about that. There was either going to be enough or not.

The next maneuver required all their attention, and he pushed fears of suffocation aside. He and Francine had to engage their uniboosts together as they clasped hands and feet, facing each other, forming a single, dual exhaust, micro-spaceship. They steered via a dance of opposing balance, leaning towards one or the other, extending legs and arms left or right, constantly adjusting the direction of thrust and the position of their shared center of gravity. At first it was tedious, and he thought beyond his ability. But as with so many seemingly complex motion problems, he let the primitive unconscious areas of his brain take over. They flew by feel. Like skiing or surfing, or just walking, he turned off his conscious thinking and let his body find its own way.

His cerebral cortex couldn't just relax and enjoy the ride, though. It still had its own work to do. They needed a course. Ultimately they had to match the station's orbit, which was circular, while theirs was still the Hohmann transfer orbit they'd come out on. This meant that they were beginning a long fall back towards close-Earth orbit. Their correction maneuver was theoretically clear; at their current point of apogee, all they had to do was thrust in a tangent direction at right angles to the Earth. But how much thrust? And where exactly did he place the Earth in his view to be firing an aggregate thrust that was at right angles?

He tackled the thrust question first. He remembered from his previous calculations on *Verdad* that their Hohmann apogee velocity was 3,600 MPH. That was compared against the station's velocity, which was easily calculated, since it's orbit was exactly twenty-four hours, and two-pi times the twenty-six thousand mile radius long, or . . . nearly 7,000 MPH!

Strangling fingers of panic clutched at his neck. How in God's name were they going to gain 3,400 MPH of velocity with their little uniboost rockets?

Think it through. There was no alternative. He assumed for simplicity that they accelerated at one gravity. That made sense, since they used one gravity of acceleration when hovering on Earth. One gravity was 32ft/second/second, or twenty-two MPH per second. Divide 3,400 by twenty-two, and you get . . . about 150 seconds—just two and a half minutes!

Will was absolutely amazed. The amount of thrust they had used just to hold them off the ground as they flew from Francine's apartment to Olympia would have translated to 30,000 MPH if they were thrusting freely through space! That was more than the escape velocity of the Earth! They could fly to Mars! . . . if they didn't mind being dead when they arrived.

He shook off these titillating thoughts. They wouldn't be going anywhere if they didn't find the station before their air ran out. They'd already been thrusting for a few minutes at maybe a quarter of a gravity. That meant that they'd already gained nearly a thousand MPH . . . but pointed hardly anything close to the tangent direction that they needed.

It was hopeless. He had to face it. He didn't have a clue as to their orbital status. He couldn't even see his watch hidden inside the arm of his suit. They were lost in space, and he didn't need a sad and clumsy imitation of a robot to tell him they were in danger, danger, danger.

And then, luck held out her capricious hand. Something caught his eye. A star moved towards them, bright and clearly visible, where all the others were nearly lost in the blinding glare of the Earth. Seconds later he lost it as the shining wanderer moved across the brilliant, illuminated face of his home planet. He held his breath in anticipation, watching the opposite side of the blue globe. There! It reappeared, now moving away from them like an arrow in flight. It had to be India Station, the sun reflecting off its metal skin.

He shouted with joy, but Francine couldn't hear through the inches of nothing that separated them. They had to catch it. It was speeding away and carrying with it any hope they had for life. He leaned his head against hers, but before he had a chance to explain, she exclaimed, thin and distant, "I saw it! Let's go!"

Using little rocket packs strapped, jury-rigged, to their backs, they were going to try to catch a star flying away at ten times the speed of sound—four times as fast as a bullet. Their initial progress was not encouraging. It was impossible to increase their thrusts in precise unison, and their course veered wildly so that by the time they were again stable, the receding space station was lost in the faint field of stars. Will had carefully noted the orientation of a particular cloud system on the Earth's sphere, though, and he now steered them back to what he believed was approximately their original course.

He realized that even this wouldn't do. Despite every sense telling them that they were rocketing along in a straight line, they were in fact still in orbit, and the non-intuitive laws of orbital mechanics ruled. Accelerating straight in the direction of the escaping space station was initially good, since this would bring them into the same circular orbit—essentially implementing the final maneuver of their transfer from low-Earth. Eventually, though, unchecked they would then find themselves moving into a higher orbit. At some point, once their velocity matched that of the station, they would need to aim inward, angling as though to dive underneath. This way, their increased orbital velocity would be countered by an Earthward vector, advancing them along with no change in altitude.

But when? He had no speedometer. He couldn't even see his watch. He would had no way of knowing when they had reached circular orbit velocity. In the end, he decided that he'd already mulled it over for the few minutes it should take them to reach at least six thousand MPH, and he steered them twenty degrees closer to the blue globe.

On and on they flew. Or, so he imagined. There was no sense whatsoever of flying through space; no trees or houses flashing by, no ground far below sliding steadily past. There was just the acceleration of the uniboosts, and that felt like he was hanging by straps from a fence watching an inexpressibly beautiful blue globe hanging motionless before him.

He realized that their chances of finding the station now were remote at best. At least they had given it their best shot. It was far better than doing nothing, waiting for hours in *Verdad* to be tortured. What he couldn't bear was to be alone tens of thousands of miles from home. People need people.

He leaned his head inwards, and a moment later, felt a bump as Francine did likewise. They were probably moving off course, but he didn't care.

"What's up with this Jenkins guy?" he called.

His own question surprised him. He had meant to ask her why she had picked India Station. The Freudian slip had been waiting ever since she'd referred to the regular Station Master by his first name when talking to Kirkenich.

"Fred?" she yelled back. "He's a friend."

"What kind of friend?"

"A friend. The opposite of an enemy."

Was she being evasive? It was difficult to tell with a conversation that was carried out in shouts. "Did Buck know about Fred?" The question sounded stupid, and he wished he could take it back.

"Is this really what you want to talk about for . . . ?"

"For our last conversation?" he finished for her.

"I didn't mean that. We'll make it. I'm positive."

"Positive is good. How much propellant do you think we have left?"

She didn't answer at first. When she did, it was almost a scream. "I see it!"

"The station? Where?"

"Above us! It's . . . just there!"

He wasn't sure if she was trying to gesture, but he didn't know how she could with him grasping her hands and feet.

"It's . . . not moving!" she continued. "We've matched orbits. Will, you're a genius!"

It was pure dumb luck, but a misconception he didn't mind prolonging.

"Cut your thrust!" he called.

It was impossible to kill both uniboosts at exactly the same time, and inevitably, they ended up in another spin. They had the routine down now, though, and within minutes he had them stabilized. The station was hard to see; he had to shield the sun with his hand. He was amazed that Francine had seen it at all.

They hadn't matched orbits exactly. The giant island in space, a perceptible structure now, was slowing pulling ahead of them.

He felt Francine push her head against his. "Come on! What are we waiting for? Let's go!"

What indeed? Was it that simple? They just rocketed over to it?

"We shouldn't rush this," he called back. "We don't want to lose it now."

But something was wrong. He realized that it had been nudging his subconscious for some time, but he'd been ignoring the warning. He was having trouble breathing. His chest pushed repeatedly against his lobster shell suit as he tried to take deep breaths. His oxygen was running out.

It seemed that they would have to rush after all.

"Okay!" he called. "Let's do it!"

He reached down and brought up his thrust to match his partner's, and then steered them towards salvation.

Fighting panic as he felt himself slowly suffocating, he kept his attention focused squarely on the space station. It was full of air. Cubic yards of it. Hell, maybe cubic miles.

So, why wasn't it getting any closer?

He told himself that it was just his imagination, born of anxiety.

No, it really wasn't getting closer. Instead, it seemed to be pulling away from them, as though trying to get away.

What the hell was going on?

And then it hit him. Orbital mechanics was non-intuitive. Accelerating *out* took you *back*. The station wasn't pulling ahead; they were moving behind.

He felt as though he was drowning. He couldn't get enough *air!*

He veered hard to the left of the station, back to their original course. He saw Francine tilt her head in, as though to protest, but then resume her position. She trusted him.

The station now moved closer. Instead of trying to escape, it was cozying up to them.

But he couldn't *breathe*!

Suddenly they veered even harder to the left . . . and kept veering.

Damn, damn, damn! He was out of propellant, and the thrust was now unbalanced. The veering stopped just as suddenly—Francine must have killed her uniboost. But now they were headed directly towards Earth, the station somewhere behind them.

Francine yanked one hand away, then the other, leaving them connected only by entangled feet. He couldn't *breathe*! He wanted to rip away the breast of his suit so that he could get a proper lung full of stale air. She squirmed next to him. What the hell was she doing? Maybe she too was out of air and this was her last, dying gasps, her death throes.

This thought sobered him. How could he help her? Could he give her some of his own air? No, there was no way.

Her thrashing seemed to have a purpose. She worked diligently at something on her legs. He understood: she was taking off her uniboost. Of course! It was the only way.

Forcing down his strangling panic, he pulled her to him and spun her around so that he could work at her back. Seconds later, her anti-matter rocket pack came free, and they held it between them like the headless torso of some victim they were fighting over. Francine engaged the thrust, and in a clumsy, wordless acrobatic dance, they maneuvered their center of gravity to swing them around back towards the salvation of the space station. At one point he felt a searing pain in his thigh. In his twisting contortions he'd come too close to the exhaust. He'd been lucky, though; had his leg actually crossed the violent steam's path, he'd be waving a bloody stub, waiting to bleed to death . . . if he didn't suffocate first.

When the station swung back into view, he was relieved to see that they had continued to move closer. It was enormous. He could see details now. What had looked like fruit flies hovering around it, he saw were in fact full-sized jump rockets, parked or waiting to dock. The station was one huge, spinning cylinder. His own universe favored spinning wheels, but a cylinder had its advantages since it provided more internal volume.

Closer and closer they came, adjusting the thrust's direction continuously as he worked his chest in and out like a bellows. The sense of suffocation was a brooding backdrop now, and had lost the edge of panic. Details of the station opened and expanded. He saw that the sides sparkled like a billion jewels, and realized that nearly the entire surface was covered in solar arrays, with the odd antenna poking through here and there. No windows. Somehow this seemed sad, to come all the way out here, twenty-two thousand miles from Earth, and not see the stars.

But now a more serious concern struck him. How the hell were they going to get in? Where was the door? Did they knock? Or, was there a doorbell? He wanted to ask his partner, but the maneuver would most certainly throw them off.

As if watching the thoughts progress through his mind, Francine turned off the thrust and pulled his head against hers. "What do we do now?" she called from far away.

Holy hell. If she didn't know . . . "Are there radios somewhere in the suits?" he called, guessing the answer.

"No!"

The suits were built for emergencies. Well, they seemed to be God-awful little use in a real emergency. "Where's the airlock?" he yelled, gasping at the effort.

She pulled her head away to glance at the behemoth. Pulling her head back against his, she said, "At each end. The ships dock there where there's no spin."

That made sense. "Let's head for the closer end," he gasped. He couldn't say more. He didn't have the breath for it.

She re-engaged the uniboost and they moved on.

He pulled air in and out of his lungs now in one long, continuous suck-and-blow, searching, searching for the last stray molecules of oxygen. He didn't care about their course anymore. He held the uniboost suit rigidly in his grip and let Francine do the steering. His thoughts seemed fuzzy, as though he was dreaming. His brain was starving for oxygen. He understood this much. He almost wished it would be over so he could be done with it.

They flew up and over the edge of a cliff. No, it wasn't a cliff, but the rim of the cylindrical station. So close. The little world built by men was just a hundred yards away. Or, was it a hundred meters? He could never keep them straight. So close, but obviously not close enough. They wouldn't make it.

Ha! *There* were the windows. They were at the ends. Maybe it kept the tourists from getting dizzy. Or, more likely, since the station's axis was parallel with the Earth's, the ends were the only areas that weren't periodically bathed in blinding sunlight.

There was apparently something floating out here in space with them. Something obviously fascinating, since all the people behind the glass were pointing outward with open mouths. It dawned on him that they were pointing at them.

The people behind the window slid away below, and Will was sad. It had been good to be near other people, even if separated by a foot of glass. He wanted to go back and press his face against the surface and wave to them.

The metal surfaces of the station rotated away, and he was once again looking at the brilliant blue globe of the Earth. He wondered vaguely why Francine was taking them back into the blackness of space. He felt her grab his head and pull it towards her. "Will!" he heard her shout from far away. "I'm out of repellant!"

Will thought about this. It seemed like an odd thing to say. Weren't they floating around in space? Why had she brought repellent? Was there some kind of space insect—a cosmic mosquito, maybe—that he wasn't aware of? This was a different universe, after all.

"*Will!*" his partner shouted louder. "Are you all right?"

"Sure," he replied.

"Will! I can't hear you! What did you say?"

"Where's the bugs?" he called loudly. It hurt his throat.

"What?"

"Bugs!" he yelled. "Where's the bugs?"

For a few moments, there was only the sound of rasping gasps as he searched fruitlessly for some wisps of oxygen, then he heard her calling again from a distance. "Will! Are you out of air?"

Air. Oh what he wouldn't give for a breath of fresh air. Mount Rainier in the fall. Air so clean, it seemed to evaporate years of Seattle smog with each glorious lung-full.

"Will! Please! Can you hear me?"

He nodded, and her head bounced against his.

"Will! Listen to me. I'm out of propellant. We're not going to make it . . . I'm sorry Will."

Propellant. Not repellant. He laughed. Words were so funny sometimes.

They weren't going to make it. She'd said that. But he knew that already. Time for last words. "I wish I'd been Buck," he said.

"What did you say? I can't hear you!"

"I wish we hadn't exchanged!" he shouted.

She didn't say anything.

He thought about what he'd said. It didn't sound right. He tried again. "I wish I had been Buck all along! I wouldn't have exchanged."

She still didn't say anything.

"I wouldn't have left you!" he added.

Her silence continued, but she eventually called back. "Will, you're oxygen-starved. You're not thinking straight."

He was indeed starved. She was probably right.

No! "I like you!"

I *like* you? How dumb.

"Will! Save your breath!"

Save his breath? Wasn't that another way of saying "Shut up"?

She didn't like him. Was she trying to break up with him? Did this mean that they wouldn't be going to the prom together? It was supposed to be *he* who did the breaking up *after* the prom. That's the way it always was.

But he didn't want to break up this time. The tables were turned. He knew it would happen someday.

They were still hugging, though. Maybe there was a chance yet to change her mind. After all, it was a clear night, and the stars were shining brightly. Girls always found stars romantic. And look at that moon! It was awfully big . . . and blue. A harvest moon, obviously. What exactly was a harvest moon? Did farmers gather crops at night? He'd better say something before she asked him to drive her home.

Too late. She was pulling away from him. He was alone. In the water. At night. A midnight swim in the sound. He'd better start swimming, then, or he'd sink. He swam . . . or tried to. He could hardly move. It felt like his clothes had gotten all wet and then froze solid.

Something grabbed him by the foot. A shark! His Mom always told him he'd get eaten if he swam with his friends, but his Dad had poo-poo'd her. He knew she was right, though, and now a shark had him.

Play dead to a Grizzly, but fight a shark. He fought. Oddly, he wasn't scared. He just knew he should fight a shark. It was no use though. The shark hung on for dear life. Maybe it was starving. Maybe it was a matter of life and death for the fish.

Were sharks fish? Weren't they actually mammals? No, that was whales. And hamsters. And people. Not all people. There were some he wouldn't consider mammals.

He laughed. He should write that one down.

Whoa! What the hell was *that*? A huge building was falling down out of the sky. A big, circle-building. Maybe it was a flying saucer. The shark was obviously an alien. The devils! Pretending for all those centuries to be fish when they were really aliens all along.

Weren't sharks mammals, though?

Alien mammals.

There were some people he wouldn't consider mammals.

That wasn't funny. That joke was old as the hills. And speaking of hills, this metal one had a hole in it. The alien mammal shark was pulling him right into it. He could see the shark now. It *was* an alien! It was silver with tentacles that looked like arms and legs, and diving tanks on its back. A shark with diving tanks. Now *that* was funny.

Too tired to laugh. He'd laugh later. Time to sleep.

Oh, yeah. Sleep.

Ж Ж Ж

He was dancing with an alien shark, which was wearing a spacesuit, fitted to support the monster's ample breasts. Although the dance moves of the voluptuous fish were smooth and seductive, Will was having a difficult time of it. His feet couldn't get a grip on the floor—in fact, he couldn't stay *on* the dance floor, but kept floating up and away.

"Hey Buddy!" the shark yelled in an uncomfortably masculine voice.

Will tried to answer, but couldn't find the words.

"Come on, Buddy. Snap out of it!" the shark insisted, now grabbing him by the head with two hands that suddenly appeared from its sides.

Will gasped. He heard himself gasp, and it wasn't part of the dream. He gasped again, and this time he felt the air lifting his chest.

He opened his eyes and stared at his savior. The man's face was tanned and ruggedly handsome. The tawny hair was disheveled and contrasted starkly with the smooth contours and precise engineering of his spacesuit. Will wondered if the man would garner disfavor, like he had, for having mussed hair, and then wondered if such an irrelevant thought meant that he was still suffering from oxygen starvation. He concluded that, like insanity, just wondering about it probably meant that it wasn't so.

The man was pushed aside and replaced by Francine's face, which looked out with concern from her form-fitting emergency suit. The plastic window had been cut and pulled aside so that it flopped back and forth as she moved.

"Will!" she cried. "Are you alright?"

It was good to hear her voice again, close and not shouting.

"I'm alive," he offered.

Actually, his cheek hurt like hell. He touched it, and his fingers came away red with blood.

"Sorry, mate," the disheveled man said dryly. "I nicked you as I was cutting open your mummy suit."

He could hardly complain, since the alternative might have been death, or perhaps more horribly, brain damage.

A loud hissing sound was followed by a door sliding aside, behind which floated a crowd of people, most in trim, cream-colored uniforms. Will realized that he must be in an airlock.

One man, plump and oily looking, pushed through and pointed an accusing finger at them. "I warned you, Wallaby" he growled, glancing at the man who had obviously come out to rescue them. "Uniboosts! You know the Protocols. You're going to rot in jail along with them."

"Take it easy, Ignatius. I'll get rid of the packs. They haven't blown yet."

An older man pushed through, sailed into the lock, and expertly tumbled, stopping himself with his feet against the far wall. Will recognized the voice of Kirkenich as he barked orders, "Steward Rye Lee—get out! Rodrigious and Whitebread—take these two to Medical. Wallaby, you sure as Satan *are* going to get rid of those blasted Devil's toys."

The Station Master clapped his hands, and seconds later Will was being pulled past the crowd and down a hallway.

He turned to look back at Wallaby, the man who had saved his life. Their rescuer had gathered together the two uniboosts and was pulling something out of his helmet. It looked like wadded-up tinfoil. He glanced up, saw Will, and winked just as the airlock door slid shut.

Francine was being pulled along beside him, both of them like Macy's Parade balloons in tow. The space station had seemed huge from outside, but winding their way through the labyrinth of passageways, it seemed absolutely infinite from inside, a universe all onto itself.

Other than a dull headache, Will felt fine. In fact, he felt a bit silly being dragged around like so much inert mass. He looked over at his companion, but her eyes were closed. She seemed peaceful, content to be in someone else's care.

After a while, they must have moved out towards the rotating perimeter of the station, for they no longer floated in free fall, and their escorts carried them under their arms like bundles of laundry. The two crewmen propelled themselves along using both hands and feet in a comical loping manner that reminded Will of old-time cartoons. Eventually the false gravity increased even more, and they were transferred to gurneys by two other crewmen who came to meet them. Will protested that he could walk, but one of the crewmen politely informed him that it was not his choice to make.

After a few minutes, they were lifted off the gurneys, deposited in chairs inside a small room, and told that the Med Officer would be there shortly. The escorts then stepped outside and took up positions on each side of the doorway.

Francine smiled at him, although she was deathly pale and drawn. Her very hair seemed to sag in weariness. Without a word, she leaned over, rested her head against his shoulder, and placed her hand on his arm. "Thanks, Will," she said simply.

They sat there for a while, and he was happy. They were alive, and . . . well, they were alive.

"I got pretty loony out there," he said.

Francine murmured agreement.

He thought a bit. He'd said some things. "I was lucid, though, when I told you that I wish I'd been Buck," he explained. "And that I wouldn't have left you," he added softly.

Francine didn't say anything. He wondered if his confession was maybe unwelcome, and she was deciding how to tell him so.

Well, to hell with it, he thought. He plowed ahead. "I know that this sounds crazy. But if you think about it, I am essentially the same person as Buck. So, why wouldn't I be attracted to you as well? Just because he—"

A clip-clop of shoes was followed by the arrival of a man of efficient bearing with a stethoscope hanging from around his neck. He took one look at them, and immediately called to the escorts. "Take her in and get that emergency suit off of her," he ordered.

"Come on, partner," Will urged gently, putting his hand on hers.

Her head flopped forward. She was unconscious.

She hadn't heard a single word of his confession.

Chapter 12

Will was a prisoner. There were no bars or handcuffs, but the uniformed man standing just outside the storage closet where Will sat on a box had made that clear when he'd tried to leave. "I'm sorry, sir," the young serviceman had said. "Master Kirkenich will be here shortly to answer your questions."

He'd tried to sleep, but there wasn't enough room to lie down, and every time he started to nod off, he jerked awake with visions of sharks doing the can-can. After twenty minutes, footsteps came down the hallway, but instead of the station master, he heard a voice he now despised. When the guard protested, Pilot Steward Ignatius simply ignored him and stood in the doorway with his hands on his chubby hips watching him, a smirk on his protruding lips.

"Well, well, if it isn't Mr. Potty-mouth. As I recall, you were urging me to stuff my proper radio protocols up my . . . what was it? My fat, pompous behind?"

"It was your fat, pompous *ass*. Not your 'behind,' you arrogant wuss. Your *ass*."

The Pilot Steward shook his head with exaggerated pity and shrugged to the guard. "The poor fool's binny as a mad hatter." Then, back to Will, he said, "I don't know what your game is, but you're playing with powers far beyond your assumptions."

"If you're referring to that other wuss, Breggart, then the power 'far beyond my assumptions' consists of a gun—excuse me—a 'peace keeper' that he uses against unarmed women."

Ignatius's smirk taunted him so that Will wanted to rip it off the bloated man's face. The Pilot Steward glanced sideways at the sound of approaching feet, and then, still smiling haughtily, moved aside for Kirkenich.

"That will be all, Rye Lee," the station master said to the Pilot Steward, who waited just long enough to demonstrate that he wasn't under direct command of station officers, then with a quick shrug, stepped just a few feet away.

Will stood up. "I want to see Francine."

Kirkenich nodded. "I understand, young man, but you'll have to trust me that she's in capable hands. The doctor tells me that she's suffering from exhaustion and loss of blood, but he's confident she'll be back on her feet in a few days. Is she your . . . ?"

"Wife?"

"Er, I was thinking perhaps fiancée."

"Neither. She's my . . . partner."

"Partner. I see."

Will waited, but the station master didn't ask the obvious next question: what venture were they were partners in?

"Am I under arrest?" Will asked.

"Arrest? No, no. I have no authority to arrest you."

"Then why am I standing in a closet?"

"Well, er, operating a ship in international space without a Pilot is in violation of protocol," he explained with a quick glance at Ignatius. "I'm afraid I have to hold both of you until somebody from the US can come and take custody."

"But I'm not under arrest."

"No, not arrest . . . but I imagine you will be when the US authorities arrive."

"Let me see if I have this straight: I'm not under arrest, just forced to stay in a closet."

Kirkenich looked pained. "I'm very sorry. There's really nothing I can do."

Will looked from Ignatius to the Kirkenich. "Aren't you curious what we were doing out there with no Pilot?"

He wasn't sure why he'd asked that. Maybe his intuition had nudged him.

"As station master, I am only responsible for the operation of the station, but of course, I am curious why—"

"I think this can wait for the hearing on Earth," Ignatius cut in staring coldly at Will.

His intuition had been right. The bloated snob was trying to keep things under wraps.

"Actually," Will said, "I'm from a different universe, and the American CID is trying to catch me because—"

Ignatius reached in and threw his hand over Will's mouth. "This man must be kept in isolation until the US takes custody," the porky steward demanded.

Kirkenich reached in and pulled the steward's hand away. "I am in command of this station, and I will decide who is kept in isolation. And in any case, in what capacity do you speak for the American government?"

Ignatius turned his steely stare on the station master, but remained silent.

"I thought," Kirkenich went on, "that the Pilot Union was a politically neutral organization? Are you acting in your capacity as the Pilot Union Steward, or an American citizen? If the latter, then it seems to me you should name a successor to your post."

The steward lifted his chin so that the layers of fat unfolded, then turned and walked heavily away.

Kirkenich sighed, and then said to Will, "It's probably best if you keep quiet for now." He chuckled. "Another universe, eh? You know, Ignatius claims you're binny."

Will smiled. "Binny is as binny does."

The station master cocked an eye. "I'll have some food brought up," he promised. He glanced at his watch and hurried off, muttering invectives about status meetings.

Will leaned out to watch him, but the guard placed his hand on his chest and gently pushed him back into his closet.

ж ж ж

"Food for the condemned," Will heard an Australian drawl announce as he jerked his head up. He'd fallen asleep after all.

Food! He hadn't realized how hungry he was until Kirkenich mentioned food. His stomach squirmed now with anticipation.

Wallaby's grinning head appeared in the doorway, and he handed Will a plastic box. Unlike the guard, the Australian wore civilian clothes. Inside the box, separated by partitions, were three portions of pureed substances differentiated by color only. The brown one might be oatmeal, the orange one possibly sweet potato or pumpkin, and the green one was beyond guessing. He grabbed the spoon, and shoveled the goo into his mouth. The tastes were bland and slightly synthetic, and he couldn't spoon them fast enough.

"The bugger's downright famished," Wallaby observed to the guard. "I've never seen anyone take so heartily to space grub."

Will shoveled while the Australian chatted with the guard. After Will had scraped the last bit of mush from the container, Wallaby took it from him and started to hand him a second, smaller one, but paused. He glanced quickly at the guard who was out of sight beyond the doorway, then looked Will in the eye, and with the same irreverent grin, shook his head.

"No?" he asked, staring at Will knowingly. "Too full, eh?"

He pulled the container back and turned to the guard. "Shame to let it go to waste. Maybe you'd like it?"

The guard asked what it was, and Wallaby replied, "Ice cream."

Will's eyes went wide, but Wallaby gave him a quick wink.

The guard remarked that he hadn't had ice cream since leaving Earth and gladly took the container.

Wallaby waited until the young man had spooned a few mouthfuls, then leaned in towards Will and said, "What did you say, mate? You need to go to the bathroom?"

Will looked at him in surprise, but the man's sun-wrinkled eyes warned him to play along.

"Oh yeah," Will said. "I have to go—real badly."

The guard peered around the corner, clearly not happy with the prospect of putting down his ice cream.

"I think I might go in my pants," Will warned, crossing his legs for effect.

The annoyed young man nodded. "I'll be done in a few minutes, and then I'll take you."

Wallaby looked at Will questioningly.

"The food!" Will cried, jumping up and holding the seat of his pants. "My digestive system wasn't ready for it!"

He bounced up and down to emphasize his urgency.

"Oh for Judas' sake," the guard muttered, looking longingly at his melting ice cream.

"I'll tell you what, mate" Wallaby drawled, "I'll take the bloke to the privy. You finish that ice cream before you need a straw."

The guard seemed uncertain, looking back and forth between his cherished dessert and his charge.

"Aw, don't worry," Wallaby pressed. "I'll keep 'im safe."

The young man seemed to waver, but shook his head.

"You know," the Australian reminded him, "dingo's don't lie."

That did it. "Okay, but you have to be back in five minutes. Five minutes, got it?"

"Sure, mate," Wallaby said, slapping him on the back. "We'll be back before you finish scratching your butt."

The guard rolled his eyes and took another spoonful of ice cream.

"Come on, jailbird," Wallaby said to Will, "let's go find out what your lower intestines have to say."

Will followed the ambling, lanky, potty-mouthed man, but once around the corner, Wallaby turned to him and confided, "Okay, mate. Ready to make a run for it?"

"Where are we going?"

"Into the wild black yonder," the Australian replied as he trotted away.

"We're . . . leaving the *station*?"

"It's hard to escape without doing that," he called, apparently confident no one could hear.

Will stopped. "Escape?"

Wallaby turned and stopped as well. "You'd rather have a sitdown and some tea with the CID?"

"What about Francine?"

"Don't worry, mate. She'll be taken care of."

Will stood his ground.

"Look," Wallaby coaxed, "we'll get her off as well. I promise."

"Just like you promised to bring me back after going to the bathroom? I thought dingo's didn't lie?"

The Australian looked hurt. "I didn't lie. I said that I was going to keep you safe, and that's exactly what I'm doing."

"How are you going to get Francine off?"

"I'll tell you what; you come along with me, and I'll explain it all. In another minute or so our young friend's going to call an alarm, and his superiors aren't going to be happy when they find ice cream all over his mouth."

Will followed his rescuer through the three dimensional maze of the station as the dingo explained the plan. The US had called to inform the station that they were sending up a military patrol to retrieve the two fugitives, but it just so happened that a medical ship belonging to Orbital Authority—a special branch of the UN—was close by, and had already offered to take them down. It also just so happened that the Pilot of this medical ship already knew that a malfunction, which he had arranged himself, was going to prevent him from decelerating out of his homeward transfer orbit so that, instead of returning to Earth, the disabled ship would continue back up to geosynchronous orbit. It also just so happened that an unregistered ship with an unlicensed pilot was right now preparing to launch from somewhere south of the equator and west of New Zealand to intercept the stricken medical ship and "save" its passengers.

"In that case," Will challenged, "why do I have to leave now?"

Wallaby stopped so that Will ran into him, and then looked him in the eye. "We're not taking any chances with you, mate," he replied. For the first time, the dingo spoke earnestly. He spun and strode off.

Will had to hustle to keep up. His feet slipped across the floor, and he was having trouble keeping his balance. It seemed as though the floor kept falling away beneath him. They were obviously making their way towards the axis of the giant cylinder, and the artificial gravity was diminishing accordingly. He noticed that Wallaby leaned far forward and swung his arms back and forth in exaggerated arcs, as though speed skating. Will tried to imitate the low-gravity gait, and was almost getting the hang of it when his guide changed tactics yet again. Their weight had reduced even further, and walking at all had become a handicap. Instead, they now used the handrails attached to the walls to pull themselves along.

Will asked Wallaby why there weren't more people out and about, and his guide explained that it was the middle of the night.

The six space stations operated on staggered day periods, and India Station happened to coincide with North American Eastern Time.

Will's arms tired, and he fell behind. He caught up when his new partner stopped to peer around a corner. The Australian turned and held his finger to his lips, and Will came to a stop behind him. He fell slowly to the floor. They weren't yet at the precise axis. He pulled himself closer and peered around. A uniformed young man was positioned next to a serious-looking door. Above it was painted, *Aft lock 2B*.

"What'll we do now?" Will whispered.

"He won't give us any problems," Wallaby replied softly. "You stay here, out of sight."

And with that, the Australian pulled himself around the corner and hailed the young man.

Will assumed that the guard was one of them, whoever "them" was, and was surprised when Wallaby gave one quick jab, and the man curled into a ball. The dingo then took a clear plastic tube from his pocket, fiddled with it a moment, and jabbed it into the stricken guard's arm. "Let's go!" he called to Will, and turned to the lock's control panel.

Shocked at the sudden violence, Will pulled himself forward and met the eyes of the guard which seemed to lose focus and then close. "Is he . . . ?"

"Sleeping soundly?" Wallaby finished for him, punching a final button. The airlock door hissed open.

"I meant dead."

"Course not, mate." The Australian turned his cocky grin on him. "That'd be cat's piss, wouldn't it? Now, grab one of those e-suits over there," he said, gesturing towards doors set into the wall.

The dingo took a silver spacesuit from a rack where it hung with at least a dozen others.

Behind the doors, stacked neatly in endless piles, Will found what he thought were folded coveralls. They were grouped into three sizes: small, medium, and large. He picked up a medium, and as it fell open, he immediately recognized the familiar faceplate window.

"No!" he cried, turning to find Wallaby already pulling on his expensive piece of equipment. "There's absolutely no way I'll ever crawl into one of these nightmare straitjackets again. I'd rather have my fingernails torn off first."

The dingo shrugged. "That's pretty much the alternative," he said, working the fasteners that ran up the front of his obviously comfortable suit. "You only have a minute to decide, though, as I'm leaving before the station personnel start arriving with crowbars."

Will eyed the rack where the other bona fide spacesuits hung. "Why can't I use one of those?" he asked, pointing.

Wallaby glanced at the row of silver beauties, and then threw Will a critical glare. "You are binny, aren't you? You would actually steal another man's suit?"

"It's okay to knock a man out, but not to take his spacesuit?"

The dingo just shook his head in wondering amazement.

Like stealing a man's horse in the old West, Will thought. He stared at the hated dark material and sighed.

ж ж ж

Will gave in to the inevitable and let his feet swing around towards the station's perimeter. The flat end of the asteroid-sized cylinder extended away into the darkness in all directions. It was like floating above an endless metal plain. The Earth's blinding white North Pole peeked above the far rim, circling endlessly along the station's edge and washing out the stars. Since the space station orbited the Earth along the equator, and so shared its solar tilt, the sun was thankfully always below this end of the cylinder's edge.

He had been pulling himself along the handholds headfirst, but the artificial gravity of the giant centrifuge tugged at him now with tenuous fingers so that it was difficult keeping his feet behind him. As his legs swung around, his mind spun dimensions as well. Whereas before he'd been floating above a plane, now he seemed to hang from the face of a cliff. The pull of artificial gravity this close to the station's axis was miniscule, allowing him to hang on with just one pinky, but his Earth instincts knew only one kind of cliff face. The fact that this cliff didn't even reveal a discernable bottom made him gasp and clutch the rung. He closed his eyes and drew in slow, deep breaths. Although stymied by the confines of his emergency suit, this helped him reorient his mental picture.

After a few seconds, he looked down past the flashlight hanging from his belt to where Wallaby had diminished to near invisibility in the indistinct light cast by the tip of the Earth's polar cap. His rescuer looked like a rappelling spider as he descended fearlessly into the deepening well of pseudo-gravity.

Will let go his grasp and allowed himself to sink. Too slow. He pushed against the handrails as they slid past to boost his speed. He knew that time was precious. His closet guard surely would have raised the alarm by now, and once they found Wallaby's unconscious victim, pursuers would pour out the lock as fast as they could cycle the air.

He glanced up, suddenly fearful that spacesuited feet might already be bearing down on him, but there was just the polar ice of Earth gliding slowly by the far rim.

Faster and faster he fell, until instead of pushing up on the handrails, he was tugging down every dozen to slow his controlled plunge. The flashlight banged back and forth between the rails and his thigh. He hoped the light bulbs of this universe were more robust than those of his own. He thought he was doing okay until he drifted away slightly and missed a rung. By the time he recovered, he had slipped to the side, a victim of the same Coriolis effect that set hurricanes rotating. He panicked and grabbed for one of the rungs, but instead, his wrist slapped painfully against five or six until he slowed enough to finally snag one, nearly jerking his arm from its socket.

He hung there a moment letting his heart slow, and then glanced up and it seemed to stop altogether. A space-suited figure had emerged from the lock and was pointing in his direction. Another head appeared and looked down at him.

Time to fly. The handholds were mounted between two rails, like a ladder extending into infinity above and below. He let go his grip and grasped the rails on each side as he fell away from his pursuers above as though sliding down a cosmic fire station pole. The rungs flashed by in a blur and he feared the velocity that was building. He squeezed his fingers as a brake and then squeezed herder until he perceived that the flashing rungs had indeed begun to slow.

Something hurt. His hands; they were getting hot! A feeble ruddy light seemed to shine through his fingers. Holy Mother of God! His hands were glowing red-hot from the friction! The fabric of the emergency suit was insulating nearly all of the heat, but one percent of red-hot was still painful . . . and getting hotter!

It was either burned hands, or catapulting off the perimeter edge of the station. He closed his eyes and squeezed until his fingers seemed to melt into the metal rails. When he opened his eyes again, the rails were gliding lazily by, and with a lunge he grabbed one and hung on as he jerked to a stop.

Above him his pursuers had grown smaller with distance, but there were now three of them, and they floated free of the station, obviously preparing to use their EVA packs to come after him.

He looked down between his feet . . . and gasped. Not ten feet below him was the station's edge. A platform waited at the end of the ladder, too small to have prevented him from tumbling off into infinite vacuum.

He slid the rest of the way down to the platform. His hands still glowed a dull red, and his fingers felt like they were on fire. He waved them up and down, and then cursed himself and the nothingness of space. With no air to carry away the heat, waving his arms did nothing. *Think!* He placed his hands flat against the station hull and let the metal conduct the heat away.

Wallaby was gone, and that was good. With luck, the dingo's head start was enough. Even if the posse above hadn't seen the Australian fly away, the traffic controllers inside were surely tracking the fancy metal spacesuit on their short-range radar.

Now for his own escape. He'd been trying not to think about his next move ever since Wallaby explained the plan back in the airlock. It had seemed hopelessly desperate then, and sheer madness now. He looked around among the crowd of suspended moored ships for his landmark. Wallaby had assured him that he couldn't possibly miss it. The dingo was right. He found it easily. The yacht looked like a huge, elongated Christmas ornament floating perhaps two miles away against a jet-black backdrop—the extravagant space toy of an aging movie star.

Stiffly in his e-suit, he crouched down to sight along the platform's bottom, but he already knew that he'd just missed an opportunity. The edge of the platform provided a convenient reference line for viewing the cylinder's tangent. The esthete yacht glided teasingly away from the target point defined by his makeshift gun sight. India Station rotated with a period of 25.6 seconds; it would be nearly a half minute before another opportunity spun its way around again.

Meanwhile, the posse had mobilized. Two of his pursuers had moved some distance from the cylinder's flat face, while the third remained near the lock, apparently standing guard in case Will decided to single-handedly storm the space station. The silver-suited men seemed to hover magically in the sky above him. From the perspective of his artificial gravity, Will had an odd thought that they should be waving their arms instead of just floating there like fish in water. Hands working waist-mounted controls, their movements consisted of distinct geometric components: shifting sideways a few feet, then rotating thirty degrees. Once they were facing sideways to him, each in turn moved forward. This seemed curious until he remembered that the station, and Will along with it, was rotating beneath them. They were heading for where he would be when they arrived at the perimeter.

He glanced at his target. The yacht was behind him. Fifteen seconds to go.

Too late. The two silver-suited men were nearly upon him, flying along, side-by-side, like twin dolls sinking face down to the bottom of a swimming pool. Tiny spurts of fire danced on their backs as they made final course corrections. A snake grasped by head and tail also danced between them. It was a cord, and they intended to snare him like a calf in a rodeo. The helmet visors reflected the white snow of Earth, hiding their faces.

The spaceman pair passed on each side up him, and an instant later the cord caught him across the chest, pulling him down. He realized that he had an advantage, though. Whereas his captors were flying free with the space station rotating beneath them, he was anchored to the small platform by centrifugal pseudo-gravity. He let the advancing cord pull him down into a crouching position, and then, with all the strength his legs could muster, he heaved himself upwards. The cord pressed in against the shoulders of the stiffened emergency suit, and slowly gave way as he overcame the two men's inertia. A second later, the cord's tension relaxed, and he quickly pulled it off and over him.

His maneuver had redirected the attacker's forward momentum, bringing them crashing into each other face-to-face. They flailed beneath him, arms waving, as they struggled to regain orientation.

Will grabbed the cord and gave it a yank for good measure, then looked around for his target. The onion-shaped ship was gliding towards the target position again.

Close enough. He should have squatted down again and sighted along the bottom of the platform for precise timing, but there was no time for that. Shouting a silent Geronimo, he stood up and pushed off with his feet against the station. The giant hulk of metal fell away, and as he gained distance, the perceived face of a cliff morphed once again into the end of a behemoth cylinder.

The two silver men gained their composure and looked around for him. Will curled into a ball as best he could in the stiff suit, the better to hide amidst the black backdrop of space as he flew away at 120 feet per second in the shadow of the space station, a human cannonball hurled from the catapult of the station's rim.

Into the emptiness he sped. The diminishing mass of man-constructed metal fell away, an island of life in the infinite sea of nothing. His pursuers, who a moment before were two adversaries that he desperately needed to avoid, now seemed his last, fading link to Earth and all the life it nurtured.

Once again he was lost in space, stuffed inside an emergency spacesuit offering preciously limited air.

Chapter 13

Will assured himself that it was just his overactive imagination. He couldn't be running out of air yet. He couldn't see his watch, but surely less than ten minutes had passed since they'd left the space station's air lock. Still, he seemed to be drawing awfully deep breaths, like when, as kids, they would breathe into a paper bag to make themselves dizzy, except that now his paper bag was all he had.

And once again he was rotating. He had come to accept that this was the norm in space. *Everything* rotated. Once off the Earth, a static orientation was a highly unlikely occurrence, usually requiring an application of energy to achieve. That old conservation of angular momentum and the vacuum of space practically guaranteed it.

But it was a real pain in the ass when you were the one angularly momentuming.

The extravagant yacht, his original landmark, had grown, slid silently past him, and was now an onion silhouette as he sped on through the tunnel of the space station's shadow. The artificial gravity of the rotating station had seemed to make "down" at right angles to the moored yacht, so that his target was off to his side. When he'd jumped free, though, he was moving tangentially to the station's rim, and was thrown off towards the yacht like a baseball off the tip of a swinging bat.

He was getting cold without the sun's heat. He wouldn't stay in the station's shadow for very long, but his air would give out long before he froze to death anyway.

Where the hell was Wallaby? If they had caught him, he surely would have explained the escape plan so that the station crewmen would come to retrieve him.

Or would he? Will realized that he didn't really know the man's motives. When Will had wanted to stay on the station until they came to rescue Francine, the dingo said that they weren't taking any chances with him. Breggart thought he was valuable for knowledge about advanced weapons technology. Perhaps this was why the Australian wanted him. If so, how did he even know about Will in the first place?

In fact, how could he be sure this man had ever intended to come to retrieve him? He knew less about the brash renegade than he did about Breggart. The only justification in trusting him was that he'd come out and saved them after they abandoned *Verdad*. But perhaps it was just Francine that he'd come to retrieve. Maybe this purported escape was just a means to get rid of the troublesome man from another universe. When he'd asked the dingo before leaving the station's airlock why they couldn't go together to his ship, he'd explained that Will would slow him down. He'd told him that the station wouldn't be able to track him since his e-suit had no metal to reflect the radar. But how much would Will really have slowed down the Australian? It wasn't like he'd be carrying 160 pounds over his shoulders.

Endless questions, and all the answers lay in the same direction as his rescue . . . which flashed by over, and over, and over as he spun on into the night. Each time the silhouettes of the receding station and pleasure yacht whirled past, he searched frantically for a rocket exhaust. Even water, he reasoned, when heated to thousands of degrees would give off light.

Finally, when it was no longer just his imagination that his air was giving out, he saw the white flicker, and relief washed through him like the fire of life itself. Multiple flickers, actually. Wallaby had already killed the main engine, and was using the baby maneuvering jets located around the perimeter, bow and stern.

Time to guide his rescue boat in. The flashlight hovered, taught at the end of its tether as it rotated with him. He hauled it in and flipped the switch. Nothing. Apparently the bulbs in this universe were no better. He swung it wide to give it a whack against his palm, and flinched as a splash of light blinded him. The bulb worked fine; he just hadn't seen the beam in the vacuum.

He tried swinging the light in a direction counter to his rotation in order to give Wallaby a steady beacon, but only managed to tangle himself in the tether. Swearing to the God of his universe, he settled for simply holding the light straight out from his navel. He reasoned that this was more effective, since it provided the dingo a strobing signal.

The winking firefly dance of Wallaby's control jets seemed to be closing in, but by this time Will was getting nauseous from all the spinning, and he shut his eyes. He was definitely almost out of air. With each breath, his chest fought against the constraining hold of his suit. He yelped with alarm when something bumped the back of his feet. He opened his eyes and saw that the impact had slowed his spin. The stars slid by more slowly . . . and then went out. No, they were just blocked by something. Something huge. Something nearly on top of him, ready to swallow him. Wallaby!

He couldn't tell how close the ship was. It was just a solid blackness against a blackness studded with stars. He reached out, but grasped only vacuum. Suddenly he was bathed in an overwhelming blast of white radiance. His eyes had adjusted to the darkness, and the ship's spotlight was physically painful. The beam of light moved off of him, and illuminated the side of the ship, which loomed not ten feet away, then narrowed until it was a three-foot spot glowing brilliantly on the metal surface. The oval light moved purposefully, gliding steadily along the ship's side. It passed over words that read, *Reaction, LTD.* As he followed the wayward illuminated circle, Will wondered whether the spotlight was perhaps mounted on a boom, and if so, whether it had to be retracted when operating in the atmosphere.

He recalled his rambling, barely connected trains of thought the last time his air ran out inside an e-suit, and worried that he might again be staggering down that surrealistic alley. He seemed lucid enough though. *Okay, what's the square root of thirteen,* he challenged himself. *More than three and . . . less than four. Thirteen is between nine and sixteen. Just about halfway, in fact. So, maybe three-point-five. No. Don't be an idiot. You're a mathematician, for God's sake. We're talking squares here; the relationship isn't linear. Three-point-six. I'll take door number three-point-six.*

Shit. It was happening again. His brain still functioned enough to realize this much.

He *hated* these damn e-suits.

He blinked, remembering where he was. The spot of light had stopped moving and remained fixed over . . . the hatchway! Wallaby was pointing to the door. Will waved his arms and legs, trying to swim towards salvation, and then stopped. *Idiot!* Think! Amazingly, the hatchway moved closer. He *could* swim in space!

No, that wasn't possible. Wallaby would be using the steering jets on the far side to move the ship towards him. Closer and closer the ship came until he could finally grab the rail that surrounded the hatch. Like the spotlight boom, the rail must also retract when in the atmosphere.

He swung his fist against the metal door, and heard a faint, distant thud as the vibrations from the concussion traveled up the bones of his arm and on to his skull and inner ear. He knew that banging wasn't really necessary since Wallaby must have a camera focused on him—probably mounted on the same boom as the light. It felt good, though.

He whacked the hatch again. It went dark, except for a small red dot that quivered nervously but sparkled with an evil glint across the ship's hull. He shook his head, trying to clear it, trying to understand what was going on.

He looked down. Wallaby had moved the oval of white light so that it was now shining on a small ledge projecting from the bottom of the hatch.

"What!" Will cried into his suit. "What do you want me to do? Let me in, goddamn-it!"

In answer, the spaceship began moving.

What the hell was Wallaby doing? Will held onto the hatch rails as best he could in his stiff-fingered e-suit. As the ship accelerated, his feet swung down, and his shins bumped against the small platform. The spot of light still hovered there. He finally realized what Wallaby was trying to tell him: *stand on the platform.*

He pulled himself up, and found instant relief once his feet were planted on a solid surface. But what in God's name was Wallaby *doing*?

Well . . . moving, of course. Far away, below his feet, he could see the space station growing visibly smaller. The dingo was making his getaway, not wasting time to cycle the airlock.

Unfortunately, this hitchhiker was just about out of air.

ж ж ж

Once again Will was looking up at Wallaby as the Australian cut away his e-suit. The first breaths of new air were intoxicating in their rich oxygen content, but this was soon replaced by a vaguely familiar odor that made him wish he had an oxygen bottle. He placed it: his college dorm. The sour smell of old food and clothes badly in need of a wash permeated Wallaby's ship. Somehow, Will found this satisfying. In a small way it helped offset the man's confident, handsome appeal.

Wallaby hadn't left Will out there on the ship's doorstep for long. In fact, he'd starting cycling the lock before he even fired up the main drive again. Within minutes the hatch had slid aside, and Will had stumbled into an airlock the size of a small closet, barely big enough for both him and his depleted hunchback air bladder. He wouldn't have fit at all if he hadn't been nearly out of air. A minute after that, the inner door slid aside and the dingo grabbed him, threw him to the floor, and began extricating him from the e-suit.

"Welcome to *Dero*," Wallaby greeted pleasantly as he cut and peeled the stiff fabric from Will. "Have a nice stroll in the night?" His rescuer worked briskly, obviously in a hurry. As soon as he'd stripped away the last leg covering, he sprang to the pilot seat, adding, "Dandy trousers you've got there, mate. Come strap yourself in so we can hightail it out of here."

Like *Verdad*, Wallaby's *Dero* had two control chairs side-by-side. Wallaby strapped himself in and gestured for Will to take the co-pilot seat. The cabin was half again as large as *Verdad*'s, and as Will stood up and made for the chair, something lying in the far corner caught his eye. Even crumbled together in a heap, the streamlined packs were immediately recognizable.

"The uniboosts!" he cried, starting towards them.

"Mate," Wallaby said, flipping switches on the board in front of him. "I hate to be an earbasher, but I'm opening *Dero*'s throttle in twenty seconds, and if you're not in your seat, you're going to have some scrapin-good bruises."

With a last glance at the old friends, Will settled into his seat and was reaching for the shoulder strap when Wallaby flipped a last switch. Invisible hands pushed him down . . . and kept pushing. He struggled to get the strap around him, and as soon as he had it buckled, the Australian flipped three more switches and Will thought the weight of the whole Earth had settled on his face. He had to take short, quick gasps of air, since he hadn't the strength to lift his chest fully against the acceleration.

What the hell kind of ship was this? *Verdad*'s top push was less than one and a half gravities. Judging from the blurring of his vision as his eyeballs were squashed, he guessed they were doing five—maybe eight—Gs.

He tried to talk, to ask Wallaby how long this would last, but only managed one strangled croak. He closed his eyes against the discomfort and focused on breathing.

He hoped the uniboosts were doing okay against the crush. He guessed that they must be built for this sort of thing; otherwise they'd have been dead already.

How had Wallaby gotten them onboard? Will had heard him tell Kirkenich that he was going to get rid of them. The dingo had taken tinfoil from his helmet as they were being carried away from the station airlock.

It came to him. The Australian must have taken the suits outside and hid them somewhere, then unfolded the tinfoil and tossed it to the stars. Radar wouldn't know the difference between a sheet of tinfoil and the metalized fabric of the uniboosts. The station operators would have seen what they thought were the uniboosts sailing steadily outward, safely away from the station.

And this also explained why Wallaby didn't take Will with him. The dingo's hands were already full between operating his suit rocket pack and hanging on to the uniboosts. He also suspected that the Australian may have simply wanted to avoid dealing with a clumsy, neophyte space traveler. Once Will had launched himself from the edge of the station, he could flail away all he wanted until

Wallaby came to pick up the valuable cargo. Or, at least, what was perceived to be valuable cargo.

The elephant standing on his chest lifted its foot, and he floated up against his straps.

"Excuse me, mate," Wallaby said, as he leaned over to peer at Will's screen. "Hand me that book, there," he added pointing off to Will's right.

He reached over and handed his new companion a copy of the same *Primary Orbits* he had used on *Verdad*. The Australian flipped back and forth through it awhile, then muttered, "Bloody hell," under his breath.

"Can I help?" Will asked.

"I doubt it, mate, unless you're a navigator."

"I'm a mathematician—I navigated *Verdad* from Earth to India Station."

Wallaby looked at him as though to confirm his passenger wasn't pulling his leg, then handed him the book. "Go at it."

"What's our destination?"

The dingo smiled broadly. "Home. Aussie-land. The big Down Under."

"Australia," Will concluded, flipping to the section on transfer orbits. "I'll get us into low-Earth orbit, and we can reconnoiter from there."

First, he had to figure out where they were . . . and where they were headed. After a series of position readings, he estimated that Wallaby's two minutes of intense acceleration had increased their speed by 20,000 MPH . . . towards the Earth. He looked up at the waiting Australian. "We have lots of propellant left, right?"

Wallaby glanced at a dial. "We're down to twenty-nine percent."

"How much delta-V does that translate to?"

"Change in velocity? Bloody-Judas if I know. You're supposed to be the navigator."

Will sighed and went back to his calculations.

"Uh, do we have a problem?" Wallaby asked.

Will looked up to find the rugged face still smiling, but his brow was furrowed. "On our present course," Will explained, "we'll continue to speed up as we fall into the Earth's gravity well. In a little over an hour, we'll pass within four hundred miles of the surface of the planet, and then head out again, never to return. At perigee, we'll be zipping along at over 29,000 MPH, well above the Earth's escape velocity."

He was surprised at his confident delivery. Eight hours ago he barely knew an apogee from a perigee.

The dingo unbuckled his belt and stretched his legs out. "I wanted to get us home ASAP. Are we going to have enough juice?"

"I think so," Will replied, chewing the end of his pencil as he reviewed his work. He looked up at Wallaby. "How were you planning on getting us down?"

The lean man shrugged. "Seat-of-my-pants." He tapped his forehead. "This old auto-pilot runs on intuition. I fly by feel."

Will just stared at the man whom five minutes ago he'd thought was this universe's version of James Bond. With careful calculation and precise timing, Will *might* get them down without falling the last mile. There was no way in hell Wallaby would have managed that 'by feel.'

"Did you bring the ship up to the station?" Will asked.

Wallaby gave him the Binny Look. "Course not, mate. I hired a Pilot. Wouldn't have been able to dock otherwise, now would I?"

"So, now we're both criminals."

"Nah. We both broke orbital protocols. *You're* a criminal, of course, but only because fussy old America considers it a serious crime."

"But not in Australia?"

"Oh, they'll probably suspend my license just for show. But I don't bother about that."

"You do have a Pilot's license, then?"

"Not that kind. Only good over Aussie territory."

"So, you've never flown a ship into orbit?"

The Binny Look again.

He now understood how his brash friend could afford to pilot by feel. Flying around Earth's surface was like pushing a ducky around a bathtub compared to orbital navigation, which was more like sailing a three-masted barkentine . . . through a crowded harbor . . . blindfolded.

"Why did you wait so long to let me in?" Will asked. He shuddered, thinking about the damnable e-suit.

"Our boy Ignatius was just waiting for me to open the hatch."

Will suddenly remembered the small red dot dancing on the ship's side. It must have been a targeting laser. "He was going to fire a missile at you?"

"He wouldn't have waited for me to open the hatch for that. Besides, a candle would have been too blatant. No, he wanted to rip up the insides of *Dero* with his com-lase."

"Com-lase?"

"Communications laser."

"That must have been the red dot I saw on the hull. But how much damage could a communications laser do?"

"A normal one? None. Once the alarm sounded, Ignatius made for the US patrol boat he uses as his personal taxi. America calls their laser weapon a communication device, but everybody knows that's just pork pie. Packing fifty kilowatts, it would have 'communicated' swiss cheese out of the inside of *Dero*'s airlock."

"It didn't seem to hurt the hull, though."

"She's pure titanium. He could probably burn a hole eventually if he could hold the beam at one spot long enough. As it was, he was just warming up old *Dero*'s skin."

Will winced, remembering the innocuous-looking red dot dancing around the hull above him. "He could have killed me."

"Would of cut you in two faster than you could sneeze. Our buddy Breggart wants you alive, though. Ignatius would've been on CID's shit list if he'd done you in."

"The station master said something about Ignatius needing to decide if he represented the Pilot Union or the US. Which is it?"

Wallaby gave him the Binny Look, but then shrugged, as though it wouldn't hurt to explain what everybody already knew. "They're one and the same, really. Old Kirkenich was just yanking the dipstick's chain. They both know that Ignatius takes his orders from CID."

"The Pilot Union is not really politically neutral like Kirkenich said, is it?"

"Does a kangaroo piss in the bush?"

"I see. But if this Orbital Authority is supposed to be part of the UN, how does the Pilot Union end up answering to America?"

The dingo stared at him, as though gauging whether his passenger was really this ignorant. "Boeing, Ford, and SCI," he finally said.

"The rocket manufacturers."

"They make the whole ship, not just the rocket engines."

"Right. Ships, not rockets. I still don't get the connection."

Wallaby looked him in the eye. "You really don't know, do you?"

"I wouldn't ask if I did."

The man who flew by the seat of his pants smiled. "The three American companies own the whole nuclear drive technology. It's almost a mistake to think of them as separate companies since they work together in a mutual wanking, a three-headed monopoly. They never sell their ships—"

"I know, they only lease them. Francine explained that part."

"Did she also explain that they only lease to countries that sign binding agreements of non-discovery?"

"Yeah. Fancy words for promising not to peek under the skirt."

"Well, if the companies find that somebody's been tampering with the seals, they pull all the ships. It happened to Brazil in '89— a one-year ban. Almost sunk their economy. Nobody's dared to try since."

"So, where does the Pilot Union come in?"

"The Big Three control the licenses. Pilots are officially certified by Orbital Authority, but because of those non-discovery agreements, the companies have the last say on who gets a license."

Will nodded. He was beginning to understand. "A symbiotic relationship. Monopolies leaning against each other. By controlling the licensing, the companies determine not only who uses their jumps, but even who flies them."

"Bloody oath. And by having exclusive rights, the Union wields god-like powers . . . under the watchful eye of the ship companies."

"How does all this explain the connection between Ignatius and Breggart?"

Wallaby gazed at him the same way his teachers had when he should know the answer. Francine had hinted at this. "The ship companies are in bed with the government?"

"More like the other way around."

It was probably the same in every universe. People were people everywhere, and corporate earnings would always find ways to pull the strings of the government.

"In my universe, it's the oil companies," Will noted.

That earned him a Binny Look. "*Your* universe, eh? Well in *this* universe, the oil companies are owned by the Big Three."

Corporations might pull the strings of government, but in Will's universe, it was never this blatant. "Why do Americans put up with it? The US is still a democracy, right?"

Wallaby looked at him, and shook his head in outright disbelief. "You're the bloody American. Why are you asking me?"

"Look, I know you don't believe me, but I really don't belong to this American society."

The Australian sighed and shrugged. "Apartheid."

"You mean discrimination against blacks?"

Wallaby wrinkled his brow and shook his head. "I'm not talking about Aussie natives, I mean American Negroes."

"Right. Negroes. How does that create a tolerance for the monopolies of the rocket companies and the Pilot Union?"

The dingo grinned, as though he found it humorous that *he* was explaining this to an American. "You have to put it in context of a global society. The US and South Africa are the only nations on Earth that practice apartheid. They obviously get a lot of criticism from all sides. Criticism tends to make a bloke defensive. You like to have good reasons, or at least good examples, to point to. Apartheid relies on the premise that people naturally fall into classes of abilities. Apartheid happens to draw the lines around racial boundaries, but any class structure becomes support for your argument."

Will was beginning to see. "The Pilot Union is a class that the whole world recognizes."

Wallaby winked. "Eighty-six percent of Pilots are white American males. Twelve percent are white European males. The other two percent are a scattering of nationalities, but none Negro."

"These are the token races."

The tanned face broke into a grin. "I like that: 'token races.' "

Will didn't explain that he hadn't originated the expression. He figured that there had to be *some* advantages to swapping universes.

"What was your business at India Station?" Will asked.

"I'm a private contractor," Wallaby replied, turning his attention to the screen in front of him.

"That could be anything. You might as well tell me you're a man with two arms."

"I am indeed a man with two arms."

"Very funny. Private contractor, as in special agent for the Australian government?"

Will wasn't sure why he'd asked that. It just popped out.

Wallaby glanced at him and laughed. "Not on your life. I keep the same distance from governments as I do with Death Adders."

Will stared at him.

"A Death Adder is a killer snake, mate. It hides in the sand until you're too close to get away. No, I test suit packs."

"Suit packs?"

The dingo grinned at him. "You don't know what a suit pack is?"

"No," Will replied resignedly, tired of knowing less than a third grader. "I don't know what a suit pack is. If I guessed, I would say it might be the rocket pack on space suits."

The grin widened. "You do like that word rocket, don't you, mate?"

Will counted to ten, but only got to three. "So I gather I was correct, then?"

This would explain the man's interest in the uniboosts.

"Right as rain, mate. I test rocket packs."

He enthused this dramatically as though imitating the professional exuberance of a disk jockey.

Will took a deep breath. The man had saved his life after all. In fact . . . "Why did you save me?"

The Australian spacesuit tester watched him a long while before answering. "Let's just say that Francine and I have a mutual friend."

Wallaby was as evasive as Francine herself. "Jenkins?"

"Kirkenich's boss? I know him. I wouldn't call him a friend, though."

"Francine obviously does."

He raised one eyebrow. "We be a bit jealous?"

Will could feel himself blushing. "That's ridiculous."

"Whatever you say, mate," Wallaby agreed, turning back to his screen.

He could feel the blush still burning on his cheeks. He changed the subject. "What does *Dero* mean?"

The dingo patted the console. "Tramp—a hobo."

"How can a suit pack tester afford to own, or lease, a whole spaceship?"

"Don't get the idea that I just put on a pack and do some somersaults. I test the operation under extreme conditions and failure modes. I do what nobody else in the company is willing to do. That doesn't come cheap. Technically *Dero* belongs to one of my client companies—"

"Reaction, LTD," Will offered.

His rescuer glanced at him questioningly.

"I saw it written on the side when you came for me," he explained.

Wallaby nodded. "Also, I make some money on the side sub-leasing old *Dero* out to—"

An insistent beeping from the panel interrupted him. He picked up the microphone, and flicked the thumb switch. "Class-three supply shuttle *Anderson-Lee* here." To Will's surprised look, the dingo laid his finger over his lips.

Crackling with static, the response came. "OA hospital *Louis Pasteur*. Schedule update. Over."

"Uh, read you. Go ahead."

"Returning to Wellington. Unable to dock at India. Over."

The enduring smile faded from the Australian's face. "Copy. Elaborate."

"License suspended pending inquiry. Alleged failure to post hours. Over."

Wallaby stared at nothing a moment, then pressed the thumb button. "Roger. Sorry, cobber. Over."

"*Louis Pasteur*, clear."

Will's companion slowly placed the microphone back onto its cradle, then slammed his fist against the panel wall.

"Was that the medical ship that was supposed to pick up Francine?" Will asked.

In reply, Wallaby let fly a geyser of curses. At least Will assumed they were curses, as they were words he'd never heard before.

"I take that as a yes?" Will asked.

"I'm going to cut that steward's throat and drink his blood."

This shocked Will sufficiently that he busied himself finishing his navigation work. The knot in his stomach, though, wouldn't let him forget about Francine's plight. How would she do with splinters under her fingernails? What if they killed her after they got what they wanted?

He glanced at Wallaby, but the dingo was preoccupied with the flashlight lanyard on the belt of his suit, flicking it back and forth hypnotically. Will put aside the calculations for their return to near-Earth orbit, and began again. After five minutes, Wallaby asked him if he was done yet. He pointed towards the paper he'd set aside and said, "I'm now working out the firing we'll need at perigee to return to India Station. Unfortunately, even if we use all the rest of our propellant, we won't be back for over three and a half hours."

"Don't bother," his companion directed, pulling some packaged food bars from a compartment. "We're going home."

The dingo's smile had returned. It was as though he'd completely forgotten about Francine.

"I don't understand. We have to save her."

"Breggart will be there and gone long before we get close. Sorry, mate." The rough and tumble man winked, as though it was just a hand at poker he'd lost. "You're rather fond of this gal, aren't you?"

"Does a kangaroo shit in the bush?"

Wallaby's eyes went wide in mock surprise at his scatological reference. "You really are from another universe, aren't you?"

Chapter 14

"In assembly language," Will explained, "you don't have the option of working with floating-point numbers like in C. Everything is done in binary—hexadecimal, actually."

His host, dusty from his wrestling match with his dog Regal, and now reclined in a chaise lounge with a can of beer, nodded. The Australian seemed perfectly matched to life on his run-down ranch, nestled in the foothills of the Great Dividing Range two hundred miles west of Sydney. "Sure, mate. I remember. Hex numbers are base-16, groups of four bits."

Will blinked. He kept forgetting that the blue-jeaned cowboy had a degree in electrical engineering. Will only knew this from an off-hand comment the rat-tag spacesuit tester had made. He'd also learned that his new friend's real name was Willobee, but that his classmates had nicknamed him Wallaby due to his slender build; apparently a Wallaby was a kind of kangaroo that was too small to qualify as a bona-fide kangaroo.

"Because of this," Will went on, "you want to set up your algorithms to work with fixed-point numbers—integers, if possible . . . look, are you sure you don't want to take a break?"

His pupil was slowly positioning his hand to catch a fly that had settled on the table next to him. "Absolutely, mate," he replied, taking a quick swipe, but missing. "I'm all ears."

And Will knew the man was. No matter how distracted he seemed, the kangaroo too-small-to-be-a-kangaroo absorbed everything he heard with almost eidetic memory. It was his host's idea that Will tutor him. The rumbled man seemed content to sit and listen to anything Will could tell him that he didn't already know.

"Okay," Will continued. "Each microprocessor has a predefined bit-width. This means that your calculations are limited to maximum values unless you define double-width operations—"

Regal pounded in from the brush, interrupting him. She whined once at her master, and then sped off again.

"She's got him!" Wallaby cried, as he jumped up and ran off after his dog.

"What?" Will yelled after him.

"The Taipan!"

He started to follow, but sat back in his chair. The Taipan was the most venomous snake on Earth. Although an antivenin existed, the nearest sample was two hundred miles away in Sydney. Inland Taipans inhabited the arid central regions of the country, and Wallaby had never heard of one so far East, but he'd gotten a glimpse a couple of days ago, and had been on the lookout since.

A hundred yards away, next to a stand of Eucalyptus, Regal watched the grass alertly, glancing up at Wallaby who trotted over. She whined and yipped when excited, but she never barked. This was a product of her genes, for she was a dingo—a real dingo—a descendant of wolves who had been domesticated by early humans, but had escaped back into the wild tens of thousands of years ago. Neither a wolf nor a dog, dingoes prowled the bridge of time between man the hunter-gatherer, and man the machine-builder. Unlike wolves, these ancient dogs lived independently in small family groups, and were agile enough to climb trees.

Will understood why Australians were called dingoes.

Wallaby had raised Regal from a pup after a rancher shot its mother. Wallaby had named her after the aboriginal word for dingoes: *Warrigal.*

Watching Wallaby talk quietly to Regal as they studied their dangerous find, Will believed that he could sit in this chair on this old, homely ranch surrounded by majestic, silent peaks for the rest of his life. After the headlong rush of adventure upon arriving naked and unprepared in this universe, the solitude of the Great Dividing Range seemed like the protective arms of a mother. He was content to never see another spaceship again. Stepping outside at night to gaze at a canopy of twinkling stars was as close as he needed to come to the alien nothingness of vacuum.

If only he could forget Francine. Since leaving her to the determined grasp of CID, Wallaby had seemed to accept that she was beyond help, and had put her completely out of mind. When Will tried to talk about her, his host simply shrugged and moseyed off to take up another repair around the house. Will tried setting her aside as well, and sometimes went an hour or more before feeling the weight of having failed her.

The thought that tortured him the most was the question he kept asking himself: would she have abandoned him? He assured himself, "Yes; of course," but his heart knew otherwise.

Wallaby started back to the house, but Regal whined in protest, wanting to stay with the new wonder. "Come on, girl," he called. "We've harassed the reptile enough."

With a last reluctant gaze, the dingo dog sprang after her master.

"You're going to let it go?" Will asked incredulously when Wallaby arrived back at the porch.

"Sure," he replied easing back into his chair. "He's got a right to live, just like the rest of us."

"But you said that one bite meant certain death. Aren't you nervous about having it around?"

"Ah, a Taipan don't want to bite you. He'd rather get away if he can—not like a bloody Death Adder. Besides, we've got *him* nervous now; he won't hang around."

Just then the radiophone beeped from the kitchen, and Wallaby jumped up and ran inside. Will could hear his host talking, but the conversation faded as he took the phone into a back room. A few minutes later, he returned and flopped back down. Picking up his beer, he said, "We need to get away from all this hustle and bustle. How about we go fishing tomorrow?"

Will looked around at the scattered stands of Acacias, where the only sound was the occasional distant screech of a Cockatoo. "Okay," he replied. "You're right. This bustle is killing me."

ж ж ж

They drove more than an hour over roads that at times seemed to disappear among the scrub. The jeep bounced and bucked like a bronco, and Will thought his butt would be hamburger before Wallaby finally pulled into a small clearing, got out, and lifted the packs from the back. Will shouldered his and followed his dingo friend down a steep path into a canyon. Far below, lay the muddy Colo River.

He wondered whether they could possibly catch enough fish to justify the effort. "Why exactly didn't we use the uniboosts?" he asked grumpily as he swatted gnats away from his eyes. "We could have been here an hour ago."

"They don't belong to us."

"Who do they belong to?"

Come to think of it, he hadn't seen them since they'd arrived at the ranch.

His companion glanced back at him. "The company that made them."

"How did Francine . . . ?"

The dingo's stern look reminded him that he wasn't supposed to talk about the woman who had saved his life. More than once. Wallaby hadn't explained exactly why, just that he wanted to "let things settle awhile."

Will had half expected to be taken into custody upon arriving at Sydney spaceport, but other than a quiet side-conversation between Wallaby and the customs agent, they might as well have been tourists coming back from a long weekend jaunt.

"Are uniboosts like the jumps?" Will asked. "Do the manufacturers only lease them out?"

"There's only one company, and anybody can buy one. They cost more than a house, though, and you need a special license. Also, you're not supposed to use them within thirty miles of a populated area, at least not until they've been proven."

"I thought Australia was supposed to be this totally free country—'the last free democracy on Earth,' as I recall Fran . . . er, someone saying."

Wallaby shrugged. "There's free, and there's anarchy. Freedom doesn't necessarily include allowing any old dill the opportunity to obliterate a whole town just because he's running on only half a brain."

Will remembered the fear in the suburban mother's eyes when he'd fallen off her fence. As he had sat with Francine on the stream bank filling his suit, he'd read the model name: *Readion.*

That sounded familiar. Where else had he seen that? It came to him. He'd seen something very similar on the side of Wallaby's ship. He'd probably misread the tiny printing on the suit. "Reaction, LTD!" he cried in triumph.

His friend's surprised look confirmed his guess.

"That's the company that makes the suits, isn't it?" Will crowed.

Wallaby gave a little "so what" shrug.

"So, how many people own one? A uniboost, I mean."

"You're infatuated with the things, mate. Maybe five."

"Five! How can the company stay in business selling *five* units?"

"They're just getting off the ground, so to speak. Besides, they're subsidized."

"Subsidized by whom——?"

The Australian gave him one of those looks that meant it was time to change subjects.

They'd arrived at the river's edge, and they dropped the packs, took out the fishing gear, and pieced the rods together. Wallaby sat on a rock and cast his line into the brown water.

"This is a good spot?" Will asked. He'd expected that they'd work their way along the bank for a while.

The dingo glanced at him. "Sure, mate. Every spot's good on the old Colo."

Forty-five minutes later, with not a single bite between them, Will was thinking that he needed to take his friend to Washington and show him *real* fishing when he noticed two other men making their way along the bank towards them. Every so often one of them made a cast, but it was more like he was testing to see if his spinner actually sank than seriously trying to catch a fish. He always made just one cast, and his companion seemed to anticipate this, since he continued down the bank even before the impatient fisherman reeled in his lure.

When Will remarked on the two's odd habits, Wallaby simply nodded without comment. After awhile, as the men finally approached their stretch of bank, Wallaby suddenly put down his pole, peered around carefully, and then turned to Will. "These blokes want to talk to you," he explained seriously. "Tell them what you know—you can trust them."

Before Will had a chance to recover from this sudden turn, Wallaby trotted away and climbed the path back up the hill, obviously heading off to serve as a lookout.

Not sure what to expect, Will turned to the two approaching faux-fishermen. Peering carefully around as well, they tossed their gear to the ground and each took one of Will's elbows and escorted him away from the river and into the thick brush along the base of the canyon wall. Once they were hidden from view, they released him and one of them, balding and sporting a round little pot-gut, extended his hand, saying, "Thank you for talking with us, Mr. Peters."

Will shook the man's hand automatically, but then recovered enough to reply, "I didn't seem to have much choice. What the hell is going on here?"

"Nothing," the man said soothingly. "We just want to talk to you."

"About what? And who are you?"

"About your resume, Mr. Peters."

"Who are you?" he repeated.

"Friends of Willobee."

Hearing his friend's real name sounded odd, as though these men weren't really his host's friends at all. "Why are we hiding?"

"You are a wanted man, Mr. Peters. You must already know that."

"The government knows where I've been. We went through immigration when we arrived at Sydney."

"Not the Australian government. The United States."

"We're not in the United States. They have authority here?"

"Of course not. They have eyes, though . . . and hands."

"They have agents here?"

"Of course."

"That doesn't say much for your government, does it?"

The man held up his hands in a gesture of futility. "It's the price we pay for living in a free society."

The man was right. The relationship between freedom and security was often an inverse proportion. Freedom required taking responsibility for your own safety, something Americans in this universe had sacrificed.

"I need to know who you are before I'll talk with you," Will insisted.

The balding man glanced at his companion. "It's really better if you don't know."

He shook his head. "No dice."

The man blinked, apparently absorbing this foreign expression, then sighed. "I'm very sorry, Mr. Peters. I'm afraid you're just not in a position to negotiate."

Will's heart pounded. Had Wallaby tricked him? What if he ran for it? Neither man looked very fit; he might be able to outrun them. Stall for now. "Information gathered under torture is unreliable and useless, you know."

The man just looked at him with a blank expression. A smile slowly spread across his face, and he laughed. "You thought we were going to torture you?"

He could feel himself blushing. "Why wouldn't I?"

"I understand," he replied with a nod. "Coming from America, why indeed wouldn't you expect that?"

He didn't explain that this America wasn't his America, where they wouldn't have tortured him . . . at least not as off-handedly. "Well then, what are you sorry about?"

The incognito man shrugged. "We won't be able to help you."

"Help *me?*"

"Well, your friend."

"Wallaby?" He glanced up the hill. Had they taken the dingo into custody?

The man smiled again. "No. Miss Sewer."

"Francine! You know where she is?"

"Not yet. That's one reason why we need your help."

His mind raced, probing different paths. They could be lying, just trying to get him to talk, or they could be genuinely trying to help. "Okay. What do you want to know?"

What they wanted to know was: first, whether he was really from another universe; and second, what he knew about advanced weaponry. Although Wallaby had been interested in everything he had to say, he'd never once asked about weapons, old-fashioned or advanced. These men who had walked down a river to get to him obviously had an ear tuned to Breggart. The spying apparently went both ways.

He told them the truth, that in his universe an advanced weapon was one that could obliterate an entire city of ten million people, leaving behind a radioactive wasteland. His interrogators agreed that this was like hitting the patient over the head with a bottle of anesthesia in order to render him unconscious. In any case, nuclear weaponry was old-art for them.

In the end, the two men glanced at each other in confirmation, thanked him, and told him they'd let him get back to his fishing. He sensed that they believed him, but that they were also disappointed. Mathematicians, after all, were probably a dime-a-dozen.

Wallaby must have seen them come out of the brush, for he came trotting down the path to meet them. "Glad to see you can still walk, mate," he said to Will.

Other than a skeptical look from the balding man, the nameless investigators ignored the dingo, and without even a handshake or farewell, continued back the way they'd come, casting their way ineffectually up-river.

"Who were those guys?" Will asked, as his friend settled himself back on his rock to watch the water flow by.

"Sorry, mate. It's best you don't know."

The less I know, the less I can spill under torture. It was becoming a familiar theme.

He sighed and sat down next to the Australian. The water gurgled and rushed off impatiently towards some unknown appointment. He was glad the mysterious interviewers had not found him useful. He decided that he was happy to sit in one spot and let the world of this universe pass him by.

If only Francine were sitting here with him.

Ж Ж Ж

The next day, Will advanced his engineer student from the abstractions of binary arithmetic to the nuts and bolts of microprocessor operation. Not being an engineer himself, Will had only vague ideas about the innards of the little machines—instruction counters, ALUs, and interrupt decoders. To his host, though, it was a whole new world of knowledge, literally.

As his ably qualified student sketched out ideas about how he might build up primitive logic components to create crude processing functions, Will realized that sometimes just the knowledge that a thing is possible is all that's required to go on and invent it. Leonardo Da Vinci's brilliant envisioned machines took centuries to become reality partly because nobody thought they could really work.

Of course Will knew that in this universe it was not yet possible to build a laptop computer, not without a few decades of integrated circuit fabrication development. But perhaps there were already some applications that could benefit from the relatively simple digital controllers possible using minitube switching components that fit ten-to-a-penny: traffic light sequencers, video programming timers . . . hell, digital alarm clocks. This universe was like his own of the sixties, poised on the verge of a digital revolution. Maybe he could team up with Wallaby to create Digital Devices, Inc..

On the other hand, this world already had space travel and less famine and poverty than his own universe. What would benefit from the introduction of a new digital age? Microcomputers might enable people to walk around oblivious to the world as they babbled to each other over super-miniaturized telephones . . . with horrible quality. Did he really want to create that monster?

"Sixty-four," Wallaby said.

"Eh?" Will replied, broken from his reverie.

"If I use six bits I get only sixty-four possible instructions for my instruction sequencer. But if I add just two more bits, I get two hundred, fifty-six. That seems a lot more useful."

"Right," Will agreed, hesitantly. He couldn't shake the disturbing image of everybody in this universe suddenly handed a cell phone. "In fact, almost all of the early microprocessors were eight-bit machines for that very reason."

He watched as his student scribbled awhile on his pad, then looked up with a grin. "My sequencer could be smaller than a briefcase."

Will sighed. He could already hear the first refrains of the siren song.

"That's only the core. You still need IO—a keyboard interface, a monitor, a printer. And what about memory? To do anything useful, you'll need a few kilobytes—"

"You mean *thousands* of eight-bit words?"

Will laughed. "My laptop came with a tera-byte."

His friend studied him, as though trying to decide if he was pulling his leg. "A computer that you hold on your lap has trillions of bits of memory—*trillions?*"

He nodded, feeling proud for the engineers of his universe.

"Piss-me-blind! You must have robots, then."

"Well . . . we have machines with articulated arms that are used in factories."

"No, mate, I mean a real robot—one that walks and talks and thinks."

"Sorry," Will said. "A man-capable robot is one of those romantic ideas that sound good, but isn't really that practical."

He decided not to mention that his universe was devoid of them not for lack of trying. He remembered the movie that was playing on Francine's television. "Your world seems intrigued by them, though."

"Intrigued my arse," his friend scoffed. "Bloody infatuated is more like it. I think we first went to Mars hoping the place would be populated by them." He chuckled and shook his head. "A trillion bits of memory that you can hold on your lap."

Will nodded. "And it costs less than a month's rent."

The perpetual grin spread into a devilish smirk. "And yet you say you only went to the moon once."

"Actually, we landed six times."

Wallaby nodded in exaggerated appreciation. "Six times, eh?"

"We also went around it three times without landing," Will added.

The dingo didn't say anything.

Ж Ж Ж

That night Will woke with a start. He'd heard something, but wasn't sure what. The sound came again, a thump, followed by a groan.

Climbing out of the bed in Wallaby's spare room, he saw a light on in the kitchen. He pattered out in his underwear, but came up short when he saw that Wallaby was standing over a man in a denim work shirt sitting at the table. The man's hair was mussed, and he looked sullen. He was holding his hands behind him, as if preparing some card trick. Will's mind shifted into gear, and he realized that Wallaby had bound the man's hands. He wasn't a guest; he was a prisoner.

"What's going on?" Will asked.

Wallaby nodded towards the seated man. "Regal snagged this bushranger trying to sneak through a window."

The dog sat nearby, watching his catch closely.

"Who is he?" Will asked, feeling impolite for talking about the man as though he wasn't there.

"My friend wants to know," Wallaby addressed the bound man. "Who are you?" His tone indicated that he didn't really expect an answer. After a few seconds Wallaby looked at Will and shook his head like a mother might towards a recalcitrant child. "I'll bet dollars to dinkums he has an American accent, though." He poked the man's shoulder with a fork. "That right, Yank?"

The man looked up at his tormentor with hateful eyes.

"If he moves," Wallaby instructed, "give 'im a good kick," and disappeared into the living room.

The bound man looked up at him, and Will felt goosebumps on his arms. He'd never before been confronted by someone who wanted nothing other than to strangle him.

Wallaby returned and handed him a rifle. "If he runs, shoot him. Try for his legs, but don't worry if you kill him. Just make sure you don't hit me."

Leaving Will nervous about holding a loaded rifle, Wallaby lifted the interloper roughly out of the chair and pushed him out the door, keeping one hand locked firmly on his arm. Will followed them into the dark night and saw that Wallaby was hustling the prisoner to the shed where he had a workshop. The dingo shoved the bound man through the door and closed it, and then walked back towards the house with Will. "You go on back to sleep," he said quietly so that the prisoner wouldn't hear. "This may take a while."

"What about this?" he asked, holding up the rifle.

His friend smiled. "Set it down inside. It isn't loaded. I just want our guest to think you're waiting outside somewhere ready to shoot him."

"What are you going to do . . . ?"

Wallaby had already turned and walked back towards the shed.

Will did as directed and crawled back into bed, but couldn't sleep, wondering what the Australian rancher engineer spacesuit tester was doing to the intruder. His friend seemed so confident, as though he'd been expecting this very visit from an American operative. Will trusted Wallaby without hesitation. He'd known him barely a week, but like with Francine, he felt an intuitive connection.

On the other hand, what did he really know about the man? Sure, he knew where Wallaby grew up and went to college, but in the course of seven days, the dingo had performed a daring space rescue, orchestrated a more daring escape, arranged for a secret interview with mysterious government agents, and captured and was now interrogating a presumably experienced undercover agent. It all added up to a lot more than sitting around an isolated ranch studying spacesuit designs.

One thing he knew for sure: he was glad the no-nonsense dingo was on his side.

His thoughts froze at a sudden sound that made the hair on the back of his neck stand up. From the near distance came a pitiful scream, a howl of despair and terror that called to some ancient part of Will's brain that once lived among ferocious predators.

Absolutely. You wanted to be on the same side as Wallaby.

Chapter 15

"My mind's made up," Will declared. "I'm leaving as soon as I can make arrangements."

Wallaby's breakfasts had become a treat he anticipated each morning, but today the scrambled-egg concoction sat on his plate growing cold.

His friend sat across from him leaning on his elbows, cheeks cradled in fists, his perpetual smile demoted to that of resigned acceptance. "It was the yank's enticement last night, wasn't it?"

"Enticement? Is that what you call it? The only enticement was that you stop."

The dingo was right, of course. The screams in the night might well have been Francine's under Breggart's own efficient hands. And Breggart surely had a hand in deploying the agent.

His friend lifted his head from its cradle and reached down to scratch Regal's ear. "He would have done the same thing to you, given the chance."

"You really think he was after me?"

Wallaby simply looked at him. The dingo refused to reveal what he'd extracted from his victim, but it was clear that he had at least confirmed this. Whoever the agent was, he'd been after Will.

"Why?" Will asked.

"I imagine the yanks still think you're some kind of military expert. They want your brain."

He had to take Wallaby's word for it. He couldn't ask the prisoner, for the man was gone when he woke in the morning. Wallaby claimed that he'd turned the prisoner over to some aborigine friends for safe keeping. He wanted to believe this since he found the alternative too troubling to consider.

"You don't even know where Francine is," Wallaby added.

Will pushed his plate away. "I'll find out somehow. You don't understand. She risked her life to rescue me from Breggart and his goons. I can't just abandon her now."

"And how are you going to go about finding her?"

"If *you* can make people talk using 'enticements,' well, I can too."

Wallaby just grinned, calling his bluff.

His friend was right, of course. He knew he'd never be able to torture somebody until they screamed in agony, even if Francine's life depended on it. "I have to try," he repeated.

The dingo picked up Will's untouched plate, and dumped the contents into Regal's dish, then set about silently cleaning up the kitchen.

"Are you angry with me?" Will asked.

Wallaby glanced at him, wiped his hands on a towel, and sat down again across from him. "Angry? No. I am tempted to knock some sense into you, though." He stared at him for a few moments, then sighed. "Look, Francine isn't the innocent young woman you think."

"I know all about her."

His friend sat back, surprised. "You do?"

"She explained that she was part of a conspiracy with fellow Washingtonians. 'Academic traitors,' she called it."

"What else?"

"That's it. 'Co-conspirators,' she called them. I assume they're pushing back against the repressive government."

Wallaby's concerned frown relaxed back to his usual grin. "Good girl, there."

Will shook his head in incomprehension.

"She told you what Breggart already knew," Wallaby explained.

Will thought about this. It actually made sense. They'd been floating around in freezing water waiting to be captured by Breggart's men.

"Torture seems to be a prime driving motive in this universe," Will said. "So who is the real Francine?"

His friend studied him. "There's a group here down under that wouldn't be too upset if the yank government were to accidentally fall."

"Sympathizers," Will offered.

Wallaby nodded. "They help out Francine's group where they can. Most of America is too busy wringing their hands in fear from bogey terrorists invented by the government. PacNW isn't so easily fooled, though. "

"PacNW?"

"Pacific North-West. Washington and Oregon. Folks there like to call themselves Washegonians. Maybe it's the distance from Washington DC. Maybe it's because they're descended from the pioneers that scrabbled their way the farthest from civilization. More likely, the wet weather just keeps them ornery towards any authority."

"These Australian sympathizers . . . do you happen to know any?"

The dingo just smiled.

"How about the two men that questioned me; are they part of this?"

"Aussie politicians are no chums of Breggart's bosses. They help where they can, but they can't afford to go too far."

"Because Americans make the rockets," Will suggested.

"And license the Pilots. You've got it, mate."

His friend sat back and eyed him. "I'm afraid Francine wasn't getting you away from Breggart because she had a tender spot in her heart for you."

Will returned the stare. "You think she was just delivering potentially valuable weapon's technology? The same reason you 'rescued' me from India Station?"

The dingo held his hands out. "Sorry, mate."

"She knew I was just a mathematician."

The Aussie just shrugged.

Will studied the grain in the wooden tabletop for a few minutes. "I'm going anyway," he finally declared. "I can't just leave her to Breggart. How can you?"

The smile faded. "Whatever information they were going to get from her, they've probably already gotten," he said seriously.

Will looked up and met the man's eyes. "Is that the only reason you would have to rescue her? To keep information safe?"

"Come on, mate," Wallaby implored. "Now you're talking like a dill."

He crossed his arms. His mind was set.

Wallaby sighed. "Where do you think you'll go?"

He shrugged. "I'll start in Seattle."

His friend sat back and massaged his face with both hands, as though he could somehow rub in an acceptance of what he was about to say. He put his hands on the table and sighed. "I did manage to get some squawks out of our parrot last night."

Will watched him, waiting for more.

"Francine's not in Seattle," he finally revealed. "She's on the moon."

ж ж ж

Will sat on the porch of Wallaby's ranch house and let the quiet beauty of the Australian outback fill his mind and soul. He wanted to soak up as much as he could; it might be a very long time, if ever, before he relaxed again among the simple pleasures of his friend's country hideaway.

He was going to the moon. It was hard to grasp. He'd already been in space—twenty-two thousand miles to geosynchronous orbit—but this was the *moon*. Somehow, perhaps because this had been the final destination, the farthest frontier achieved by men of his universe, the moon seemed to be *really* leaving Earth.

His friend had tried to talk him out of it, and Will understood full well that there was only a slim chance at best of success. But now that he'd made the decision, he felt a peace that floated above the constant bed of anxiety born of dangers, known and barely imagined, that lay in a rocket rescue venture to the moon.

The *moon*.

And, he reminded himself, it wasn't a rocket, but a "ship."

Wallaby's turnaround had surprised Will. Once he'd convinced Wallaby that he wasn't going to change his mind, his friend had embraced the whole idea as though it had been his own. For a while, Will wondered if Wallaby was going along just to watch after his charge, but it dawned on him that his host would be defying every authority in Australia, including the shadowy organization that was somehow connected to Francine's group in PacNW. His "charge" knew no more about weapons technology than could be found in any encyclopedia, and was worse than useless to the Australians. If anything, they'd probably be happy if he went to the moon and never came back.

But Wallaby . . . why was he defying his superiors? Will could come up with only one answer, the obvious one: the dingo cared about him.

In any case, they were going at it together, and Will couldn't have been more pleased. They even had a plan. His friend had pulled out a massive book of detailed moon charts, and showed him where Breggart was keeping their damsel in distress. The Americans had built a large facility within Kepler Crater, purportedly for conducting dangerous nuclear drive research, but no one knew for sure, as it was strictly off-limits. Even though the moon had been established, like in his own universe, as international territory, protocol allowed national claim to man-made structures. Under "enticement," Wallaby's parrot had even squawked the entry code to the Kepler facility.

Will heard the rising and falling pitch of an engine negotiating the uneven dirt road. A billowing plume of dust was approaching just beyond the closest ridge. Wallaby must be back already. His swashbuckling partner had gone off to arrange the services of a Pilot, an acquaintance of his who would get them off Earth and up to Tahiti Station. The union member would then just happen to be occupied while they took off for the moon against protocol in *Dero*. Wallaby must have had good luck to be back already. In fact, he must be excited about the good fortune, for he was tearing along faster than his usual reckless driving.

Will watched as the battered jeep topped the rise and tore for the house. Something wasn't right. The wild, speeding vehicle cried urgency, not excitement.

All four wheels skidded to a stop. His friend jumped out and, grabbing him by the arm, pulled him inside.

"What's wrong?" Will asked, as Regal whined his own concern at his master's obvious distress.

"I'm afraid you're on your own, mate," his partner explained, reaching up into the back of the top shelf of the cupboard. "We've had a turn of events." He pulled down a manila envelope, which he tossed in the wood stove.

"What happened?"

Wallaby watched to make sure the envelope was burning. "Looks like I'm taking a fall. Our little escapade on India Station has caused quite a ruckus among the government wumps."

"They're coming for you?"

"Hot on my heels, mate."

Will steadied himself against the back of a chair. He felt dizzy. They'd had it all worked out. This time tomorrow they would have been on their way to the moon. It wasn't fair.

On the other hand . . . "This is a surprise?" he said. He turned to Wallaby. "You helped me escape from custody with half the space station on our heels."

"The surprise," his friend said, holding him by both arms and looking him in the eyes, "is that my own blokes are giving me up for roasting."

"Why?"

His friend's grin had turned sardonic. "I don't know, mate."

Will sensed he was lying, that he did know, but wasn't saying. "This is binny!" Will objected. "What kind of friends do you have?"

"It's not their fault." Wallaby let him go and called Regal over. "And don't talk like a yank. It's unbecoming."

"But it's not fair—"

His friend wasn't listening; he had squatted down and was hugging Regal, talking quietly into the dog's ear.

In the distance, Will heard the roar of another motor. It sounded big and angry.

With a last, prolonged hug, Wallaby stood up. "We've got to hide you," he said, striding off into the living room.

Will found him prying at a board in the wall next to the fireplace. Unable to get a purchase, he picked up the poker and jammed the point into the crack. With one solid yank, the board popped off and fell clattering to the floor, revealing darkness beyond. "Here you go," Wallaby said gesturing towards the opening.

"I won't fit," Will warned, stepping forward.

"You're not that chubby."

He almost was. Wallaby had to push him through, tearing his shirt in the process. Inside, he found a narrow space between the living room wall and the cement foundation, just enough room to stand. Outside, the engine stopped as Wallaby's pursuers arrived.

"You have to get out of here!" Will whispered hoarsely as Wallaby lifted the board back into place, drawing down the darkness to his Cask of Amontillado catacomb.

"No deal, mate," he heard his friend reply through the wall as he gave the board a few taps with the poker to drive the nails back home. "Like I said, I have to take the fall."

A minute later Will heard the muffled voices of several men, and Wallaby's response: he told them that he'd come back to say goodbye to Regal. One of the men's voice sounded familiar. He said he knew that Willard was here, so Wallaby might as well stop with the games. It was Breggart! The CID agent still thought that his name was Willard.

"Be my guest," Wallaby offered. "Have a look around."

And have a look around, he did. Will heard Breggart slamming doors, and tossing things aside, sounding angrier and angrier as the minutes ticked by. He finally came into the living room, but there wasn't really any place for a person to hide. Through the narrow crack, Will saw the lean face with the precise, pencil-thin mustache searching the room for a clue and, despite his enemy's slim build, Will cowered, terrified he'd be found. Through all the talk about torture, it was these merciless eyes that he'd imagined watching coolly as red-hot irons were laid sizzling against his skin and the smell of burning flesh penetrated his nostrils.

The agent suddenly walked forward, as though he'd realized exactly where Will was hiding, and he fought the urge to curl up into a ball. He saw a blur as Breggart walked by, just inches beyond the wall, and then heard him rattling something just a few feet away at the fireplace.

"What are you doing?" asked another voice, this one with a distinct Australian accent.

"It looks like there's space in here," came Breggart's voice right next to Will.

He looked over and nearly shouted in alarm as he saw an evil eye peering in through a space between the wall and the fireplace bricks.

"Oh, come on," the Australian voice said. "Enough is enough."

Will realized that the darkness of his haven was hiding him.

"I want to pull these boards away," Breggart declared. "A man could hide in here."

"You're not going to tear Mr. Willobee's house apart. It's enough that we're handing him over to you without due process."

The evil eye withdrew. "I will search this house as I see fit," the agent asserted.

"We're done here," the voice of Australian authority stated firmly. "You'll get your Willard when we catch up with him, but if you are not in the car in three minutes, you will be leaving for the US without Willobee."

"In that case," he heard Wallaby's voice say dryly, "I encourage you to tear the wall apart. The bloke may just be in there. Take your time, in fact."

Will heard Breggart snort and then storm out of the room.

"Nervous little man, isn't he?" Wallaby commented, and then Will heard footsteps receding, and minutes later the roar of an engine, which revved, rumbled away, and quickly diminished with distance.

Will waited for what seemed like at least ten minutes to make sure they didn't come back. He pushed against the board in front of his nose, and after a few grunts, it fell away and clattered to the living room floor. Regal sat there, as though patiently waiting for him to finally emerge. Will squeezed out and squatted down to rub the dingo dog's neck. "It looks like we're on our own," he said.

The wild dog just looked up at him with sad eyes. He seemed to understand that his master was not coming back, and shared Will's sense of melancholy.

First Francine, and now Wallaby. He was all alone in a universe not his own.

He stood up, walked out to the kitchen, and gasped in shock. A man sat at the table watching him. He wore a suit and tie, but Will recognized him. The man's hat sat on the table in front of him revealing his balding pate. "You!" was all Will managed to say, since he didn't know the name of the man who had interrogated him in the bushes along the Colo River.

The man nodded. "Hello again. I assumed that if I waited, you'd eventually emerge."

"You knew I was here?"

"I guessed as much."

"Are you going to . . . ?"

"Turn you over to the yanks? Not likely. I'm not out to pander to Breggart."

"What do you want, then?"

"I'm not sure myself. I didn't want to leave you here dangling, though." He stood up and extended his hand. "Jenkins," he said. "Fred Jenkins."

Will shook the man's hand, his mind churning. That name; he'd heard that name. "The station master!" he cried.

Jenkins smiled. "You know me, then."

"Francine was expecting you to be at India Station."

At the prisoner's name, the station master's eye twinkled. "Did she call me Uncle Fred?"

"Uh, no. You're her uncle?"

"Not at all. Old chums with her father. We were roommates in college." Jenkins studied him a moment. "You know, we couldn't decide what to do about you, whether to let Breggart take you."

"Who's 'we'?"

Francine's 'uncle' just smiled.

"I understand," Will said. "Everybody's part of some secret society. So, what has your covert gang decided to do with me?"

Jenkins sat back and put his hands in his pockets. "You've become something of a liability, you know. The yanks think you hold valuable knowledge, and they're doing everything they can to get their hands on you."

"But you know otherwise."

"Presumably. On one hand, it's useful to have them distracted by you, but on the other, we'd prefer that their attention . . . well, let's just say we'd prefer if they weren't looking too closely in our direction."

"Sounds like what you'd really like is for me to lead them off somewhere on a wild goose chase."

Jenkins smiled. He liked that idea.

"Is that why you're here? To tell me to get lost?"

The station master watched Will a moment and finally just shrugged.

"In that case, why don't I just carry on with my original plan without Wallaby?"

Jenkins snorted. "You mean gallop off on a chivalrous crusade to rescue Francine?"

"To put it sarcastically, yes."

"You might as well save yourself time and just give yourself up to Breggart. You wouldn't have gotten within fifty miles of the yank's facility at Kepler Crater. They'd have tracked you on radar all the way from Earth and would either intercept you, or more likely, simply shoot you down once you came close."

"Wallaby didn't think so."

"Sometimes Willobee's bravado countermands his intelligence. I'm sure he understood the futility. Most likely he had some other plan. But we'll never know."

Will wondered if Jenkins meant "never know" literally.

"I would have thought you'd have come up with some way to take advantage of the fact that the US thinks I'm valuable."

As soon as the words left Will's mouth, the idea struck him like a gong. "Trade me!" he cried.

"You mean for Francine?"

"Yes! If they want me that badly, they'd go for that."

Jenkins leaned forward, propping his chin on his thumb and curling his forefinger over his upper lip. Although the agent sat staring at him, Will had the sense that the man was far away, his mind searching one avenue of possibility after another. He finally sat back with a resigned sigh. "Won't do. Won't do at all."

"Why? I know Breggart would go for it."

"That's exactly the problem. You'd never hold out, and Breggart would learn too much."

"What could he learn? I don't *know* anything."

He tried not to think about the process that would allow them to conclude this.

"The only person I know is Wallaby, and they already have him. All I know about you is your name . . . and that Francine calls you Uncle."

"Oh, they already know who I am. That's not the problem. No, I'm afraid it just wouldn't do at all."

Will let it go. The man apparently thought that Will knew something that he didn't even know he knew. He really hated this whole spy-vs-spy stuff. He was a mathematician. Numbers could be subtle and slippery sometimes, but they never went out of their way to deceive you.

"So, what will you do?" Jenkins asked.

Will got up and paced around the kitchen. Regal came in to see what the commotion was all about, and Will knelt down and took the dog's head in his hands. "What *will* I do, old girl?" he asked, gazing into her eyes. The dog gave out a little high-pitched yelp. "Well," he said, standing up. "There's my answer. I'm going to stay right here and take care of Wallaby's best friend."

Jenkins stood up as well, pulled a business card from his wallet, and handed it to him. "Very well. Give me a call if you need help. Dial that number and tell the receptionist that you'd like to solicit Merlin for your twenty-fifth wedding anniversary party. She'll contact me."

After Jenkins left, Will looked at the card. It read:

Sydney Magic, LTD
Materials and Services for Deception and Amusement

ж ж ж

Will and Regal spent the next couple of days taking whatever solace they could from each other's company, but the retired ranch was destitute, an empty haven without their friend and master's wit and laughter.

He found a hammer in the workshop to replace the board next to the fireplace. First, though, he humored his curiosity and searched out a flashlight. Inside the narrow space he found nothing but the cement brick foundation on one side, and the wall studs on the other. A foot to the left was the chimney bricks, while three feet to the right was a plywood partition. He placed the board in its slot and hammered in the first nail, wondering why the builder had included that plywood partition.

He paused. Why *did* they build that plywood partition? He walked down along the wall. A shelf had been hung at chest level. On it, Wallaby displayed various souvenirs he'd picked up from other countries. Will tugged experimentally at the shelf, but it only rattled a bit. It was secured to the wall by three decorative wood brackets underneath. "What do you think, girl?" he asked Regal who sat watching him curiously. "Does your master have another hiding place in there?"

The dog whined, probably just wanting to know when her master was returning.

Will was tempted to take the claw of the hammer to the wall boards when he noticed a smudge of fingerprints on the middle bracket. He wouldn't have seen it if he hadn't been leaning over, studying the bottom. He checked the end brackets, but they were clean. Somebody had been handling the middle one. He gripped it and pulled, but it didn't budge. The smudge marks were high on the left side of the bracket, and low on the other, as though . . .

He placed his thumb and curled forefinger over the marks and rotated his hand, as though opening a doorknob. The bracket didn't turn, but it did give slightly—more than it would have had it been screwed to the wall behind it. He put more muscle into it, and felt the smooth resistance of hidden linkages sliding.

It *was* a doorknob.

The bracket turned, and he felt something give, as though coming free. He took the shelf between his fingers and pulled. He was expecting a door to swing open, and was taken by surprise when the shelf fell forward along with a three-foot section of the wall to which it was attached. Wallaby's souvenirs fell clattering, and Regal bounded away with a yelp. The wall section and shelf were heavy, and he let the whole piece slide sideways to the floor.

There, lying in their erstwhile secure hiding place like pup rabbits squinting up from their uncovered lair, where the miraculous devices that had set Francine and him off on their adventure seemingly so long ago. Somehow, right under Will's nose, his friend had smuggled the uniboosts to the ranch.

Chapter 16

Will saw that he was slowly sinking. He nudged the throttle up a bit. Two hundred feet below, Regal whined and yelped and ran around in circles. She was concerned for him. Or possibly afraid that he too would fly away and leave her all alone.

He hadn't been able to resist the uniboosts. Ever since their escape to *Verdad*, he'd dreamed of flying again. Their exodus from the university's jump ship hardly counted, as flight through space was the very definition of non-flying, simply an abstract manifestation of Newton's laws of motion.

Here in the Australian outback, though, with wind in his hair, and the birds swooping *below* him . . . yeah, this was flying. Was he a bird? Was he a plane? No! He was superman—

Suddenly he was spinning in a somersault like he did when trying to land next to *Verdad*. In his exuberance, he'd tipped too far backwards while looking at the billowing cumulus clouds above. Swallowing a cry of panic, he leaned against the spin and was soon stable again. He had demonstrated yet again that riding a uniboost was more like carrying a heavy load on slippery ice than flying like a bird.

Now he had a problem, though. Regal insisted on positioning herself immediately below him, maybe thinking she would catch him when he finally realized that people can't fly. And fall he would eventually when his water propellant gave out, with far more serious consequences than merely a couple of broken legs. But if he tried to land, he'd scald and maybe kill her with his hellishly hot exhaust.

He briefly considered landing on the roof of the house, but realized that he'd probably blow off all the shingles. A tree? The whipping branches would blind him or worse. In the end, he decided to simply outrun the dingo dog. He leaned forward, increased the throttle, and accelerated away from the house. Regal took off after him, and although the dog made a valiant effort, soon tired and fell behind. Once Will had a couple of hundred yards on the dog, he eased the throttle and brought the uniboost down, raising a storm of dust.

Outrunning Regal was easier than he'd thought. And he wasn't even using maximum power. He remembered calculating that, once in orbit, a uniboost could reach escape velocity with power to spare.

With power to spare.

What if . . . no, it was crazy.

But what *if*? He looked down at the metalized silver material covering his legs and waist. Wallaby had used a small sheet of tinfoil to imitate the radar image. But that was for the short-range radar used by the station control crew. It might not be visible to longer range systems.

Regal caught up to him, panting but happy that his new companion was alive and back on solid ground. "Come on, girl," Will shouted, pulling off the suit. "We've got some planning to do."

He jogged off towards the house, and the dog watched him a moment before starting the long trek back.

Ж Ж Ж

"I'd like to hire Merlin . . . it's for my twenty-fifth wedding anniversary," Will explained into the phone.

He was self-conscious playing this spy game. He half expected her to ask him who the hell Merlin was. Instead, she paused the barest moment before replying. "Very good. Do you have a number where he can reach you?"

Exhaling with relief, he gave her Wallaby's telephone number.

Ten minutes later, the phone rang. It was Jenkins, and Will explained his plan, except that as he described it, he realized that it wasn't a plan at all, just an idea, and a pretty goofy one at that judging by "Merlin's" reaction. When Will finished, the station master was silent for many heartbeats before commenting, "Well, that's certainly ambitious. I don't know what to say. It's sort of like those blokes who go over your Niagra Falls in barrels. You really think you'll have enough propellant to reach the moon?"

"I can carry some reserve."

"What about air? And what about the cold? You'll freeze to death if you don't suffocate first."

"I can take reserve air as well—oxygen. The sun will be shining on me the whole time. If anything, I'll be *too* warm."

He heard a sigh. "I have to confess that I'm torn," Jenkins said. "You'll be committing a very effective suicide, circumventing the messy bother of a dead body in the process. On the other hand, there is the tiniest chance that you might actually be able to help Francine."

"What's there to be torn about?" Will countered. "You said that I had become a liability anyway. You've only come up with good reasons for me to try it."

"There is one other that counters the idea."

"What's that?"

"I'd rather like to see you alive."

"Well, thanks for that."

"As I understand it, you are the Buck of your universe."

"Or he is the Will of this one."

"Francine cared deeply for Buck, and although the whole thing is a bit difficult to keep straight, it would seem that she must therefore care about you as well."

Will didn't know what to say, other than, "Maybe."

"So, there you have it," Jenkins concluded. "Damned if I do, and damned if I don't."

Will waited, not sure what other argument to make.

"I'm returning to the station tomorrow afternoon," Jenkins finally said. "Can you be ready by 9:00 a.m.? I'll pick you up."

Will smiled to himself. "Sure. I'll be ready."

He hung up the phone. Regal sat watching him, her eyes sad, as though she understood that even he was now going to abandon her.

"Don't worry, girl," he said, kneeling to rub her down. "I'll come back."

He sure hoped so.

ж ж ж

"Don't worry about the Pilot," Jenkins assured him. "He's totally focused on his navigation. He won't even notice that you've left the ship."

Will understood what his travel chaperone was really saying. This was the Pilot that Wallaby had arranged to take them on their aborted rescue mission. Australian-born, he knew when to avert his eyes.

"I hate these things," Will muttered, holding the limp emergency spacesuit like it was something long dead and rotting.

"You could still use Wallaby's."

They'd brought it along. His friend was in American custody or worse, so it wasn't really like stealing his horse.

"No," Will concluded reluctantly. "If I'm lucky enough to make it all the way to the moon, I won't want to be shot down the last mile. Transparency to radar is probably the only advantage of the cheap e-suits."

It was bad enough that the uniboost would reflect some of the radar transmissions; no need to add yet more.

Will had already stripped down to his underwear, and now he worked his way into the suit, once again finding it extremely difficult in free-fall as the jump ship coasted along its Hohman orbit towards India Station. Jenkins helped him, handling himself in the weightless environment as though he'd been born into it. These e-suits were a different model, boasting a detachable clear plastic faceplate. This allowed him to continue talking, and breathing, until the last minute. He already had his two five-gallon containers of extra water tied together, and he attached the line to his belt.

He climbed into the uniboost and tackled the last of his entourage of aids: the auxiliary air supply. This had been the toughest hurdle, almost scuttling the venture until he hit upon the solution, ignominious as it would appear. The problem was how to couple the spare air supply into a spacesuit designed only for one-time use. Unlike its hundred-fold more expensive, full-featured cousins, the e-suit had no port for an auxiliary air hose. What it did have, however, was an access hole in the belly used for testing the suit. The owner was supposed to periodically inflate the suit via the hole to confirm that it still held pressure. Given time, he could have made some sort of adapter to fit the hole, but as it was, he had to use the only thing he knew of that already mated exactly: other e-suits.

Jenkins helped him inflate Wallaby's supply of suits, stringing them together with light line. They had six, and when they were done, the small airlock was jammed with humpbacked inflatable dummies. It was nearly impossible to move among the jostling, mindless crowd, and by the time they'd sprayed the sealer on them all, he was exhausted.

And he still had 230,000 miles to travel to the moon.

Lastly, they pulled a flexible net around the whole platoon of dummies. This would keep them from wandering around and committing suicide if they happened to pass through the uniboost's exhaust.

"Any last words?" Jenkins asked, peering at him from around the huge bundle of inflated e-suits.

Will looked down at himself, at the haphazard pattern of white brush strokes. He was still afraid of roasting. "How about a last splash of paint?" he suggested.

The station master shook his head. "You'll freeze, my friend."

He nodded. It was time to go. He was just stalling. He positioned the faceplate, but before he sealed it, Jenkins called, "Whoops! Almost forgot this," and pulled himself back into the cargo area beyond the airlock. Seconds later, he returned with the "paddle." This was a miniature hand-held rocket used to maneuver while EVA—a space paddle. Will would need this later when his auxiliary water was gone.

"Thanks," he said, tying the lanyard to his belt. "I would have sailed on past the moon, the first person to go solo into orbit around the sun . . . dead."

Jenkins extended his hand. "Good luck, son. I'm afraid you're going to need a good bit of that."

"Thank you," he replied, shaking the station master's hand. "I'll call you when I have Francine back safe."

Jenkins smiled. "That's the spirit."

And with that, the only person who knew where he was going fought his way around the dummy-bundle and was gone.

Will positioned the faceplate and pressed the seam all around, sealing the suit. A moment later, a red light came on at the control panel on the wall, indicating that Jenkins was ready inside. Will pressed the big orange recessed button that started the pump, evacuating the air lock chamber. A few minutes later, the red light began blinking on and off. He could leave any time.

He suddenly felt a rush of panic. What the hell was he doing? Jenkins was sure he'd be dead before he ever reached the moon. Coming from somebody so competent, the belief was hard to ignore. Will had gone through all the options dozens of times. If there were another, more reasonable, way of rescuing Francine, he'd have thought of it. He punched a bright red button and the outer door slid aside revealing the brilliant disk of the Earth gliding past under the slowly rotating jump ship. Whispering a silent farewell, he pushed himself out.

Two seconds later something spun him around and he rebounded back, the two water containers jostling a wrestling match against his back. His gang of e-suit dummies was jammed in the airlock door, all trying to push through together. He planted his feet against the ship and tugged at the netting. Squeezing against each other, the dummies, now taught with pressure in the vacuum, popped out, and suddenly he was floating free, the rotating ship falling away from him and his bag of buddies. He was on his own. Again.

He stiffened the uniboost suit and moved the buddy-bag above his head, where, cursing at the inflexible suit fingers, he pulled the netting as tight as he could. He then tied the bundle to his forehead where, hopefully, he could keep his air supply out from under the searing exhaust. Next, he lashed the two water containers together, and held them to his chest. For now, they would serve as ballast. With one glance back at the jump ship, he reached down and carefully engaged the uniboost's thrust the tiniest amount. This, his shakedown cruise, would also be his maiden voyage.

The acceleration became apparent as the buddy-bag tautened, pulling back slightly against his head, and the plastic containers took on a tiny amount of weight. As an experiment, he held them out farther, shifting his center of gravity. He smiled as the universe slowly rotated, the Earth and jump ship dutifully sliding past, over the top of his head.

It might just work.

Using the containers as attitude control, he oriented himself so that the three-quarter moon was immediately above him, and then increased the thrust in increments. It took some getting used to. Each time he reached down to adjust the throttle, his center of mass changed and he veered away from his target path. And each time it became more difficult to bring his entourage back to position as the water containers became heavier and heavier.

At one point, he glanced down and saw that the jump ship was lost in the glare of Earth, and for a moment panic again clutched at his throat. Like it or not, he was committed.

He had planned to thrust continually at about one and a half gravities, but once he reached what he thought was that much, he realized that he would never be able to hold the containers in position for any length of time. He'd calculated that, with the orbital boost he'd gotten from Jenkin's ride, it would take about four hours to reach the moon: two hours of acceleration where he'd reach a maximum speed of just over 140,000 MPH, when he'd approach .03% the speed of light, and then another two hours to slow down so that he didn't impact the moon with enough force to create his own new crater. After some experimentation, he found that he could tie lines to the containers and support them from his head. This had the added benefit of counteracting, somewhat, the backward pull of the buddy-bag. Instead of tired arms, though, his neck quickly cried out in pain at the abuse. He moved the container harness to the base of his neck and settled in for the long haul.

He couldn't see directly above him, so every once in a while he had to tilt backwards to check on the moon's position. Thus, his path to the moon was an inefficient squiggly line weaving back and forth, but ultimately converging on Earth's airless partner. The Apollo astronauts of his universe had spent four days getting there, but of course, they had only the benefit of primitive chemical fuels. He, looking like a spaceborn hurdy-gurdy man with a sack of inflatable dolls slung over his shoulder, had at his disposal the nearly limitless energy of complete matter annihilation. He just hoped he had enough propellant. He had calculated it, many times. He was confident . . . at least he had been, sitting at the kitchen table of Wallaby's ranch.

He relaxed into what he was coming to associate with solo space travel: mind-numbing boredom. The moon seemed to be getting larger and the Earth smaller, but it could easily have been just his imagination. He'd wondered about hitting debris. At 140,000 MPH, a grain of sand would obliterate him, but Jenkins had scoffed. The perturbations caused by the moon's gravity would sweep away any orbiting pests. One-in-a-thousand odds, the station master had claimed. Right now, one-in-a-thousand didn't sound all that reassuring.

Time passed. It could have been five minutes or a half-hour. He'd debated whether to bring a watch along, but decided that it would just be something else dangling from the emergency suit waiting to get tangled up with something. Since he couldn't accurately gauge the uniboost's thrust and acceleration, knowing the time really didn't gain him anything.

Sitting in Wallaby's kitchen talking to Jenkins, his scheme had seemed bold, if fairly outlandish. Now, actually attempting to cross a distance equal to ten trips around the equator in an emergency suit designed for a one-time, ten-minute excursion, it was nothing if not totally, unquestionably, indubitably bizarre—indeed, binny. He would guess his turnaround point—when he'd point his feet towards the moon to begin the long fall—by holding out his hand and comparing the size of the moon to that of the Earth. He'd run through the trigonometry a dozen times, and had made two ink marks on all of the suit's thumbs: one mark for his home planet receding at thousands of miles-per-hour, and one for her satellite daughter. When the two fit precisely within their marks, he was halfway. He was flying by the rule of thumb in a most literal way.

He had all the energy he'd ever need; it was now a matter of propellant.

A dread settled in his stomach, something he'd known he would have to deal with, but dreading just the same. He was having difficulty breathing. The suit's air should last forty-five minutes. It couldn't possibly have been that long already. It occurred to him that it wasn't a lack of oxygen that was causing the problem, but heat. The sun was as intense as on any equatorial beach—more so, since there was not a scrap of air to diminish its rays.

He had prepared for this. In fact, he'd probably been a bit smug when explaining his solution to Jenkins. The remedy was simple, and in his mind, illustrative of genius. He had painted wide swaths of white paint across the front of the suit, leaving the backside its natural black. When facing directly away from the sun, like now, he would absorb the maximum amount of radiation and overheat, but if facing towards the nuclear heat source, the paint would reflect the radiation, and he should actually get cold. He could regulate his temperature by positioning himself somewhere in between.

Genius.

All he had to do now was . . . turn . . . somehow . . . around.

Shit.

He could position the water containers to move his center of gravity and change the thrust's direction in almost angle, but it was nearly impossible to use them to rotate around the uniboost's thrust axis. After several minutes of wild gyrations he managed, somehow, to impart to himself and his baggage a spin. Although not intended, this was an improvement since it distributed the sun's radiation across his whole body and reduced the overall heat load.

Except that now the universe spun around him, making him dizzy. He closed his eyes, only opening them periodically to check his navigation. The buddy-bag, now a little satellite of his own, pulled against his head in a constant centripetal force.

God, he hated flying through space.

ж ж ж

It wasn't his imagination now. Each breath was a desperate effort to fill his lungs with as much volume as possible. He was definitely running low on oxygen. He wanted to hold out as long as possible, but the consequences if he got loopy could be disastrous.

Time to sacrifice one of his buddies. He killed the throttle of the uniboost, and his spin morphed into a wild tumble, nearly emptying his stomach. He was forced to use some of his precious paddle fuel to gain stability. Loosening the net bag, he grabbed a dummy at random. He imagined it screaming silently in the vacuum at its fate, while the rest of the dummy prisoners cried final farewells to their doomed companion.

Maybe he'd waited too long after all.

All he had to do now was open the test access port on his stomach, let all the stale air blow forcefully from his suit, and attach the sacrificial buddy-dummy before he suffocated horribly.

Easy as pie.

There was another problem that had been building, though, ever since he'd left the ship. He had to pee. Despite the hours and hours of planning, he'd somehow failed to consider this. In contemplating the hurdles that had to be crossed in leaping a span of vacuum fifty times as far as Columbus' historic journey using just the push from ten gallons of water, this had not surfaced. Importance is often a matter of proximity. He knew how Alan Shepard had felt, lying in his Mercury capsule waiting to become the first American into space in a capsule with no toilet facilities. Like America's first astronaut, he didn't have much choice in the matter. Whereas Shepard relied on the super-dry oxygen in his suit to quickly evaporate the urine, however, Will decided to blow it out like some space whale spouting from its blowhole.

He relaxed and let his bladder drain. He found that the feel of warm liquid spreading outward around his waist and down his legs was embarrassing. Dread of going number one in ones pants was instilled long before memory took hold. It served as incentive, though, to get on with what nearly scared number two out of him as well.

Holding the sacrificial dummy in place, he popped the access hole in his suit. Instantly, intense pain stabbed both sides of his head, as though pencils had been jammed into both ears. Arthur C. Clarke had successfully dispelled the myths about instant exploding death from exposure to vacuum, but it still hurt like hell.

Desperately, he hugged his dummy and, aligning their stomach holes, squeezed while simultaneously twisting. He'd practiced aboard the ship, but if he failed to get this right the first time . . . well there wouldn't be a second time.

He felt the satisfying click of successful mechanical connection, and a moment later his suit once again filled with air. Fresh, oxygen-laden air. *Hot* air. He hadn't thought to protect his dummy buddies with white paint.

Something else he'd failed to think about during his hours and hours of planning.

The pain in his ears abated little by little, and he was able to admire the golden cloud that surrounded him like an army of microscopic fairies. The spray of his pee had frozen instantly as it blew from the warmth of his suit.

He almost regretted engaging the uniboost and leaving his glittering jeweled cloud behind. He wondered idly if his pee would eventually make it to the moon, perhaps passing him by as he decelerated, but then realized that the uniboost's exhaust, hotter than the surface of the sun, would quickly reduce his offering to individual atoms.

He increased the thrust and adjusted the water containers so that he was once again pointed at the moon. There was less room to maneuver his ballast, as he now had a dummy lying sideways across his belly like a Siamese twin. *Enjoy our time together*, Will silently told his brother, *because once our air goes stale, you're history.*

ж ж ж

Forty-five minutes later, a half hour before turn-around, he bid the first dummy farewell, and twisted the next one into place, trying to ignore the excruciating ear pain. The anxiety that accompanied the anticipation of expected pain at least circumvented the shock. This was the shock that came when he took the first breath of new air. It felt like it had been drawn directly from a blast furnace. How could it *get* that hot? He knew the answer: without an atmosphere to carry the heat away, the energy from the sun was effectively trapped in the black suit material. His buddies were experiencing their own local global warming, except that it was more like global roasting.

He glanced back at the buddy-bag, now depleted by two. Sure enough, the remaining four were visibly larger, their material stretched by the hot, expanded air so that they looked like they'd been eating way too much pizza.

Hold on, fellows, he thought. *Just another 135,000 miles to go.*

Chapter 17

As close as Will could tell, the Earth and moon appeared to be the same size. If so, then he was now only 50,000 miles from his destination, a little more than three-fourths. Turn-around had gone smoothly, and now he had just discarded dummy three for number four, leaving two left, embracing each other desperately inside their ever-shrinking net bag. Since he only needed one more victim, he was in fine shape. Although filling the uniboost from his water containers had been a lively and somewhat spectacular exercise, with the water bubbling madly like a boiling caldron as soon as he unscrewed the cap, only a small amount actually escaped, so he knew he had a comfortable margin there as well.

His long fall towards the moon was his only real worry. In order to conserve resources, he had accelerated right up to what he gauged was the halfway point. He knew his accuracy was only good to within five percent—maybe only ten. If he had erred too long, beginning the deceleration too far past the halfway point, then he'd end up with residual forward velocity when he reached the moon. And ten percent of 140,000 MPH was still enough to make his, albeit smaller, crater.

Uncertainty and plenty of time to imagine consequences weighed on him, so he increased the thrust. Better to be safe. If he slowed too much, well, he had plenty of air for the extra time it would take to get there.

Now that he was down to one water container, though, keeping on target was trickier with the reduced ballast since he now had to hold his arms out farther, and they were cramping with the effort.

Suddenly, one of the dummies pressed against his neck, rotating him forward so that the Earth, looking so small and far away, swung into view. Below him, he saw an expanding gray cloud falling away.

What the heck? He reduced the thrust to a whimper and pulled the buddy-bag around from behind him.

There was only one dummy left! The other was limp and deflated. He could see a tear had been blown from the side. The material had finally given way under the pressure.

He understood how the Apollo 13 astronauts must have felt when they realized their command module, their ride home, had blown all its fuel.

I only need one more, he reassured himself desperately. *I'm fine.*

But fear clutched at his heart. If one had blown, the other could follow any minute. He had to do something.

Reduce the heat load; get the temperature down in the last dummy. He had no way to release a controlled amount of air.

He pulled the dummy around into the shade provided by his own body. His lone buddy bulged at every seam, and felt as hard as a rock. The sun continued to move slowly around, though, shining once more on the dummy's black fabric. Damn it! The curse of space: he was spinning again.

And also still hurtling towards the moon a hundred times faster than a bullet. Unchecked, he'd be blasting out that small crater in about forty minutes. He increased the thrust, but keeping the last dummy in the shade while positioning the ballast water container to stay on target proved maddeningly difficult. Instead of watching the moon expand under his feet where it belonged, he continuously found his destination wandering away to one side or the other. He was then forced to reduce thrust in order to juggle things and bring it back into line. The result, of course, was that whereas he needed to apply at least as much thrust during the last half of the trip as the first, his interruptions meant that there was indeed a new, small crater waiting with his name on it.

It looked like Jenkins may have been correct after all. He was seemingly committing suicide.

As an experiment, he opened up the uniboost to full-power. He was hoping to feel the pressing weight of two, or even three, gravities, but it didn't feel like any more than the 1.5 he'd been using all along. He had already been maxing it out.

He was in trouble.

A persistent and growing pain seared his back, like the night after he'd fallen asleep on his stomach on the San Diego beach. His troubles were compounding. By keeping the last dummy in his own shade, he was exposing his own dark side to the sun. Now *he* was overheating. He should have painted his backside white instead, but that was all hindsight now.

Doing his best to ignore the sweat running into his eyes, he concentrated on keeping the moon under him. The heat became unbearable, though, and he set himself slowly spinning again. The dummy would have to share the pain.

The moon seemed alarmingly large now. Where before he'd watched with anticipation for it to get closer, he now had the urge to reach out and push it away. Under the oblique light of the sun across the three-quarter-full surface, features he'd previously only seen in pictures stood out in sharp contrast, highlighted by the shadows they cast. Off to the left side, he could clearly see Kepler Crater. Only twenty miles wide, it was rendered obvious by its spray of white ejecta which spread across the dark volcanic plains of Oceanus Procellarum to its left, and Mare Insularum to the right. Kepler's namesake seemed lonely sitting there, nearly three hundred miles from the nearest settlement, the main lunar base set up by the Orbital Authority in Coperincus Crater.

Likely enough, isolation was precisely the reason America had chosen the site. When he had asked Wallaby why Breggart would have taken Francine all the way to the moon, his friend's guess was that the remote isolation would allow undisturbed interrogation. Despite American arrogance and disregard for international sensibilities, there were, after all, clear UN-dictated guidelines for treatment of prisoners . . . on the Earth.

The crater-pocked orb grew until it seemed to fill his view, while the Earth, in comparison, seemed tiny and every bit its quarter million-mile distance. He wished to God he had some means of measuring his speed and precise location. He really wanted to know if he was going to die soon. Actually, that now seemed almost certain; more like *when* he would die.

Whatever the consequences, he realized with a terror-fueled wail building at the back of his throat that he couldn't just let himself fall to a pulverizing impact on the moon like the early Ranger probes. Holding the half-full water container out as far as he could reach, he pitched forward until the rugged gray surface spread out before his face as though he was a skydiver falling spread-eagled before pulling the ripcord—except that he was still thrusting at maximum power, accelerating now sideways.

It was a gamble against a gamble. Instead of continuing to thrust directly against the moon, hoping to stop before smacking the surface, he decided to try to miss the moon altogether. If he couldn't stop in time, maybe he could whip around.

The moon's diameter was about two thousand miles, he reasoned. That meant that he had to move a thousand miles sideways. At one-and-a-quarter gravities of thrust, it would take . . . about eight minutes. Those craters and mountains seemed to be coming at him awfully fast. Did he really have eight minutes?

All he could do was keep his uniboost aimed accurately and wait. With each breath, he wondered if he was ticking down the last ones.

And they were deep, unsatisfying breaths.

Christ, oh Christ. He was running low on oxygen. He couldn't possibly afford to switch now, though. Every second of directed thrust counted.

He tried to calm himself and conserve his air. Could a condemned prisoner calm himself while walking the last mile to the chair?

The lunar landscape began to slip by underneath him as he gained sideways velocity. But it also continued to expand, as he was no longer decelerating. Faster and faster it moved by, and larger and larger became the craters. He realized that he had one small advantage: as he moved sideways, he gained precious distance due to the moon's curvature.

This close, it now felt like he was flying over the rumpled moonscape that now flashed by almost too fast to see. *Well, silly*, he thought, *you* are *flying*. But it felt like he was a bird. A space-bird. One that flew in vacuum and used the fabric of space-time continuum, whatever the hell that was, for motive power. Grabbing his last buddy by the neck with one hand, he spread his arms wide, a space faring Boeing 787, a water container on one wingtip, a dummy—excuse me, fellow—a *buddy* on the other.

The universe spun. What the . . . ?

He shook his head and took a couple of extra deep breaths. It was happening again. His brain was sputtering along on only a couple of cylinders. He couldn't afford to wait; he had to change out his last dummy, impact or no.

With practice came adeptness. In less than a minute, he pulled off dummy number four, slapped and twisted the last one into place, belly-to-belly, and re-engaged the thrust. The new scorching hot air brought instant clarity.

He tried to ignore the shades of gray flicking past below too quickly to discern detail, but he began to catch flashes of individual distinct shapes: a circular crater here, a peak there. The uneven ground thickened until he was once again rushing headlong over familiar cratered moonscape. In his mind, he scanned Wallaby's moon charts. He guessed he'd crossed the relatively featureless expanse of Mare Tranquillitatis and was now over the rough territory to the east, nearing the visible edge as seen from Earth.

No need to hang on to expended dummy number four. He tossed it downward. If he was going to die, obliterated against a crater wall, well, the dummy would go first. He watched it fall away, down and behind as he continued to accelerate, but suddenly it disappeared. It just disappeared. One second it was there, as clear as day, and the next . . . gone.

A passing peak must have caught it. He was obviously lower than he'd feared. He tensed, even though he knew he'd never know what hit him when his turn came to be molecularly deconstructed. And then, just like that, everything went black.

Not quite everything. Behind him, beyond his feet, crisp, brilliant lines jagged through the darkness. Above the glowing white border, the achingly beautiful blue sphere of the Earth hovered; below him was utter blackness. It came to him. He'd crossed the terminator, leaving the dayside. The crisp white crinkly lines were the last visible peaks and crater walls reflecting the sun already fallen below the horizon. Dummy number four had simply fallen into the shadow first.

He was hurtling through the moon's night. Drenched with sweat, he was dehydrated and close to heat exhaustion. He might still smack into the side of a moon mountain, but for now, respite from the merciless sun was a great relief.

ж ж ж

He was freezing to death. Space was nothing but incessant rotation and extremes of temperatures. He swam in a freezing sea of his own sweat. Confined inside the suit, it didn't evaporate. He could be thankful for that, since it would have drawn even more heat away. But it was still damn uncomfortable.

He had no idea how long he'd been hurtling through the blackness. As his eyes adjusted, the stars shone forth in a splendor that no man sees within a quarter-million miles of Earth. With no atmosphere to diminish the light that had traveled hundreds of thousands of years to reach him, and no telltale reflections of the sun to dominate, the far-distant suns blazed in all their revealed glory . . . or would have if the faceplate of his suit wasn't splattered with droplets of sweat.

The ghostly light of the stars provided just enough illumination to reveal that there was *something* passing by beneath him—very fast. It was not enough, though, to gauge how high he was. He'd turned off the uniboost. If he hadn't made a spectacular explosive contact by now, he probably wasn't going to. The moon's pull would wrap him around the backside, and if he kept thrusting, he was afraid that he might accumulate too much velocity. Like a racecar speeding along too fast to make a turn, he'd be hurled out the other side and off into space again, with no propellant to get him back.

In fact, he was thinking he should probably turn around and slow down, effectively firing his retrorockets. He was too chicken, though. Not in the dark. Not without seeing what the hell he was doing.

He shivered. It was *cold!* And getting colder by the minute. It was hard to imagine that less than an hour ago he'd nearly died from heat.

Space. Bah!

Something caught his eye, something had flashed ahead of him.

Praise the Lord! It was the sun, the glorious warm sun, shining on peaks ahead. He was going to live after all. For a while, anyway.

As the daylight terminator became clearer, he could tell that he was indeed going too fast. He was gaining altitude, leaving the moon on a parabolic orbit that would take him . . . off into the solar system somewhere.

He turned on the uniboost. Nothing. He should have felt the pull of acceleration. *Damn, oh damn!* He could guess what happened. The water in the uniboost tank had frozen solid. Something jerked him. He jerked again, and then felt the wonderful push of solid thrust. The annihilating positrons were thawing the ice.

Happy to be alive, he was nevertheless totally drained, first from heat exhaustion, then from hypothermia. He considered heading straight for the UN base at Copernicus Crater. He would find water, and warmth, and fresh air, and food, and a place to lay down and sleep, and maybe even a smile from a friendly stranger. He had earned this. He had probably made some sort of solo flight record. He might even be welcomed as a hero, a celebrity.

But he knew he couldn't. He hadn't set out to gain popular success. He'd risked his life to save someone else's.

Suddenly he was blinded by nuclear light, and he flinched and shut his eyes until the faceplate window automatically adjusted and darkened. God bless Wallaby for not buying the cheapie e-suits.

He had studied his friend's moon charts until he saw the terrain in his dreams, but he didn't recognize anything below him. He realized that he hadn't yet come around to the side visible from Earth, the area he'd memorized.

Suddenly he was over the smooth surface of solidified lava. Far off in the distance, north and south, he saw the edges of this vast ancient magma flow. He might be over Grimaldi, a three-hundred mile wide area that the early astronomers couldn't decide was a crater or a mare. Minutes later, he left the flat plain and was again over cratered badlands, but soon he burst onto another lava plain, this one seemingly endless—Oceanus Procellarum. He was confident now. Kepler Crater was less than four hundred miles to the northeast.

He no longer had his water container. He had used the last of the propellant soon after passing into the night side, and tossed the empty container to the darkness. Bereft of his ballast, he used the paddle now to turn forty-five degrees. As he arced north, he continued to slow down and lose altitude. When he guessed that he was only a mile high, he angled the thrust a bit downward to maintain his altitude. Soon, he rotated himself completely upright and reduced the throttle. The uniboost now just balanced the moon's gravity, and he continued north and east on momentum.

Ahead, he saw the distinct line of a crater wall. It looked to be about the right size. As he came closer, though, he saw that it was too shallow to be Kepler. Feverishly he replayed the charts in his mind. Encke! It had to be Crater Encke. Kepler would be sixty miles north and a bit west. He turned and gained some altitude, anxious to see his destination. There, just rising over the confusingly close horizon of the moon, it appeared: the nearly perfect circle of steep crater walls.

Crater Kepler.

He'd made it. Against all odds, against every expectation, he'd made it . . . assuming his propellant held out.

He let himself sink until he was barely a hundred feet above the dust and gravelly rubble. No sense giving them a chance at catching him on their radar. Then he leaned over hard, and brought the thrust to max. Thirty seconds later, he guessed he was about halfway, and used the paddle to lean backwards, slowing down like a baseball runner sliding into home plate.

As the mile-high wall of the crater rose above the horizon, he began to suspect that he might have done it again. In his eagerness, he may have accelerated too long. The ground rose slowly as he neared, and the crater wall morphed into a giant, sloping wall. It was obvious that he had indeed overshot the mark, and he gained altitude to clear the rim. Up he floated, the crater wall rising quickly now beneath him. With barely fifty feet to spare, he glided over the rim, and the crater spread out below him. In his mind he'd imagined a deep bowl, with perhaps a single sharp spire at the center. Instead, the interior of the young crater was a vast twenty mile-wide plane of jumbled rocks, boulders, gravel, and dust. Indeed, the far wall was barely visible above the close horizon.

Although not a majestic spire, there were still the remnants of a central peak, looking like someone had dumped a huge pile of excess cement to dry ten miles away across the plain. He knew from Jenkins that the American base lay there. The yanks believed that the crater provided protection from spying and clandestine approach. And Will could see the logic; any vehicle would have to clear the crater wall, and would be obviously visible by both radar and sight.

Unless you happened to arrive without a vehicle.

He sank back to the crater floor, and let his momentum carry him forward. With no atmospheric drag, he could continue forever. His breathing was becoming strained, though, and having no reserve dummies left, he leaned forward and picked up the pace. Again he underestimated his speed, and had to lift when he arrived at the central peak. He came to a stop near the very top, and looked around. Jenkins had explained that the American's base was mostly underground, insulated from the temperature extremes, but he still expected *some* kind of structures.

Yes! There, just visible on the crater floor below the tumbled moon basalt of the peak, he saw a small farm of dish antennas, and beyond, almost invisible, gray metal against gray moon dirt, two squat ships sat daintily on their tail fins.

The uniboost faltered, and he jerked like a puppet whose master has sneezed.

Bad news; his propellant was almost dry. Time to get down, fast.

He moved a quarter mile to the edge of the moon rubble comprising the peak, and the base opened below him, storage tanks and open-frame ground vehicles . . . with mounted guns. There were no people, though, and that was a relief. But he also didn't see a door that might lead down into the underground facility.

He was breathing very deeply now, that desperate search for stray unused oxygen with which he was becoming all too familiar. What if he couldn't *find* the door?

He glided over the edge, and let himself sink, peering around for something that looked like an entrance. Seventy feet from the surface, the uniboost gave one last gasp, and he was suddenly weightless. He fell face downward and watched the ground, crisscrossed with a myriad of footprints, come at him. In the reduced gravity of the moon, a seventy-foot fall was like only twelve feet on Earth. But a belly-flop on hard ground from twelve feet was a serious fall.

The twenty-eight seconds it took to fall seemed like forever, long enough that he thought he should be doing something. But there was nothing to do except close his eyes and hope for the best. Just when he'd decided that some miracle had spared him, he struck the moon at seventy miles-per-hour.

The shock rattled his brain, and the universe spun, and he was looking at the American's moon base spinning around him, followed closely by the blue ball of the Earth. The second time down, he fell on his back, knocking the air from his lungs, and this time he stayed there, gasping stale air, and slowly realizing what had happened. He'd forgotten about the last Siamese dummy attached at his stomach. Like a heroic soldier, his last buddy had taken the fall.

The Spread-Eagle had landed.

He lifted his head. He lay next to a sheer wall, and embedded in it was a door.

He had fallen onto the Americans' doorstep.

Standing up slowly and painfully, he checked his brave buddy, and although smeared with moon dirt, the dummy seemed intact.

He wheezed long, unsatisfying lung-fulls. Not much time left. He had the entrance code, but passage through the door would almost certainly be monitored from within. The plan that he and Jenkins had worked out called for him to break a communication cable so that his clandestine entrance would be mistaken as personnel exiting or reentering in the course of repairs.

No time for that now, though. He needed air. Any minute now he might go loopy, and God only knew what would follow.

He unstiffened the uniboost, walked to the door, and found the keypad. The numbers were blurry. His faceplate was still smeared with dried sweat, but the blur came and went in waves.

He was losing it—loopy time had arrived. Peering closely, he carefully punched the five-digit code. A second later, the door slid soundlessly aside, revealing a well-lit room the size of a bathroom. He stepped inside the airlock. What now? A closed inner door waited invitingly before him, but the outer door remained open to the vast vacuum beyond.

"Close, sesa-me!" he called into the stale stink of his e-suit.

Uh-oh. The tiny rational part of his brain groaned.

He noticed a large, green button next to the outer door. If he pushed it, the outer door might close.

On the other hand, maybe it was a booby-trap. Maybe it would blow up the whole facility. "Hah!" he yelled. "Do you take me for a fool?"

Push the button, the rational part urged, growing weaker by the second. *Go ahead. It will be okay.*

"Okay," he replied. He reached out and punched it with his knuckles, then cringed, waiting for the mighty explosion. Instead, the door slid shut, and a yellow light above the inner door started to blink. It blinked on and off, on and off, on and off, mocking him like his brother poking at him when they rode in the backseat of the family car. If he protested, his brother only cackled with glee, having won the contest. He could take it. He wouldn't give his brother the satisfaction. Blink away, you jerk. But the resentment built. If he gave his brother a good punch, well, then he'd stop. But then his father would also get mad. Suddenly the inner door slid open to reveal his whole family standing there watching him. "Hi," he said, raising his hand in greeting. "What are you doing here?" His words sounded muffled, as though somebody was holding a pillow over his face.

Open up your faceplate, the rational part whispered. *It will be good.*

Family members were talking, but he couldn't make out the words. Why were they mumbling?

Open up your faceplate!

Faceplate? He put his hand to his face, and sure enough, something was there.

He remembered. It was an e-suit. It was an emergency if you had to wear one. A real, horrible emergency. Time to get out of it.

Using his fingers, he popped the seal, and the clear plastic window peeled away and flopped to the side. Air washed over his face—air so clean and brisk, it felt like a clear winter morning when the sun shone, glinting off frost-encased blades of grass.

With each delicious inhalation, the muddled mind-fog cleared. He was standing at the threshold of the American moon station airlock, and five US crewmembers stood in front of him, staring.

Blaine C. Readler

They were making faces, as though he'd just handed them a rotting rat carcass.

The youngest of them finally spoke. "It smells like . . . urine!"

Chapter 18

This wasn't in the plan; he was supposed to sneak in undetected.

"Where did you come from?" a lieutenant, the apparent leader, asked.

"I came from Earth," Will replied. He had the urge to follow with: *I come in peace; take me to your leader.*

"No, I mean where did you come from before arriving here, at this facility?" the lieutenant reiterated.

He shrugged. "Earth."

All five just stared at him.

Will turned so that they could see the uniboost.

"You are trying to tell me," the officer challenged, "that you came all the way from Earth on a . . . a . . . ?"

"On a uniboost. Yes."

They just stared.

"It wasn't easy."

Still they stared.

"I wouldn't do it again."

After a few more seconds of incredulous stares, the officer pointed and asked, "What's that?"

He looked down and saw that the man was pointing at dummy number four, the last brave platoon member bobbing sideways across his stomach. "My air supply."

The officer blinked. "You're Willard, I presume."

"My name is actually Will . . . but how did you know?"

"We've been watching for you on arriving ships."

Jenkins had explained that the moon was like a small town; it was easy to find out who came and left.

"If you didn't know I had arrived, why were you waiting here at the airlock for me?"

In answer, the officer waved him forward. Will had to turn sideways to get dummy four through the airlock door. The lieutenant then pointed into a side room off the hall. Inside, Will saw a monitor station with screens that were obviously radar displays, and others that showed video camera feeds. Most were internal scenes, but a few were of the moonscape outside. An operator was working at one terminal, studying a loop that he played over and over. It showed the stark gray-on-gray moon dust immediately in front of the outer door. Suddenly, two dark figures attached at the belly fell downward across the screen, and then a couple of seconds later they bounced, spinning, back into view, one now flailing wildly.

"That's enough, Cybulski," the officer told the operator. "We've found the intruder."

The man looked up from his station at Will, and his eyes went wide, the bottle of water he was drinking remaining suspended before his open mouth.

Will turned to the officer. "How did you know to watch for me on arriving ships in the first place?"

The man studied him a moment before answering. "We'll ask the questions, if you don't mind."

"Breggart," Will muttered. One of the lieutenant's eyebrows lifted a hair, and Will knew he'd hit pay dirt. "It was a trap all along! The bastard was counting on Wallaby to catch . . ."

He stopped himself; no sense giving anything away yet.

A voice came from behind him—a familiar and despised voice. "You were going to say that the 'bastard' was counting on Willobee to capture that operative?"

Will spun around, hampered by the flopping dummy four. It was indeed the CID agent, attached to the throat he'd wanted to squeeze between his fingers ever since meeting him in his Uncle's basement. Although dressed like the other men in a drab jumpsuit, his gelled hair and Rhett Butler mustache set him off from the crewcuts and clean-shaven faces.

"No," Breggart continued, walking forward and scanning Will up and down as though sizing him up for auction sale. "The operative was indeed supposed to kill you. Leading you here to me was just a fallback plan. One that worked admirably well, however, thanks to your . . . rather bumbling ingenuity."

Will stared at his enemy in horror. "You sent him to *kill* me?"

Breggart gave a dismissive shrug. "We couldn't afford to let somebody else have exclusive access to you."

Will glanced at the lieutenant, who watched him stone-faced, then back at Breggart. "You've captured my brain, but there's a price for my cooperation."

"I think I've paid quite enough already. How do I know you even have anything worthwhile to offer?"

He was afraid this might happen, that Breggart would call his bluff. "Phasers," he blurted.

Surely they hadn't independently developed the same television shows in this universe. He wished he'd given this more thought beforehand.

Breggart eyed him curiously. "What is a phaser?"

Will waved his hand nonchalantly, as though everybody in his universe carried one. "A hand weapon. It uses an energy beam."

"An energy beam," Breggart repeated, sounding both sarcastic and curious at the same time.

"Right. It's powered by dilithium crystals."

At least, that's what he thought Scotty always called them.

"Dilithium crystals? I never heard of that. Caruthers!" he called to one of the men. "You're a chemist. What is a dilithium crystal?"

One of the men stepped forward. "Uh, lithium is the lightest metal. The word dilithium refers to a molecule composed of two lithium atoms, but lithium by itself isn't stable—it wants to combine with oxygen to form lithium oxide. In the lab, we have to store it in oil or it rusts."

"So, there's no such thing as a dilithium crystal?"

"Not that I know of."

Breggart turned back to Will. "Well?"

Will snorted. "If it was that obvious, you would have already discovered it."

"How does one go about making, or finding such a thing?"

Will returned the stare. The piercing eyes seemed to bore into his head. "I told you," he parried, "there's a price."

The CID agent examined his fingernails. "I'm waiting," he said after a few moments without looking up.

"I want to see Francine."

He suddenly realized that if this had all been set up as just a trap, then she probably wasn't even here. Breggart stared at him a moment, and then a smile spread across his face. "Why not?" he agreed. He turned, and walked down the hallway.

The officer nodded at Will to follow, and then fell in behind along with two other men.

Will was surprised at the size of the base, considering that it had been carved out of moon rock. After three turns, Breggart stopped, opened a door, and gestured for him to go in, smiling like he was showing off his renovated den. The room was small and bare with just one chair. In the chair, Francine was slumped, head down, apparently unconscious. A man with slicked hair, obviously one of Breggart's deputies, stood next to her. He looked at Will with alarm and suspicion.

"It's okay," Breggart assured the man. "Willard has joined us as another guest."

Will knelt down next to her. "Francine," he said, softly. She didn't move. He placed his hand gently on her shoulder, and then terrified at what he'd discover, he placed his palm against her neck. It was warm, and he knew she was alive.

At his touch she stirred, and then moaned. He knelt down farther so that he could look up into her face and saw that she was barely recognizable. Her eyes were swollen nearly shut, and her lips were cut in multiple places. Dried blood covered the rest of her face.

He jumped up, swaying to steady himself in the unfamiliar moon gravity. "You son-of-a-bitch!" he yelled at the man standing guard, who met his gaze impassively. He wanted to punch the bastard, to hurt him as badly as he had hurt Francine. But he'd never punched anybody in his life, and his arms didn't know how to do it on their own. Instead, he pushed the man, or at least tried to, but the man grabbed both his wrists as though he'd been standing there waiting for that exact moment. The grip was strong and hurt.

Instead of struggling to get free, Will pulled himself close, within an inch of the man's nose. "I'm going to kill you," he said softly, seriously, earnestly.

"Perhaps," the man replied. His breath reeked of garlic. The barest hint of a smile formed. "That remains to be seen," he added, pushing Will away so that he had to double-step to keep from falling down. "What is certain, is that you will feel a great deal of pain first." He nodded at Francine, his best, proud example.

She'd finally woken and lifted her battered head. Will wanted to cry in pity for her.

Don't let him them get to you, he warned himself. He turned to Breggart. He was lucky that they'd forgotten to search him. "Time for reckoning, you bastard," he declared, reaching around to open a small pouch he'd been carrying around his waist.

Francine's torturer stepped forward to intervene, but Breggart held up his hand. He looked amused as he took his gun out and aimed it at Will.

The little doodad Will took from the pouch was his ace in the hole, his plan B if he wasn't able to sneak Francine away. The compact device was a secret weapon that Jenkins had anguished over giving him, and had made him promise to destroy rather than allowing it to get into Breggart's hands. He pointed the device at Breggart and pressed the thumb button. The handle shifted under his grasp, as though not a solid piece.

"My reckoning is administered with a video camera?" the CID agent taunted, grinning.

"Not just any camera," Will proclaimed, feeling a surge of confidence. "The whole world is now watching."

"Really?" Breggart replied, feigning incredulous surprise. "And how would that work?"

Will swung the camera to capture the torture victim, now looking at Will with growing comprehension and amazement. "This little baby is breaking into your com feed to Earth," he crowed, turning it back towards Breggart. "A receiver in Earth orbit is intercepting and relaying that signal as a live global feed. Say hello to Earth, Mr. American CID agent Hank Breggart."

In his excitement, he'd made up the part about the live feed to all of Earth. Actually, what Jenkins had really said was that they continuously monitor and record America's Earth link, and that they could use the footage later as political leverage.

The dapper man sighted his gun at Will's head, smiling with open amusement. "All of Earth, you say? My, I should make sure my hair is combed."

Even Breggart's smug arrogance couldn't be this bold. Will felt a sinking sensation in his stomach.

He heard footsteps, and the roly-poly form of Ignatius appeared next to Breggart. Will moved the camera on his other nemesis. "Smile," he said, trying to maintain his bravado. "You're on Candid Camera."

The Pilot Steward glanced nervously from Will to Breggart. "What's going on?"

"Say hello to Earth, fatso," Will said.

Ignatius stepped back and put his hand up to shield his face. "Is it true?" he whispered to Breggart.

"Don't be a fool," his cohort replied, nodding at the camera.

Will glanced down at the small device as well. There, hanging from an open crack, were pieces of circuitry. It must have been under him when he'd made his crash landing; it probably took the blow and spared the uniboost from blowing. He pushed the thumb button a few times. A light that was supposed to indicate operation remained dark, an unseeing eye of the dead and departed. It looked like Jenkins wouldn't have to worry about Breggart getting his hands on it.

He looked up at a sneering Breggart and a relieved Ignatius. "Okay," Will admitted. "You win. I'll make you a deal: I'll agree to tell you everything I know about my universe, if you'll let Francine go. There's a New Zealand geological survey team five miles east of the crater wall. They'll take her."

Breggart nodded. "We've had our eye on them. That's how you were going to escape?"

Will stared at him. The answer was obvious, but he still hated to admit all the details of his plan.

"Of course it was," the CID agent answered for him. "A very generous offer, but I'm afraid I'm going to have to decline. I think I'll have my cake and eat it too. In fact, now I have two pieces of cake to eat."

"Do you really think you can get useful information out of me by torture?"

"From my experience? Yes. Why did you think I let you see your colleague . . . or, should I say girlfriend? First we will have some fun with you, because we can. Then we'll really get down to business on Miss Sewer. You risked your life to try to save her. It was inept, but that's beside the point. I don't think you'll let us actually kill her."

The bottom dropped completely out of Will's stomach. He'd lost indeed. Even if he spilled everything he knew, they would think he was just holding out.

"Look, I promise," he pleaded. "Let her go, and I'll tell you everything."

More than everything, he thought. *I'll make things up.*

Breggart tsk-tsked. "Begging is unsightly . . . even on someone as pedestrian as you."

Anger boiled Will's blood. He now understood how any animal, even a rabbit, would fight back when there was no alternative. And he had no alternative. It was fight or watch Francine die.

But fight with what? His bare hands? Breggart had a gun, and the goon behind him had already demonstrated his physical prowess.

He needed a weapon that was bigger than both a gun and three men. He needed a bomb. A bomb. He *had* a bomb! A really *big* bomb!

He just had to figure out how to detonate it . . .

He looked around at his uniboost pack, then at his foes. "In my universe," he said, stepping to the side so that he could address all three at once, "I belong to a religion."

Ignatius and the goon looked at him like he was short on oxygen, but Breggart, who knew his origin, watched him warily.

"We believe that there is no greater service to God than to die doing His will. Sending Satan's puppets—that's you, by the way—off to hell ensures my place in heaven."

Before they could react, he flipped the throttle on full and then reached around and grabbed a lever on the side. "I pull this," he said, looking Breggart in the eye, "and the uniboost blows."

The CID agent searched his face, but Will held his gaze. "You're bluffing," Breggart declared, "you wouldn't kill your girlfriend."

Will smiled, and then laughed. The cackle sounded demented even to him. "Hah! Who's pedestrian now? You idiot; that's exactly how I can guarantee we'll spend eternity together!"

He glanced at Francine. She seemed alert now. Through her swollen eyelids she watched him intently.

"He's bluffing!" Ignatius cried. "He can't force a uniboost to explode."

"He's right!" Will cried, putting his best dementia into it. "Come and find out for yourselves!"

"Do it, my love!" It was Francine. "Do it now, before they stop you! This is our only chance to be together!"

Good girl! He struggled to keep from smiling.

"Have you ever seen a uniboost up close?" Breggart asked. He was looking at Will but speaking to Ignatius. He seemed nervous.

The steward sputtered. "It just doesn't make sense that the designers would build in—"

"Do it!" Francine bellowed. "*Now!*"

"WAIT!" Breggart cried.

The room was silent.

The agent took a deep breath. "Okay. We'll take Miss Sewer to the New Zealand crew."

Before he could agree, Francine said, "What about Will?"

Breggart shook his head. "He stays."

Francine sat up straight. "Do it, my love. It's better than being parted again. I'm ready."

He smiled at her and nodded slowly.

"OKAY!" Breggart shouted. "Judas!" he added, pushing the fingers of both hands through his hair. Ignatius watched sullenly. He wasn't buying it.

He had to act quickly before Breggart changed his mind. "You, Mr. Thug," he said to the goon. "Help her. Breggart, Ignatius— you two go first. To the airlock."

Mr. Thug looked to Breggart for confirmation before helping Francine to her feet. She was so weak that her torturer had to practically carry her. It seemed to take forever just to get her into the hallway. When Will stepped out behind them, he saw that Breggart was talking on a phone attached to the wall. "Hey!" he shouted. "Put it down!"

Breggart held it a moment, then hung it up. "I was arranging suits," he said calmly. The drip of sarcasm was gone. He was a man trying to handle someone insane . . . and in love.

As they made their way slowly down the labyrinth of halls, he noticed that Ignatius had disappeared. Well, good riddance.

A crowd of curious base personnel waited at the airlock.

"Get rid of them," Will told Breggart.

The CID agent called to them to leave, but the base officer wanted to know what in Satan's name was going on.

"He's threatening to blow his uniboost," Breggart explained.

"And I'm just looking for some reason to do it," Will added. "You've got twenty seconds to get everybody out of here."

The officer, faced with a man who claimed to have come all the way from Earth with an inflated e-suit stuck to his belly, didn't need convincing that he was also capable of blowing himself and the entire moon base to smithereens. Eighteen seconds later, the airlock area was clear.

Breggart had apparently been telling the truth: two very nice spacesuits, one small, one large, hung next to the airlock door waiting for them. He would finally get to try the real thing on for size . . . except that he decided not to. He would have to take off the uniboost, and that was just too risky. He was lucky he hadn't removed dummy number four, as he'd need the air. He looked down at his faithful companion bobbing gently on his stomach and sighed.

Will stood to the side as Breggart and Mr. Thug helped the woozy Francine into her suit. The process went quickly despite the obvious pain it caused her. At one point, Mr. Thug looked questioningly to Breggart, but the agent shook his head quickly. Once they were done, Breggart opened the airlock door and grudgingly motioned them through.

Will didn't like that silent little exchange between the CID men. Something was up. "Nice try," he said, bluffing that he knew.

Breggart just stared at him.

"I'm going to count to three: one . . . two . . ."

His foe made a disgusted face and gestured to Mr. Thug, who took a canister off a rack and slipped it into the back of Francine's suit.

They had intended to send her out without oxygen. By the time he would have realized what had happened, they'd have been outside where the outer door might have weathered the uniboost explosion. He looked at the smug agent and very much wanted to practice teaching his fists to punch, but decided to just get the hell out of there.

As he helped Francine into the airlock, though, he looked at Breggart and spat, "Eat my shit."

The agent's eyes went wide for a moment at the unaccustomed language, but quickly regained their cold control. In fact, the supercilious smirk had returned.

At the last moment Will realized that he had come very close to eating his own shit. He remembered that the uniboost was empty of propellant. He hurried over to the monitor room and took the water bottle from the operator. "Thanks," he said, then hurried back to the airlock. Breggart watched him the whole way.

The inner door closed behind them, and a blinking yellow light indicated a button that wanted to be pushed, so he pushed it. Immediately, he heard an air pump motor kick in.

He reached over and grasped the Death Lever he'd been threatening to pull, and pulled it. The propellant fill tube fell out, and he stuck it into the bottle and pumped. He hoped it was enough to get them over the crater wall, and five miles to the waiting New Zealand field team.

That supercilious smirk. That damnable smirk. He just knew it meant something.

He realized he was having difficulty breathing. *Shit!* He'd forgotten to close his face plate, and Breggart knew it. He quickly pressed it into place, closing the seal. *Great!* he thought. He was starting off already low on air, and he couldn't afford to recycle the lock. They had probably watched him pull his Death Lever on a monitor camera and knew he'd been bluffing. He had to get the two of them away as fast as possible.

In fact, he was half expecting that Breggart would somehow abort the lock cycle from within, but either he didn't have the means, or wasn't quick enough, for with an eerie silence, the outer door slid open. Framed in the hatchway, he once again saw the blue globe of the Earth hovering above the stark, airless horizon: home, a quarter of a million miles away.

He helped Francine out onto the bleak moonscape. Through her faceplate, he saw her swollen eyes watching him with what he thought was fondness, but could have been just as likely fatigue. He wrapped one arm around her, pressing her against dummy four, and engaged the throttle with the other hand. Inches from his face, she squeezed out a painful wink. They lifted from the ground, throwing a cloud of moon dust into the non-air, and something solid and shockingly painful slammed into his thigh. In confusion, he lost his grip on his damsel as she was yanked away.

The uniboost carried him up, and when he looked down, there was Ignatius, struggling to contain a thrashing Francine. The bastard must have come out through a different entrance. The loathsome Pilot Steward looked up and his blubbery lips smiled as he lifted his gun and fired off another shot. This one slammed into his foot, sending him spinning. The uniboost suit was tough and stopped the bullets, but eventually Ignatius would land a shot in his unprotected chest or head. He had no choice but to rocket away, leaving Francine in the defiling grasp of the man he now hated most in this universe.

Up, away, and over Kepler's crater wall he soared, as tears of rage and frustration streamed down his face. Minutes later, laboring for air in his already depleted emergency space suit, he located the New Zealand team's moon-rover, and shortly afterward found himself sitting among the scientists as they watched in surprise, alarm, and sympathy. He ripped open the seal of his faceplate and let loose with a stream of every curse he knew as he wiped the tears away with an offered handkerchief.

After a while, he settled down, and someone handed him a steaming cup of coffee. As he took it, his host remarked, "They said you were American."

"I am," he replied, smothering a sob.

The man blinked and said, "You sound like an Aussie."

All the other men nodded in agreement.

Chapter 19

Not knowing what else to do with Will, the Australian government sent a clerk to drop him off at Wallaby's ranch. Although Regal was beside herself to see him again, Will wished her master had been there as well to hand him a cold beer. He'd been gone less than two days, and that long only because it took a whole day for Jenkins to arrange a special shuttle to come fetch him from the moon, as they didn't want the Americans Shanghaiing him on a regular commercial jump.

Considering that the Aussies viewed him as a liability, he knew he should be grateful. He should be happy just to be alive. Jenkins even hinted that once things settled down, he might become something of a celebrity for his solo moon flight. When Will had asked what "things" needed to settle down, the station master had reminded him that the Americans would have to verify his arrival to validate the stunt, and then he quickly changed the subject.

But Will wasn't happy, alive or not. Burned in his mind, like the after-image glance at the sun, was the picture of Francine's brutally battered face gazing at him with the gratitude of the condemned snatched from the guillotine. And he'd let her down; he'd let her go. A thousand times he'd asked himself why he hadn't held on to her more tightly, or even braved Ignatius' bullets to get her back.

The third day alone in the empty house with Regal he made up his mind and dialed Sydney Magic, LTD and asked for Merlin. When Jenkins called him back, Will told him that he was going to contact Breggart to arrange an exchange. As a courtesy for all his help, Will wanted to give the station master a heads-up . . . and, by the way, could he borrow some money? Prepared for an argument,

Will was surprised when, after a few moments of silence, Jenkins told him to sit tight, that he'd be back in touch within the hour.

Two and half very long hours later, the phone rang, and Jenkin's told him simply to stay put, that he'd be there in six hours. He was coming down from India Station.

Dusk was falling when, five hours and thirty-six minutes later, Will heard the distant throbbing rumble of a helicopter. Regal sprinted back and forth, excited at the unusual visitor, but then cowered behind Will as the downdraft of the landing chopper threw blasts of dust past them. The landing skids had barely touched the ground when Jenkins emerged, and hanging on to his hat, ran for the house.

"You need change for the fare?" Will called above the subsiding roar.

Jenkins simply smiled and gestured for them to go into the house.

Will put on water for tea, and asked if the copter pilot would be joining them.

"I'm only going to be a few minutes," Jenkins replied.

"You came twenty-three thousand miles and commandeered a helicopter for a few minutes of talk and a cup of tea?"

His guest shook his head. "I was coming earthside anyway. I have other business that's come up. I wanted some private words with you."

A radio link from synchronous orbit was essentially a broadcast to anyone on Earth who cared to listen. Without advanced digital technology, Will realized, sophisticated encryption was hardly an option.

"Why the secrecy?"

"We're going to help you do the exchange, but there's more to it than simply getting Francine back."

Will took his time pouring the hot water. There was always some catch. "Getting her back is not enough?"

"I know this seems cold and calculated, but believe me, Francine would understand. In fact, she would have chastised me for taking so long to decide."

"Decide what?"

Jenkins studied him, as though weighing how much to tell him. "I need you to keep Breggart occupied during the exchange."

"Why?"

Jenkins shook his head. "I'm sorry. I can't talk about it."

"I should have guessed. They can't torture out of me what I don't know. It's becoming my mantra. What do you mean by 'occupied,' and for how long?"

"Breggart carries a sky-phone—"

"A spy phone?"

"No. A *sky* phone. It's actually a radio that can make a phone connection via low earth-orbit satellites."

Will nodded. "We almost had them in my universe, except that cell phones won the race."

Jenkins sighed. He didn't have time to be sidetracked.

"Why doesn't everybody carry them?" Will asked.

His guest gave him the Binny Look. "You don't understand. They communicate via satellites . . . in orbit."

Will shrugged. He was obviously missing something.

"There's only so many channels. There are maybe a hundred sky-phones in the whole world."

Will understood. Lack of digital technology again. Without all the encoding and multiplexing, they would indeed be limited in how many could operate at the same time.

"Okay," Will continued. "So Breggart supposedly has one of these . . . wait! I remember! He had this clunky thing hanging from his waist. It looked like a walkie-talkie from WWII."

Jenkins nodded. "That was probably it. You have to keep him from using it."

"Why would he use it?"

Jenkins sighed again. "I can't tell you. Just don't let him use it. You have to do whatever you can to keep him from using it. Do you understand?"

Will shrugged. "For how long?"

Jenkins eyed him a moment. "You'll know."

Will sensed that he wasn't going to get any more information.

Just one more thing, though. "Can you promise me that you will try to get Francine out safely? Whatever spy game you're planning here, I need your word that Francine will be safe."

The station master smiled and nodded. "I promise that we will do all we can to get her out safe and sound. I know you don't believe it, but I want her back as badly as you."

Will gazed into the man's eyes. He had a sense that he could indeed trust him. He stuck out his hand, and the station master who was more than a station master took it and shook it firmly.

ж ж ж

"That's right," Will said into the phone, "I want to speak to Hank Breggart."

The female operator at the Virginia CID office told him to please hold a moment. "I'm afraid Mr. Breggart is not in the office," she said after a few seconds. "Can I take a message?"

"No," he insisted, nervously scratching Regal's ear. "I need to speak with him. Believe me, he'll want to talk to me."

"I told you," the woman replied a little testily, "he's in the field."

"He has a satellite phone, doesn't he?"

"You mean a sky-phone?"

"Right, a sky-phone."

"I'm sorry, that's CID confidential information."

"CID information," he repeated. "Meaning that lowlifes like me aren't entitled to know."

"That's right," the operator said expectantly, as though he had some other point he was leading up to.

"Look. Just get hold of him and tell him that Will—no, Willard wants to talk to him."

After he gave her the number at Wallaby's ranch, she said, "I'll see what I can do."

"Okay, you see what you can do, but believe me, I wouldn't want to be you if he finds out he didn't get the message pronto."

There was silence on the line for a few moments, and then she said, "Is there anything else I can help you with . . . Willard?"

She said "Willard" as though it was the funniest name she'd ever heard. Maybe it was.

He waited inside the house within earshot of the kitchen phone. Without cell phones, answering machines, or even cordless phones, the people of this universe still understood the meaning of "catching a call," like his father's generation. It was two long, eternal hours before the phone rang.

"Hello, *Will*," said Breggart's voice. "What can we do for you?"

"I'm ready," he replied, not sure how to interpret the use of his real name.

"For what? A long prison sentence? Getting bored sitting around Willobee's place?"

"You know what."

"You don't mean some sort of exchange, I hope. I'm afraid you blew your last chance on the moon."

"Look, let's cut the games. Release Francine, and I'll tell you everything I know."

"Miss Sewer is a dangerous criminal, guilty of multiple serious offenses. Why, for goodness sake, would I ever give her up?"

"What happened to 'innocent until proven guilty'? Look, Breggart, I don't know what you're holding out for here. I offered to give myself up; what more do you want?"

"Maybe I already have everything worth having."

He was getting an uneasy feeling. "Go on."

"It seems there was some misunderstanding about your background."

"What do you mean?"

"A university mathematics instructor? An academic whose weapons knowledge consists of what he's read in popular magazines?"

His heart seemed to stop. Those were the very words he'd told Jenkins in the bushes next to the Colo River. For a brief, doomed second he envisioned Jenkins as a CID mole, but realized that the station master himself wouldn't have to be the spy. Anybody who sat in on meetings where the subject was discussed could have passed on the information.

"How do you know I was telling the truth when I said that?"

"Simple. You wouldn't have jeopardized the life of the sweet young woman you seem to hold so dear—'My love,' I believe she called you?"

He heard a rushing sound in his ears, and the kitchen seemed to spin. This was it, the end of the game. He would never see

Francine, or Wallaby, again. "I'm from a whole different universe," he blurted, pleading.

"Assuming that's even true, so what?"

"That has to be worth something."

"I don't see why. A kitten from one litter is as good as one from another."

"That's not necessarily so."

His mind shifted into overdrive, trying desperately to keep the CID agent on the phone. "There could be genetic differences not immediately obvious. One litter could be prone to kidney failure."

"You are implying that my universe is flawed?"

Yes! he wanted to shout, *In a very big way!* Instead, he said, "I'm saying that any number of differences between universes could be useful in ways not immediately visible."

"Let's think of one. Maybe you have better coffee makers? Perhaps that might contribute substantially to national security?"

"I've had your coffee, and yes, our coffee is better. In fact, our machines automatically make the coffee in the morning."

"That requires just a timer. Hardly something worth releasing a dangerous terrorist like Miss Sewer for."

"Our machines measure the water temperature and . . ." He wasn't going to impress Breggart with coffee makers. "Our controllers turn on video recorders at set times to record television programs, and they monitor your house when you're away, and sound alarms if somebody tries to break in, and they can change the temperature in your house before you come home from work, and they can call you—wherever you are—to let you know that your house is on fire—"

"What do you mean by 'controllers'?"

He hesitated. How could he make this sound impressive? "Digital logic . . . with servo-activated feedback loops. And memory—lots of memory."

"Memory? Like, thinking?"

The agent's tone had changed. Instead of sarcastically superior, it was now intrigued.

Will played the nibble. "Like intelligence, artificial intelligence."

"A 'controller' can think and do all this?"

His foe thought that he had been describing just a single controller for the whole house. What would that be? What was Breggart envisioning, if anything? The perfect household gadget? Rosie, the Jetsons' robot maid?

And then it hit him. He remembered the television at Francine's, and Wallaby's joke about why this universe went to Mars. Like his own world of the fifties, they were still tickled by the possibility. They hadn't had the chance to discover just how difficult it is to duplicate the capabilities of a human, even a drunk and stupefied human.

"All this and more—much more," he enthused. "Those tasks require hardly any thinking at all."

"You're describing a robot."

"That's exactly what I'm describing."

The agent was silent at the other end of the line. "This is too farfetched. How can this be possible, when our scientists don't have the first idea how to design one?"

Will summarized the conversation he'd had with Francine about the diverging paths their two universes took when Shockley invented the minitube instead of the transistor. Through it all, Breggart let him talk, interjecting only for clarifications. When he finished, the CID agent was silent. After many moments, he finally said, "How do I know you're telling the truth?"

Will knew he had set the hook.

Ж Ж Ж

The bulky case sat on Will's lap, blocking his view out of the van, but he wasn't about to let it out of his sight. Inside lay the result of nearly a week of round-the-clock effort by himself and a crew of six engineers and technicians that Jenkins had arranged. His sponsor had seemed barely curious about what was forming inside the Sydney lab, only that whatever cockamamie contraption they were brainstorming, it had to—absolutely *had* to—be ready on time. On time was today, and it was therefore by definition done. They'd only been able to implement a tenth of the features Will had originally envisioned, and he hoped to hell that Breggart would be sufficiently impressed.

They arrived at the Sydney space port, and the driver made for the secure area reserved for the Australian Air Force. Jenkins had told him that the government did not officially recognize his organization, whatever that was. When Will had asked him why, therefore, they were going to depart from a military base, the station master had simply changed the subject.

Once through the security checkpoints, they wound their way through the maze of Air Force spaceships laid out in various stages of maintenance, towards a far, isolated corner, where a small private jump waited for him. Jenkins was talking with someone, so Will decided he'd use the bathroom before they took off. He glanced around, and not finding anything obvious, tried to catch Jenkin's eye, but his project sponsor was immersed in paperwork. Instead, figuring he might find a bathroom inside, he made for the nearest building, a corrugated metal storage shed. The door was locked, but he saw that it hadn't completely latched shut, and it swung inward when he pushed it. Darkness waited inside, and he felt along the wall with his hand until he found a light switch. The facility was indeed used for storage. Piles of crates and boxes loomed all around and above him. He wandered through the maze, and found the bathroom near the rear.

When he was finished, he headed back towards the entrance, but a scattered jumble of crates caught his eye. The rest of the supplies were piled neatly, but these were lying haphazardly, open and empty, as though the contents had been extracted in haste and their containers abandoned. The logo printed on each crate was an arrowhead in flight. Forward motion was conveyed by droplets streaming away behind. It all seemed familiar. Droplets . . . he remembered! This was the same logo he'd seen on his uniboost while they were filling it next to the stream. What he'd thought was a heart was really an arrowhead. He turned several crates over and finally found a shipping label. The return address was Reaction, LTD.

"Will!"

It was Jenkins, standing in the doorway, and he looked upset. "Come on! It's time to go!"

"Did you see these . . . ?"

The station master had already walked away.

Will caught up to him at the jump, where the pilot was waiting for them. Before he had a chance to ask about the crates, Jenkins handed him an envelope, explaining briskly that the papers would get him through Seattle customs where CID would be waiting for him. Will didn't want to depart on bad terms with the man who'd been helping him, so he resisted pressing him about the Reaction labels. There was one thing, though, that had been nagging him for the last week.

"One question," he said, shaking Jenkin's hand in goodbye. "You weren't willing to let me exchange myself for Francine when I first arrived in Australia. Why now?"

The balding man's face softened, and he smiled. "Events turn and priorities shift."

Will laughed. "In other words, I don't get to know."

His sponsor and link to all things espionage nodded and placed his hand on Will's shoulder. "Everything will become clear eventually."

As Will followed the pilot into the portable elevator, Jenkins called after him. "You may find somebody you recognize! And don't let Breggart use that sky-phone!"

Will took his place in one of the six empty passenger seats and watched through a window as the elevator was rolled away. From somewhere below him came an ominous rumbling as fusing nuclei heated water to temperatures found on Earth only inside the fireballs of colliding asteroids.

Everything will become clear eventually.

He wondered how much optimism that presumed.

Chapter 20

As it happened, he didn't need the papers Jenkins had given him. A black CID sedan was waiting as he exited the portable elevator at the Seattle-Tacoma airport. Apparently, the Counter Intelligence Department took precedence over the lowly functions of customs and immigration. A man in a suit and sunglasses, which color-coordinated the sedan, approached and asked him if he was William McKinney, then escorted him via a firm grip on his upper arm to the car, where he was guided into the back seat. Inside was another agent who could have been a twin. Without a word, the man reached out his hand. Thinking it an unexpected but pleasant gesture, Will grasped it to shake hands, but was surprised when he suddenly found handcuffs snapped around his wrist. The other end was attached to the agent's own.

"Nice to meet you, too," Will remarked, but the man ignored him, staring impassively out the front window.

Will concluded that they didn't need his robots after all; they apparently already had their own.

The first agent put Will's case in the car's trunk, and they drove away, leaving the pilot to wait for Francine. They made for Seattle, a city now alien and unsettling. He recognized the Smith Tower, built in the early part of the twentieth century, but the stately pyramid peak was nearly lost in a crowd of strange skyscrapers, as though it had been transported off to some foreign land. In a sense, it had. He searched the northwest skyline, but there was no Space Needle to be found. Built for the 1962 World's Fair and tolerated with fondness by Seattleites of his universe like a show-off child, he ached to see it now.

As the driver turned into a garage beneath one of the unfamiliar tall buildings, Will glimpsed a bronze plaque with the words *Federal Building*. A guard peered at the ID the driver held up, then lifted a barrier for them to enter the dark depths, where they parked in a reserved spot. They took a nearby elevator up eighteen floors. People stepped on and off along the way, glancing quickly at Will's large case in the driver's arms, then at the handcuffs binding Will to his escort, and finally looking quickly away, as though to relieve him of unbearable embarrassment. Off the elevator, down a hall, a left turn, and seven steps to an unmarked door. The driver knocked, peered in a moment, and then nodded to Will's escort who unlocked the cuffs.

"Will I see you again," he asked as the other agent handed him his case. He was babbling out of nervousness. "Maybe dinner and a movie?"

The taciturn man ignored him, which was just as well. He took one deep breath, and then stepped through the door. The case blocked his view, and he had to turn sideways to see around it. The room was empty except for a few chairs and a folding table. The single, large window probably would have provided a spectacular view, but only allowed diffused light to enter through nearly closed blinds. Breggart was there, leaning with his butt against the table, arms folded across his chest. He was alone.

"Where is she?" Will asked, clinging tightly to the case.

The slim CID agent nodded towards another door at the back of the room.

"Bring her in," Will demanded.

Breggart just watched him with the eternal mocking smirk. The sky-phone sat perched in a holster at his hip like some futuristic version of a wild-west six-gun.

The thirty-pound case was getting heavy. "I'm going to leave," he threatened, even though he knew the two other agents would be waiting right outside to stop him.

"You'll get your girlfriend. Let's see the robot first."

"I've already explained: it's not a complete robot. That would take months to build." He leaned the case against the wall to take up some of the load. "Look," he reasoned, "this prototype won't do you any good without my knowledge. You need my cooperation. The only way you're going to get that is for you to start cooperating as well."

His enemy waited long enough to annoy, then called out to somebody. Seconds later the back door opened, and Francine stumbled through, her hands bound behind her in cuffs. She didn't look any worse than two weeks before on the moon, but not much better, either. At least she didn't seem to have any fresh wounds.

He didn't have much time to study her, though, for another prisoner came stumbling in behind her.

"Wallaby!" Will shouted with joy.

This was what Jenkins meant about recognizing someone. The station master must have arranged for both to be exchanged. Unlike Francine, his dingo friend showed no obvious marks of physical battering. A different form of abuse, though, was apparent in the impassive face and glazed eyes. He didn't even seem to recognize Will in his drugged state. Maybe Breggart was more careful about visible torture with non-US citizens, or maybe they just hadn't gotten around to the more direct approach yet.

Two other men walked in behind Wallaby. One wore the ubiquitous black suit, the uniform of Breggart's flunkies, but the other was dressed casually in baggy clown pants and open shirt. This second man seemed embarrassed by the rough handling of the prisoners whom the flunky shoved forcefully into chairs.

"Okay," Breggart directed, nodding towards the case. "Your turn."

Will set it down carefully on the table, undid the latches, and lifted off the top. As he pulled out the packing, the man with the baggy pants leaned over, curious to see. Will stopped and extended his hand. No sense being shy now. "Hi," he said, "I'm Will McKinney, a mathematician from another universe."

The man shook his hand, blushing. "Uh, hi. My name is Brent. I'm uh . . ."

"He's a professor from the university," Breggart finished for him. "He's an expert in systems electronics."

Uh oh. Maybe it was time to get nervous.

Will pulled out the rest of the packing, lifted Rosie from her transport home and set her on the table. Engineers always give names to their projects, and Will chose that of the Jetsons' maid.

Although initially skeptical, once he explained the premise of the cartoon show, his crew embraced the moniker with enthusiasm. Will concluded that engineers were the same in every universe and possibly across all species.

Rosie had no legs or arms, and her torso was just a plain metal box, but she did have a head of sorts. A smaller box sat on top, sporting ears, or maybe antennas, that were really microphones mounted to each side in order to provide directional differentiation. A glass screen made up her face, now dark and featureless. Rosie's head was made to swivel in a semicircle, and she was originally designed to automatically turn to face whoever was talking to her. They never got that part to work, though, and he had secured her so that she faced only forward. He apparently hadn't done a very good securing job, for it had come undone during the trip, and Rosie's head now flopped back and forth as though she was dead, or maybe drugged like Wallaby.

Will prayed that the flopping head hadn't caused wires to come off inside. If he had to open her up to make repairs while Brent, the electronics expert, watched . . . well, he just had to hope for the best.

"I'm told that this is supposed to be a, umm . . ." Brent seemed embarrassed to even say it.

"A robot," Breggart finished for him. "At least, it's *supposed* to be." To Will he said, "You know, you don't get to just walk away if I'm not satisfied."

"Don't worry," Will replied, positioning Rosie's head to look forward. "You'll be impressed enough to gladly let my friends go free just so that I'll help you."

His creation refused to face forward, so he left her staring blankly to the side at the equally blank Wallaby. "Like I explained, this isn't a complete robot. It's just the core brain."

"Using," Breggart confirmed, "what did you call it? Logics?"

"Digital logic. My universe's specialty."

He reached behind her and flipped the power switch. Her glass face sprang to life with lighted characters. A series of indecipherable patterns flashed quickly, followed by the words *yes*, *no*, and finally a lone question mark.

"I didn't have time to build the speech synthesis circuitry," he explained, "so the brain communicates using displayed words."

Breggart seemed intrigued now that Rosie showed some life. "Do I . . . just talk to it?" he asked, bending over to peer at the glowing question mark.

"Uh, yeah," Will replied. *Sort of.*

Sporting a silly smile, the CID agent glanced up at Brent. Into the glass plate, he said slowly, "Who are you?"

"Um, I should explain," Will interrupted, gently pulling Breggart back a little ways. "The brain hasn't had a chance to get . . . acclimated. Watch." Turning to face Rosie, he spoke forcefully. "Rosie! Are you a robot? Please answer." He spoke her name with deep authority, but his tone was almost pleading when he uttered "answer."

After a few seconds, the question mark was replaced with the word *yes*, which glowed for five seconds before reverting back to the question mark.

Breggart spun his surprised gaze towards Will, as though expecting that he would catch him holding some sort of control box. He just stood, though, smiling with arms crossed over his chest.

The agent turned back to Rosie. "Who am I?" he asked loudly.

"Hold on," Will said, pulling the agent back again. "It takes a while for it to get used to different voices." He faced the robot again. "Rosie! Is this man's name Fred Flintstone? Please answer." This time, he pleaded with both "please," and "answer."

A few seconds later, the word *no* appeared.

"Rosie! Is this man's name Hank Breggart? Please answer."

Rosie returned the word *yes*.

Breggart was speechless at first, obviously impressed. "Ask it," he finally ordered, "what's four plus four."

"Er, we've got a little catch, here," Will confessed. "Rosie's word generation block is still developing. For now, you'll have to limit the questions to yes or no answers."

He'd given this a lot of thought, but this was the best he could come up with. Breggart looked disappointed at the limitation, but Brent's brow was furrowed in doubt.

Will asked Rosie if four plus four was five, then ten, and finally eight, always starting with her name, and ending with a plea to respond.

She answered *no, no,* and *yes,* and Breggart nearly danced with excitement.

There was a quick rap on the door, and one of his escort flunkies stuck his head inside. "Uh, sir, I think there's something you should—"

"Get out!" Breggart yelled. The flunky looked shocked at the outburst. "Wait until I call you!"

"Ask it," Breggart enthused, gaining back both his composure and excitement, "my mother's name—wait, no. I know, ask it if my mother's name is Shirley."

"Uh," Will said. "It can't possibly know that. It only has information that we've fed to it."

Brent finally joined in, still looking dubious, "But it should be able to make calculations."

"Well . . . sure," Will replied.

The electronics professor pulled a slide rule from his pocket and slid the center piece back and forth a couple of times. "Ask it the natural logarithm of thirty-three."

Will stared at the man. He could probably get close, but that wasn't going to be enough. He hadn't counted on Breggart bringing help. "It doesn't know logs yet."

Brent shook his head, as though one of his students had given an excuse he'd heard a thousand times already. "How about trig?"

Will sighed.

"What's with the math?" Breggart asked.

Will realized that he had an unlikely ally in his foe. Breggart *wanted* Rosie to be a real robot.

"It's not the math itself," Brent explained. "I just want to ask something that Mr. McKinney wouldn't know himself."

Oh shit! Wouldn't it be his luck that Breggart would bring somebody with an actual brain?

The CID agent thought a moment, then looked questioningly at him.

He shrugged. What else could he do?

"Maybe we should look inside," Brent offered.

Will felt his heart pounding in his throat. "You wouldn't understand the technology."

"That may well be true," the electronics professor replied.

"Then, what's the point?" Breggart asked.

"Well," Brent continued, scratching his head in thought, "intelligence implies complexity. After all, our brains contain billions of neurons, with trillions of synapse connections. Surely some degree of complexity would be apparent, no matter what the technology."

Breggart looked at Will again. The implication was obvious. It was up to him to defend himself. He had climbed into the hot seat when he'd agreed to the exchange, and they were now turning up the heat.

Will looked from Breggart to Brent, and back to Rosie. He had no choice. From a small tool kit he'd included in the case, he took a screwdriver and started to work on the screws holding an access panel on the back of Rosie's torso. The big outside window was next to him, and through the fine slits between the blinds, he caught movement. He stopped and looked up. He couldn't tell what it was, but there was something gliding by outside. If it were a helicopter, they should be hearing it.

"Quit stalling," Breggart barked. He seemed angry, apprehensive that his precious robot might not be all that he was hoping for.

Will went back to work on the screws, and the cover clattered off onto the table. He stepped back, letting them see what he'd revealed. There, extending the full width of the exposed innards, was a matrix of tiny fibers arranged in an apparently random pattern. Underneath lay a shiny metal surface dimpled with a myriad of curious indentations.

Brent squatted down to take closer look. "What *is* it?" he asked.

Will saw movement again through the blinds. This time he thought he recognized the shape. He leaned over and flipped up one slat. It took a moment to convince himself of what he was seeing since he'd never watched a uniboost in flight from a distance. A man hovered three hundred feet above the ground holding a serious looking gun. The flier wore a helmet and some sort of body armor, bulging at the chest. As Will watched through the slit, the man aimed downward and fired, then soared away. At first he thought it might perhaps be the Seattle police, but remembered that uniboosts were illegal in the US. Then he saw another flier off to the side, and *another* beyond that! There was a whole army of flying soldiers!

And suddenly he understood: the empty crates at the Sydney spaceport with Reaction, LTD shipping labels; Jenkin's insistence that he be ready with Rosie by exactly this day; his sponsor's reassurance that he would know when . . . oh shit! The sky-phone! He was supposed to keep Breggart from using it. The rebel colleagues of Francine and Wallaby would have cut the phone lines, leaving Breggart with the only means to call for help. In a world with no cell phones, where urgent information is faxed, a single link to the outside world via a satellite could mean federal reinforcements arriving hours sooner.

At that moment the door burst open, and the flunky shouted, "Sir! We're under attack!"

"What in Satan's name are you talking about?" Breggart roared.

"Insurgents, sir! And the phones are all dead!"

Breggart threw one piercing glance at Will, and then scrambled to get the phone from the holster at his waist.

Brent stood frozen in shock. Wallaby peered at them, dazed and confused, as though if he concentrated, he might make some sense of it all. Francine was watching Will. Her battered face was smiling. She nodded to him.

He looked around. Use a chair? The flunky stood not fifteen feet away. He scanned the rest of the room, and his gaze rested on Rosie.

Breggart had the sky-phone out and was fiddling with it. Will wrapped his arms around his creation and hefted it off the table. Turning to Breggart, he called, "It's all yours!" and tossed it.

Taken by surprise, Breggart tried to catch the metal beast, but it was too heavy, and it fell with a crunch to the floor. The CID agent looked at his empty hands, and then down at the sky-phone lying on the floor, a tiny voice buzzing like a mosquito from the connected party. He looked up quickly at Will, and their eyes locked for a brief fraction of a second before they both sprang for the phone. Breggart had his hand on it when Will's foot came down with all his weight. The agent rolled away holding his hand and howling in pain. The satellite phone looked dead, but Will gave one last stomp for good measure. It responded with a satisfying crunch.

Somebody from behind grabbed him painfully around his neck. The flunky. It didn't matter now. It was just a matter of time until the insurgents secured the building.

Brent bent over Rosie. Her torso was twisted, and one side had broken completely away. The electronics professor reached in and extracted the curious metal substrate supporting the fiber matrix. It was round and about ten inches across, and once removed, looked exactly like the bottom of a metal bowl. The electronics expert looked up questioningly.

Will flipped his thumb towards Wallaby. When he spoke, the words came out hoarse from the flunky's grip. "My friend's dog," he said. "It's her water dish."

Chapter 21

Will sat in the rickety lawn chair between Francine and Wallaby on the porch and threw Regal's water bowl out onto the dusty yard, then waited as the indefatigable dingo dog retrieved it. It seemed to him that the dog was happier to see her dish back than Wallaby.

"You swept up Regal's hair," Francine repeated with wonder, "and glued it to the bottom of her bowl?"

Her face was coming along slowly. The doctor assured her that she'd be good as new in a month or two, but Will didn't believe it. It was just hard to imagine how all the damage would heal completely. Scarred or not, she seemed not to care, just happy to be here on Wallaby's ranch. For himself, Will couldn't have been happier either.

"I did it on impulse the last night before leaving. It just occurred to me that Breggart might want to look inside before giving you up, and I remembered we had all that open space right under the access panel. I figured he wouldn't know hair from transistors. I never guessed he'd bring along an electronics engineer."

He glanced over at his co-conspirator. She was looking at him fondly through eyes that were no longer swollen, just black and blue. "You really had no idea the war was starting that day?" she asked.

"I really and truly had no idea the shortest war in history was about to start."

The world news media was calling it the Washegon War of Cessation. For himself, he wasn't sure one battle that lasted less than a day and involved fewer than a hundred casualties qualified as a war. Washegonians referred to it as the uniboost scuffle. He finally understood why the solo rocket-pack designers had assumed that the rider would be balanced by something carried in front. That something was a gun and ammo stash.

"Which means," she concluded, "that you were actually giving yourself up in exchange for me and the old soaker here."

She nudged Wallaby, who grunted. He'd pretty much recovered from the nasty cocktail of drugs they'd given him, but he was tired, and would have still been in bed if they hadn't dragged him out.

"I didn't know that Wallaby was part of the deal until he stumbled through the door."

She took his hand in hers. "Which means you were giving yourself up just for li'l 'ol me." She smiled at him and batted her eyes. "Will McKinney, you're my hero."

He felt himself blushing. Embarrassment steered him to change the subject. "Apparently you didn't know about the revolt as well—either that or you didn't . . ."

They hadn't talked about her torture yet, and he was aghast at himself for broaching the subject so crudely.

"I knew," she said. "I just didn't know when."

"So . . ." He couldn't say the words.

"Did I squawk?" She looked at him soberly, then off to the far hills. "I don't remember telling Breggart, but there's a lot of time there I don't remember anything at all."

"I'm sorry . . . I shouldn't have said anything."

"It's okay," she said brightly, squeezing his hand. "It's over, and whether I talked or not, it doesn't matter now; we've won."

We've won. He'd never been much for games, the absolute win or lose of it, where nothing was really gained other than a leg up over your rival. But now, after all they'd been through, it sounded grand.

They'd won.

The enduring pioneer spirit of the Washegonians played the key role. But that by itself wouldn't have been enough. The world had grown tired of America the bully. Boeing, based in Seattle, had seen the writing on the wall, and had signed secret deals with the transition government that was now in power until elections could be held. Selected representatives of the UN—Russia, France, and

China—had been engaged, and the Security Council had held an emergency session to immediately recognize the new nation of Washegon, passing a highly controversial, and still contested, special provision to override the US's veto.

"What about . . ." He nodded towards Wallaby.

Will didn't think the ranch owner was listening, but the dingo grunted and said, "Didn't know."

Will and Francine looked at each other. Those were the most words their friend had volunteered all morning.

The Aussie nodded, as if agreeing with himself. "S'why I took the fall."

"What'd he say?" Francine asked.

Will understood. "He's saying that he didn't know what was coming down. That's why they let him take the fall when Breggart came after blood. Jenkins probably didn't want to draw too much attention. It was better to let Crocodile Dundee be thrown to the lions than lose the chance they'd been working on for so long."

"Crocodile Dundee?" she asked.

"He's from my universe. An historical Australian hero. He saved all of Australia from media obscurity."

"Really?"

He looked at her. "Yes."

What the hell; it was true.

"Is Breggart dead?" she asked.

She had seen their foe get shot when he pulled his gun on the trooper who came through the window. But that was the last she'd seen for a while, since she was butting her head against the flunky who was choking Will, and the lunk had indeed let him go, only to slug her one, knocking her out cold.

"Jenkins says he's going to pull through just fine. In fact, I apparently did more damage stomping on his hand than the bullet did."

"Too bad," she muttered.

"That the bullet didn't hurt him more?"

She laughed. "At least that. No, I meant that it's too bad he's going to pull through at all. What's going to happen to him?"

She hadn't heard much news at the hospital. "They tried to use him as currency to exchange for some dissidents the US is still holding outside Washegon, but—get this—CID didn't want him. They're apparently using him to take the fall on the whole affair. He's going to stand trial at the World Court on charges of torture and assassination."

She nodded dourly, clearly preferring that the monster had been killed. "What about Ignatius?" she asked, with an equally despising tone.

He sighed. "There's a large faction that wants to lynch him first and ask questions later, but unfortunately, the interim Washegon government has decided to take the responsible route. They have enough on him to keep him on a tight leash, and he's useful right where he is in his steward position. Rumor has it that they're going to force him to split off a faction of pilots. The new union would be associated with Boeing. If they can pull it off, the pilot/ship-builder monopoly would finally be broken. I heard on the news last night that Reaction, LTD is already talking with Boeing about a joint venture: anti-matter powered ships for exploring the outer solar system; maybe even probes to the stars."

She didn't look happy at the prospect that Ignatius would escape unscathed.

"You may get your chance to confront him yet," he consoled.

At this, she finally brightened. "What do you mean?"

"If he gives them any trouble, you're probably their best witness. He abducted you on the moon, after all. Once outside the pressurized facility, we were technically in international territory."

She looked at him and grinned mischievously. "We can't be too rough on him. We need something from him as well."

He looked at her questioningly.

"Corroboration," she explained.

"About what?"

"Your solo flight to the moon. Don't you want to be a celebrity?"

"Bah!"

She nudged him. "Oh come on. Washegon needs some heroes for the media. In a few years, they'll have you chopping down cherry trees in your youth and throwing coins across the Sound."

"Bah!" he repeated. "Humbug!"

The morning sun was getting warm. It felt fine after the chilly night, but they'd have to find some shade before long.

"Auto-pilots," Wallaby grunted.

They both looked at their dingo friend.

"He lives!" Francine observed with feigned wonder.

"What about them?" Will asked.

"Only way," Wallaby said.

"To do what?"

"Break the unions."

Will stared at the Aussie. There was more going on in the weather-tanned head than he had been letting on.

"What's he mumbling about?" Francine asked.

"I think I know. I was teaching him some basics of digital processing, and explained how we—my own universe—use computers to calculate trajectories."

Their near-comatose host took a deep breath and stood up, stretching his arms out wide and yawning. He shook his head, as though shaking off water. "The bloody leaches are going to continue to suck blood as long as we need them for orbital navigation."

Will and Francine exchanged shocked glances.

Wallaby looked down at them. "I'm not drugged anymore, mates."

"Two minutes ago you could hardly speak," Will objected.

The dingo stretched again. "Had to wake up. Haven't had me coffee yet," he said, walking inside to take care of that.

"I still don't understand," Francine said.

Will smiled. His Australian friend would probably forever be fooling him with his rough outback demeanor. "Remember how I calculated our orbit out to India Station?"

"Of course."

"You could have done it as well."

"Sure . . . at least, I think so."

"I'm a mathematician and you're a physicist, and that was about the easiest maneuver in the book. What chance would most people have without years of special training? It's not just the fact that Pilots wield a monopoly with their union. They really do offer an absolutely essential service. Wallaby is saying that they are always going to hold the world hostage until that power is replaced, and computers are the only way to dilute it—dissolve it, eventually."

Her eyes were wide with comprehension. "This digital stuff really can take the place of a Pilot?"

"Oh, not completely, but it can take over all the number crunching chores, so the job becomes no more difficult than flying an airplane."

She was staring off at the hills.

"Earth calling Francine," he quipped. "It's not going to happen overnight. It took my universe decades to develop the technology."

She blinked and looked at him. "What about your robot?"

He laughed. "Rosie? She wasn't a robot; she was a ruse. She has less smarts than an amoeba. I knew I didn't have to build a real robot. I can't, anyway. Nobody can—at least, not the kind I saw on that television program in your apartment. I just needed to fool Breggart long enough to get you free."

"You mean, it wasn't really intelligent?"

"No more intelligent than Clever Hans."

"I remember reading about that. He was a horse that lived early in the twentieth century. People thought he could do arithmetic until some psychologist figured out that Hans was simply reacting to visual clues from the trainer, and the trainer didn't even know it."

"I should have named it Hans instead of Rosie."

"I think I'm getting it," she said. "That's why the electronics engineer—Brent—wanted to ask Rosie a question that you wouldn't know the answer to."

"Yeah. He was on to me. The difference between Hans's trainer and me was that I knew I was giving her the answers."

Francine grinned. "That was hogwash about how Rosie could only give yes and no answers because her 'word generation block' was still developing. That sounded lame even to me."

He chuckled. "Lame?"

"I didn't use it correctly?"

"No, you used it too well. You sound like a teenager right out of my universe. I think I'm corrupting you."

"How did you communicate with Rosie? It was the way you asked the question, wasn't it?"

"Yep. Jenkins' whiz kids put in high-tech FM sound filters."

"Frequency modulation?"

"Very good, Madam Physicist."

"Ha!" she cried, catching on. "You always ended a question with, 'Please answer,' and you used a rising tone sometimes."

"You get a cigar. They tuned it to my voice, but I still had to practice until I was nearly hoarse. There were actually two filters. I always began a question by saying 'Rosie' loudly. That was for the first filter, which primed her to respond to the encoded answer. She waited until she heard the rising tone. If I used it with just one word, Rosie lit the 'yes' word, but if I used rising tones on both words, she said, 'no.' It probably seems pretty simple, but believe me, it took us a week of very long days to get just that much working."

She pouted. "I'm disillusioned. I thought my knight in shining armor was a robot genius."

He felt his face getting hot again. "I know low level assembly language," he offered, "and that's where your universe needs to start. This is what our engineers were sweating over while yours were sending men to Mars."

From inside, he heard the phone ring, and then Wallaby talking to somebody. Seconds later, the door banged open and he stuck his head out. "Mate, you'd better get in here!"

"What's the matter?" he asked, alarmed at his friend's tone.

"It's your uncle—Uncle Bill."

For a moment Will froze in confusion. Had his great uncle figured out how to make a one-way exchange? Unless . . . "Do you mean Uncle William?"

"You have two? Yeah, sorry. The bloke actually called himself William."

Will blinked, re-orienting himself. Still, it was great to hear his "other" uncle had come through captivity alive.

When he picked up the handset, he had to remind himself that the voice at the other end really wasn't Uncle Bill, or at least, not exactly. "So, how did you do with Breggart?" Will asked.

"I plan to return his favors someday, but all that will have to keep. There's something that's come up, and it's extremely urgent."

"What? Has the US retaken control?"

"No, nothing like that. I just got back home this afternoon, and as I was cleaning up, I found another note that Buck left. He put it where I wouldn't find it right away on purpose. I don't think he counted on me being in jail for a month, though."

"Another note?" Will asked, dazed.

"He explains that if you're not able to make the return exchange in the days after you arrived, then he would wait awhile and try one last time."

Will felt as though he was back in space floating weightless with nothing solid to hang on.

"When is it? This last time?"

"I'm afraid it's tomorrow morning, 7:00 AM sharp."

"Tomorrow . . . uh, that's your time?"

"That's right—uh, wait. It's after midnight here. No I mean 7:00 AM *today.*"

"But, but that's in . . ." He tried to figure out the time zones, but couldn't remember if they added or subtracted.

"It's six hours from now," the old scientist clarified.

"Six hours! You're ten thousand miles away!"

"I know. That's why it's urgent."

"It's not possible to get there in that much time . . ."

He remembered that this universe had sub-orbital jumps that made the trip in two hours. "I'll be there, Uncle William. You just be ready with the capacitors charged."

He ran back to the porch, dragging Wallaby along. "I need to get hold of Jenkins!" he cried. "He owes me one last favor."

Francine shook her head in dismay. "What are you talking about?"

"I'm going home! Home! To *my* universe! Where people talk on cell phones all day long, and there still gets to be a first man on Mars!"

His friends just stared at him. They were probably confused, struggling to absorb the news.

"What about the navigation computers we need to break the pilot union?" Wallaby finally asked.

"You don't need me. You understand enough now to get the ball rolling. You know how it goes: sometimes we just need to know that something is possible."

Francine reached out and placed her hand on his arm. "I'm happy for you, Will."

She didn't seem happy at all.

ж ж ж

Will was back in his uncle's basement. It was like stepping into a dream. No, it was like stepping *out* of a dream. The last month now seemed like one long adventure that was already becoming the great story to be recalled and retold fondly. He was Dorothy returning to Kansas, Bilbo setting off from The Lonely Mountain for the Shire, Tarzan, leaving London to return to the jungles of Africa.

Well, maybe not the last one.

He could feel his heart pounding as he took his place, naked, under the familiar rod hanging from the ceiling. His interim uncle stood ready at the controls, smiling warmly as they both watched the big clock sweep away the final seconds.

Francine had come along. He had thought that she would have been embarrassed to see him naked. He thought that *he* would have been embarrassed. But he wasn't. It somehow felt right for her to be there at such an important time. For her part, she didn't seem shy about the show. Quite the opposite, she seemed to watch him with rapt attention, as though mentally recording everything she could.

She glanced at the clock, and then gave him a small wave. "Goodbye, my hero knight," she said softly.

In less than a minute she would be gone. Forever. When he got back home, he'd have to deal with Alicia. He knew now that it would never work between them.

He also knew that this had the appearance of the same old Will, the same old Buck—not able or willing to commit. But his heart told him that she was not the woman for him. He knew this as surely as he knew the moon circled the Earth.

"Ten seconds," his uncle recited, quietly.

If there was a parallel version of him in this universe, then maybe there was a version of Francine in his. He could seek her out. She might have a different name, so it might take a while, but he would find her.

"Five seconds."

He emptied his lungs, and stood straight and still.

What if she was already married?

"Four."

What if she didn't even exist?

"Three."

He swiveled his eyes to look one last time at her.

"Two."

There, sparkling in the light from the control panel, was one pure tear rolling down her cheek.

"One!"

He sucked his lungs full of air as the basement exploded with brilliant light and a shower of sparks, his own personal fireworks heralding the life he'd chosen.